# PUZZLE ME
# A MURDER

# PUZZLE ME
# A MURDER

## ROZ NOONAN

Kensington Publishing Corp.
www.kensingtonbooks.com

KENSINGTON BOOKS are published by

Kensington Publishing Corp.
900 Third Avenue
New York, NY 10022

All Kensington titles, imprints, and distributed lines are available at special quantity discounts for bulk purchases for sales promotion, premiums, fund-raising, educational, or institutional use. Special book excerpts or customized printings can also be created to fit specific needs. For details, write or phone the office of the Kensington Special Sales Manager: Attn. Special Sales Department, Kensington Publishing Corp., 900 Third Avenue, New York, NY 10022. Phone: 1-800-221-2647.

KENSINGTON and the KENSINGTON COZIES teapot logo Reg. US Pat. & TM Off.

Library of Congress Control Number: 2024934882

ISBN: 978-1-4967-4671-9

First Kensington Hardcover Edition: August 2024

ISBN: 978-1-4967-4673-3 (ebook)

10 9 8 7 6 5 4 3 2 1

Printed in the United States of America

# PUZZLE ME A MURDER

# Chapter One

"I'm going to kill him," said the woman seated in the grim shadows of the kitchen nook.

"Good morning." Alice Pepper yawned as she entered the kitchen and flicked on the pendant light over the oak table. "I can see we're going to pick up where we left off last night."

Alice noticed that her friend was still smartly dressed in a black pantsuit with a gold-and-bronze-striped shirt that complemented her brown skin. Probably never made it to bed. Most likely she'd sat here through the night, dozing off and stewing over the betrayal.

And yet, Ruby looked fabulous. Her hair and makeup were impeccable, as always. Her lips were taupe colored with a subtle sheen, and a layer of gold eye shadow highlighted her chocolaty eyes. Even in desperate times, Ruby Milliner maintained her polished appearance.

Alice paused by the table. "Honey, you look fabulous, but I have to ask. Did you get any sleep at all?"

"I won't rest until he's breathed his last stinking breath."

"That's one way to work through it."

"This is not a therapeutic exercise, Alice. I'm going to kill him. A slow, painful death, that's the plan." Ruby turned a puzzle piece in her hand as she stared blankly toward the mountains. "It's not like I didn't warn him. I told him I'd rip him apart if he ever messed around."

"Coffee first." Fastening her robe, Alice caught a fuzzy image of herself in the glass of the wide window. Her cap of gray hair sat flat against her skull, and her face seemed to be all angles—long nose, jutting cheekbones, pointed chin. Add a white kerchief to her jaw and a ball and chain to her six-foot-tall frame and she could have played the ghost of Jacob Marley.

Not that any woman looked her best on a few hours of sleep. Not her fault.

Last night Alice had planned for some solid sleep. Today was her meeting with the mayor, an important chance to plead her case. She'd been winding down around ten p.m. when Ruby had arrived in crisis mode.

Alice yawned. She was running on a half-empty tank, which was not a good look for a woman who was no longer on the sunny side of sixty. "No one should be up this early."

"I never went to sleep," Ruby muttered. That explained why her shiny black locks fell over her shoulders and curled gently at the ends. Or wait, was that a wig? With Ruby, she was rarely sure, unless she was sporting an elaborate hairstyle of twisted braids or sculpted colored hair. As owner of Ruby's House of Wigs, she had hundreds of hairpieces at her disposal. Wigs that transformed her from diva to entrepreneur to hippie mama. Alice often envied Ruby for her variable looks.

"He robbed me of a good night's sleep." Ruby's voice was slightly hoarse. Poor thing. "The thief!"

Alice headed to the counter that housed three methods of coffee-making. Coffeepot, Keurig, or Nespresso?

Definitely a Nespresso morning. Fast and strong.

"So what's the best way to kill someone?" Ruby held up a puzzle piece, as if it held the answer.

Alice let out a weary breath as she filled the water well and started the brewing. "I don't know. A ghost gun? Poison?"

"I hate guns. And poison won't work. I'm too good a cook for anyone to believe I poisoned my husband."

"Debatable," Alice said under her breath, not wanting to engage. Murder was not the usual topic of conversation when Alice kept company with her friends in the kitchen nook that offered a view of the green Willamette Valley below and whitecapped mountains in the distance. Most days they used the table to assemble puzzles as they sipped coffee or iced tea or something stronger. Most days the gals enjoyed conversations meant to crack each other up.

But this morning, Ruby had only one thing on her mind.

"Although they seem to use poison a lot in mystery novels," Ruby went on. "Or maybe I should go with something that involves suffering. He should have time to feel remorse."

"Far be it from me to stop you from killing George. But the plotting will go better with caffeine involved." Alice placed a steaming mug in front of Ruby. The coffee aroma began to work its magic as the second cup filled and Alice considered her day. Ruby needed her support, but there was no way she could miss this morning's meeting with Mayor Tansley Grand. The town council had recently voted in a 10 percent cut to city services, and Alice was ready to fight for her library. Well, the library wasn't actually hers. It was a public library; the most used library facility in the state of Oregon. A wonderful library, and Alice was determined to defend it with her last breath.

When Alice placed a spoon and sugar bowl in front of Ruby, the cell phone sitting there chimed a few times as messages popped onto the screen. "Look at that," Alice said. "It's probably George begging you to forgive him."

Ruby frowned at the screen, then looked back at the puzzle piece in her hand. "Nope. He hasn't responded since last night. Running scared, because he knows I don't get mad. I get even."

Tough talk for a woman who was on the board of West Hazel's women's shelter and a founder of the local animal rescue league. Alice took a deep sip of her espresso shot, loving every note of flavor. A second sip helped her realize that Ruby's was a problem without a quick solution. "Look, honey, I've got a few minutes, and then I'll need to scram for my meeting. But remember all that deep breathing from yoga? Good air in?"

"Yeah, yeah, sure."

"You just keep focusing on the puzzle. It'll keep your mind off things. And I'll be back this afternoon. Promise me you won't make a move to kill George until I get back."

Just then Violet breezed into the kitchen for her morning ginger shot. "Who's killing whom?" she asked. "Oh, Ruby. I thought I heard voices. You're here early."

"I've been here all night, and I'll tell you why." As Ruby explained she'd caught her husband cheating, Violet grew tense, putting up her hands, as if to create a barrier. "I hear you, and I feel your pain. This must be difficult for you, and I'll discuss your options later. However, in this moment I need to be surrounded by positive energy. Parent-teacher conferences today."

"Of course. Don't let me ruin your day." Ruby picked up her cell, which was still chiming with messages.

Alice shot her sister a disapproving look. "A little empathy, please."

"My heart is breaking," Violet said, patting her chest lightly. "But I do have a school to run. So . . . off to work I go."

*It must be nice to let the pain of others roll off so easily*, Alice thought as she watched her sister leave through the garage door. Maybe Violet was lucky to be so obtuse. Alice had always been cursed by compassion for lonely hearts. She wanted the folks around her to be happy, damn it.

"What's with these people?" Ruby scowled at her phone. "I've got a bunch of texts from Imani. George's assistant Nicole keeps asking me to call. And so does my neighbor Tiger. Whom I wouldn't mind calling. Not *the* Tiger, but he's just as hot. What the hell does he want this early in the morning? Everyone wants a call back, and the sun's barely up."

"That is strange," Alice agreed. "Especially Imani." Imani Jones was Ruby's assistant at the wig company. "She knows you don't take calls before ten."

"Everyone's crazy this morning." Ruby planted the phone screen side down on the table and went back to trying puzzle pieces.

"Aren't you going to call them back?"

"Eventually. For now, they'll just have to understand that I'm taking a mental health day. An Ugh-my-husband-is-a-rotten-cheating-scoundrel Day. You can call the shots like that when you own the company."

"You're right." Alice took a seat at the table and cupped her warm mug. "Take some time for yourself. And what have we here?" For the first time she glanced at the puzzle, not an image she recognized. "Did you bring this puzzle?" she asked Ruby.

"No. It was already sitting on the table. And it's a weird one, right? A nice break from all those little white children picking flowers or ice skating in any-white-town, USA."

Alice chuckled. "Oh, honey. We haven't done one of those for a while. But this one is quite unusual. Part graffiti, part drawing of a maid sweeping stuff under a carpet. Actually, a carpet of graffiti."

"I got it for you, Gran," said a voice behind them. It was Alice's granddaughter Taylor, a twenty-two-year-old hipster who was currently squatting in the basement. Tall and lithe with long coppery brown hair, Taylor reminded Alice of herself when she was young. Back in the seventies, Alice had marched with her mother in a huge antiwar protest on the streets of Manhattan. Peace, love, and rock 'n' roll. Simpler times? When you're freckled and fourteen, you view the world through a simpler lens.

"Do you like it, Gran?" Taylor asked as she crossed to the fridge.

"Well, thank you for the gift, dear." Alice knew Taylor couldn't afford it, being behind on her discounted rent. "It's certainly unusual. Where'd you get it?"

"A thrift shop." Taylor leaned into the fridge. "It's a Banksy."

"Oh, right, that graffiti artist," said Alice.

Ruby tapped her chin with a shiny lacquered nail. "Never heard of him, but I kinda like it."

Taylor emerged from the refrigerator with a pie plate half full of quiche. "Is this vegan?"

"It is not," Alice said.

"Whatev." Taylor found a fork and started eating.

Ruby squinted down at the nearly assembled puzzle. "Your Banksy is kind of gritty and rough, isn't he?"

"That's Banksy's style. He's big on messages that have social impact."

"The message being clean your room?" Alice suggested.

"I think it's more a statement on the way the Western world tries to sweep important issues under the carpet. Banksy created this piece in 2006 when AIDS was a crisis. I think he was saying that AIDS was everyone's problem, though much of society tried to ignore it." Taylor shot Alice a probing look. "You need to catch up on your pop art, Gran."

"You're right," Alice agreed. "I'll get on it today." A good librarian stayed current. Always learning.

"Whoa, you guys did this puzzle pretty fast." Taylor stood over them. "I dropped it here just a few hours ago, when I got home and found Ruby sleeping on the table."

"I was meditating," Ruby insisted. Alice wondered what the folks at the senior center would think about Banksy. She suspected Aunt Gildy would be delighted. Alice and her friends often traded puzzles with the senior center. It was a good way for everyone to save money, and it was such a pleasure to deal with Stone Donahue, the manager of the center. Nothing serious, of course, but light encounters with Stone always helped to get the heart pumping faster.

"So if you don't mind me asking, why were you sleeping on the kitchen table last night?" asked Taylor.

"I offered her one of the guest rooms," said Alice.

"I was working through some things." Ruby's doe eyes focused on Taylor. "My George did me dirty. I came home early from a business trip and caught him having an affair."

"What?" Taylor gasped and took a seat at the table. "No! Tell me everything."

As Ruby spun her tale of woe one more time, Alice got up to escape. Taylor was a good listener, and right now Ruby needed to keep venting.

"Will you ever forgive him?" Taylor asked.

"That man has only called me once since I caught him. One call! If that's all he thinks of me, he doesn't want forgiveness. He wants some pain, is what I think."

Alice left them talking about vengeance and slipped off to her suite to shower and dress. That was the beauty of Alice's house on the summit, or Alice's Palace, as her ex had dubbed it when she'd held on to it in the divorce settlement. The old craftsman house on Sunset Hill had been extensively renovated to include a handful of en suite bedrooms in the 1990s. The previous owner, some tech prince who'd fled Silicon Valley for more affordable digs, had remodeled the place with a plan to bring his genius staff up to the Portland area and lodge them here. When those plans hadn't worked out, Alice and Jeff had gotten a good deal on the house.

A good deal that recently had required a second mortgage. Money was tight, but Alice would give up food and water before she'd let this house go.

The dryer fluffed up her hair a bit too much, and now she resembled a fuzzy silver chick. She paused to adjust her light summer jacket over her long black dress. She had chosen the basic black dress with a geometric print jacket to convey just the right combination of professionalism and art appreciation for her meeting. Back in the kitchen she found Taylor and Ruby staring at Ruby's ringing phone.

"The cops are calling Ruby," Taylor reported, pointing to the caller ID.

"The police? West Hazel's finest," Alice said, proudly thinking of Taylor's twin, Madison, who was a rookie cop. "Aren't you going to answer?"

"I can't talk to anyone right now." Ruby handed the phone to Taylor. "You answer."

"I'm good," Taylor said, backing away.

Alice was losing patience. "Someone answer the phone."

"Trust me, you don't want me talking to the cops." Taylor disappeared back down the basement stairs, leaving Alice to worry about her latest illegal antics. Of Alice's twin yin-and-yang granddaughters, Taylor had a well-earned reputation as the hellion.

Fortunately, the ringing had stopped, and Ruby placed her phone back on the table. "Go away," she told the phone as if it were a pesky insect. "If it's so important, you can leave a message."

Just then Alice's cell rang, and she saw that it was a call from Taylor's twin. "It's Madison," she told Ruby. A recent college graduate, Madison was a rookie cop with the West Hazel Police. Alice began the call with: "Honey, I can't talk—"

"Is Ruby Milliner with you?"

"Yes, she's here, dear."

"I figured as much." Madison sounded a bit cold. "Open your door, Gran."

"You can come in, honey."

"I'm here in an official capacity, so I think you need to let me in."

With a dramatic sigh, Alice ended the call and opened the door to find Madison waiting on the porch in her dark uniform pants, Doc Martens boots, and crisp white shirt with departmental regalia—badges and patches and that cold weapon on the hip. Smart and low-key, this girl knew how to get a job done. Unlike her twin, who couldn't hold on to a job. "It lifts my spirit to see you looking so smart in your uniform," Alice told her. "Calm and dedicated. You are exactly what West Hazel needs."

Madison grimaced as she moved past Alice. "She's in the kitchen?"

"That's right." Alice followed behind, wondering why her granddaughter was so pale and stiff this morning. "Licking her wounds. I'm afraid she caught her husband fooling around with another woman last night."

The news didn't seem to penetrate Madison's tight demeanor. "George?"

"That's the lily-livered cheat," Ruby said, lifting her coffee mug. "I was trying to surprise him, seeing as this weekend's our anniversary. I left my beauty convention in Vegas a day early, thinking he'd be happy to see me. The show was supposed to end Tuesday, but I hopped a flight back to Portland last night, all buttered up for my baby. Turned out the surprise was on me when I walked in on some blond floozy chasing my husband through the house. My man, who was buck naked, by the way, except for some weird Renaissance mask."

This seemed to stop Madison in her tracks. "This was last night?"

"Indeed, it was."

"Did you recognize the woman?"

"I couldn't see her face, on account of the mask she was wearing. Some sparkly thing with feathers and rhinestones. And I can't be sure, but I think the blond hair was one of my wigs. And she may have been wearing one of my negligees, too!"

Madison absorbed the information with a careful breath. "This explains a few things."

"Of course, Ruby was so distraught, she came straight here," Alice explained. "It was late—ten or eleven, I think—and we talked for a while. I insisted she stay the night, though I don't think she got any sleep."

"I'm still fired up," Ruby admitted. "At the moment I'm rounding the corner from sorrow to anger and starting down vengeance avenue. Thinking up ways to kill him. You know the song, "Fifty Ways to Kill Your Lover.""

Alice cocked her head to one side. "Not sure that's how the song goes."

"It's not," Madison said, "and you're too late."

Ruby slipped another puzzle piece into place. "Too late for what?"

"I'm sorry, Ruby, but I've been sent to notify you that your husband is dead."

# Chapter Two

"Are you talking about my George?" Ruby looked up from the puzzle. "I don't believe it."

Alice was equally dubious, but then she noticed the taut strain on Madison's face. That was not a mask of calm; Madison was trying to suppress her own freak-out.

"Our patrol officers found him on the bedroom floor," Madison said quietly.

In the loaded pause that followed, Alice and Ruby stared at each other, doubt and dread heavy in the air. The silence was sliced by Ruby's sorrowful wail.

"Oh, Ruby." Alice went to her friend and slipped an arm over her shoulders. "Honey. I'm so, so sorry."

Alice stayed by her friend as Ruby slipped from disbelief—"It couldn't be him!"—to shock. "Oh, no! Oh, no! Oh, no!"

And then the questions began. "Are you sure he's dead? I mean, is he not breathing at all? Maybe it's not even him!"

"One of the paramedics was able to identify him. Turns out he's on George's bowling team. He's really gone."

Ruby took a bunch of napkins and pressed them to her face. "How did it happen?"

"He may have fallen off the exercise bike and hit his head, but that's just one theory. The coroner will do an autopsy, of course." Madison winced. "I might be telling you too much. I've never done this before. I'm so sorry."

"You're doing okay," Alice reassured her. "It's a terrible situation."

"Where is he?" Ruby dashed away tears with the balled-up napkins. "I need to see him. Is he still at the house?"

"He should be." Keeping her gaze trained on Ruby, Madison remained on task but sympathetic. "But I wouldn't advise going over there. You don't want to see—"

"I need to go to him!" Ruby was digging through her handbag, tossing aside a tissue pack, lipstick, a leather case for sunglasses. "Where are my keys? I can't find my keys."

"Ruby." Madison touched her arm. "You're in no shape to drive."

"Then I'll walk. I can walk. I'll run." Ruby's house was only a few blocks away, but the image of her shocked, desperate friend rushing through the streets broke Alice's heart.

"I'll drive," Alice said, grabbing her purse. When she turned to shepherd Ruby out, Taylor stood by the stairs, her round-eyed expression of shock revealing that she'd heard, too. "Are you coming with?"

Without a word, Taylor grabbed the tissue box from the desk and followed to the garage.

"This is not a good idea," Madison called, hurrying after them.

No one answered because everyone understood. Even if it was too late, Ruby had to be there to see for herself the tangible signs of death. Without another word, Madison jumped into the backseat beside her sister.

As Alice started to back the car out of the garage, Ruby dabbed at her eyes with tissues and articulated the gazillion questions in the air. How did George die? A heart attack? A stroke? He wasn't even sick. Yes, he was on beta-blockers and some kind of blood thinner medicine, but he'd never had any big issues. Had the stress of having his affair discovered proven to be too much for his heart? Or maybe he had died in the saddle with Blondie?

"Let's not go there yet," Alice said, turning the last corner onto Ruby's street. Although the road was passable, it was littered with so many emergency vehicles that Alice had to park a few doors down. Their car inched past police cars, an ambulance, a firetruck, and a dark sedan with a cherry light on top. Ruby's charming, cedar-shingled, two-story home with its wide, wooden sitting porch seemed to cower under the strain of strange visitors.

"What are all these people doing at my house?" Ruby asked.

"They're here to process the crime scene and collect the . . . to take George away," Madison answered.

"A crime scene? What crime?" Ruby railed. "I thought he fell off the damn exercise bike."

"Just in case something nefarious happened," Madison said. "I mean, it's just a precaution."

Ruby shook her head in disbelief as the other women huddled around her and ushered her toward the house.

A dusty black station wagon with blacked out windows had been backed into the driveway; its rear doors were open. At first Alice wondered what sort of tools the police might store in the dark recesses, and then it dawned on her that the open compartment was for a corpse.

It was the coroner's wagon. This was real.

Looking quite official in her police uniform, Madison held her hands up to stop them at the front door. "Before you go in, you have to promise to stick near me, and don't touch anything. This is an active crime scene."

"I keep hearing about this crime no one can explain, and it's pissing me off," Ruby said. "What happened to my George?"

"It's procedure. Since he appeared to die alone, we need to investigate to make sure he died of natural causes."

"He died alone!" Ruby sobbed and plucked another tissue from the box in the crook of her arm.

Alice rubbed her friend's back, wishing she could offer true solace. "Ruby, honey, do you want to wait a few minutes and pull yourself together?"

"Nope." Ruby shook her head. "Let's get this over with."

Madison opened the door of the house Ruby had shared with George Byrd for the past few years and pointed the way. "Just stick with me, please."

Ruby and Alice pressed toward Taylor, who was closest to the door. But as Taylor stepped over the threshold, she paused, looked up the staircase, and pressed her hands to her cheeks.

"I can't do it." Taylor backed out, bumping into Ruby.

"Whoa, girl." Ruby braced herself against the doorjamb. "You're about to knock the stuffing out of me."

Alice placed a hand on her granddaughter's shoulder. "What's wrong?"

"I can't go in there. I keep thinking of George. What if his spirit is lingering? Sometimes people linger. Sometimes they're really pissed." Taylor shivered in the summer sunlight. "It's too creepy."

"It's just George," Ruby said. "And from what they're telling me, if he's dead and gone, he's not going to say boo to you now."

Taylor crossed her arms. "I can't. I just can't do it."

"So stay out here." Madison led the way inside, muttering under her breath: "It doesn't always have to be about you."

"I can't help how I feel," Taylor protested.

"Of course, honey," Alice said, guiding Ruby past Taylor. "You just wait here."

"Okay," Taylor said. "But I might wait across the street. Or down the block."

As if a few yards would be a barrier to a rogue spirit? Alice didn't understand the mystical world Violet and Taylor inhabited. Too many invisible elements, psychic portals, and porous veils to parallel worlds.

"Believe me, George the ghost would not venture too far from the couch and TV." Ruby reached back to hand Taylor the tissue box. Then she smoothed the collar of her blouse and set her chin. "Let's do this."

"She's so immature," Madison muttered under her breath as Alice stepped into the front entryway. Although Alice tended to tamp down the tension between the twin girls, she was immediately distracted by the fleet of law enforcement that had taken over Ruby's house. Everyone was wearing paper booties and gloves, which Madison was applying to her own boots and hands. One tech spread black dust on surfaces, having made a hell of a mess on the lavender wall along the stairs. A photographer was snapping shots on his way up the stairs, which curved up from the vestibule and split right and left, providing a balconied hallway to the upstairs rooms.

"Do you want to go wait in the kitchen?" Madison asked. "Detective Bedrosian will be here soon, and you can talk to him. He's just finishing up at another crime scene."

"I want to see my George." Ruby's doe eyes gazed up the staircase. "Is he still up there?"

"I think so." Madison had to hop to keep her balance as she pulled on a blue shoe cover. "But you can't—"

Ruby was already climbing the stairs.

"—go up . . . Ruby, wait!" Madison grabbed a pair of booties and followed Ruby up. "You need to cover your shoes."

Too late. Ruby was near the top, moving like a fashion model in her black wedge sandals.

Alice let out a sigh as she watched their ascent. She'd seen dead bodies before—her parents' mortal shells, and a few funeral home displays that were waxy and disheartening. If George had been in bad shape, Ruby might get a look at something she couldn't unsee.

Talk about being haunted.

But right now, Ruby needed a bit of protection from her own curiosity. Resolute, Alice slipped on a pair of booties from the basket by the door. Slippery little devils. Stepping cautiously, she hiked up her dress and trudged up the stairs. The hub of activity was through the main bedroom, in a wide hallway outside the walk-in closets. Madison detained Ruby at the edge of the scene, where three workers were gathered near the exercise bike. At least Ruby was calmer now, though she continued to rattle off questions and her glazed eyes suggested that shock had set in.

Moving closer, Alice overheard the workers near the bike discussing the bloodstains on the carpet there. A dark puddle that had set into a stain, a little tacky in the darkest region. "Minimal splatter," someone said. Alice figured that was a peaceful sign. In mystery novels, splatter was usually a sign of violent action.

Had Ruby seen the blood? She hoped the workers were blocking her view. Was that where George had fallen? It was near the bike. And where was George?

Fortunately, his body wasn't in sight.

Over at the bedside, the tech got a shot of a discarded blond wig on the floor, then photographed a satiny black mask with rhinestones and peacock feathers left on the edge of the bed. Leftovers from last night's tryst, based on what Ruby had witnessed. As soon as they were photographed, another worker lifted them with long tongs and bagged them. Evidence of some role-playing, for sure. Foul play? Probably not.

Over by the closet entrance, Alice spotted a long black bag on the white carpet. The bag was oblong and uneven, as if it contained snowboarding equipment. A body bag.

She'd found George.

"Wait!" Ruby's voice was louder now. "What's that stain on my white carpet?" As she moved closer to the huddle of investigators, one woman lifted her head and stood up straight.

"Who are you and what are you doing in my crime scene?" The middle-aged gal was of solid build, and the set of her shoulders indicated she was not someone you'd want to tangle with. Dressed in jeans and a western shirt with braiding and pearlized snaps, she looked like she might have just left a rodeo, though her air of authority made it clear that she owned this space.

"This is my house, and George is my husband," Ruby said, stepping forward and leaning down to reach for a fat blond braid—a hairpiece—that lay on the rug.

"Don't touch anything!" The western gal surged forward to block Ruby's motion.

"But it's my hairpiece. And this is my house."

"Honey"—Alice winced at the braid on the floor—"you don't really want that thing back now, do you?"

"Actually, I don't. But it's mine," Ruby insisted.

Western Gal heaved a sigh. "Who let this woman in?"

"She's with me, Jane," explained Madison. "This is Ruby Milliner. She's the wife of the deceased."

"Yeah, I got that the first time, but she shouldn't be in here." Jane pressed her iPad to her chest and straightened to face Ruby. "Listen, Ruby. I'm Dr. Jane McCallister, the county coroner. I'm sorry for your loss, ma'am. This is a difficult time for you. But you really don't want to be here. Why don't you wait downstairs while we finish up?"

"I can't. I need to see him."

"Not a good idea. This is not how you want to remember him, and he's on his way out of here," Jane said, turning away. "That's your cue, Miguel."

Two of the forensic guys scrambled to lift the body bag onto a stretcher.

Dr. Jane barked more orders as they lifted George's body and headed toward the door. "After you transport the deceased to the morgue, make sure you do one more thorough search for hair and fibers."

"No, no, wait!" Ruby insisted. "George can't go. I have to see him. I have to know. Maybe it's not even him. You might have some other poor stiff in that body bag."

"I get it, Ruby. You need to know," Alice said, trying to think of a quick way to dissuade her friend. The blood-stains on the carpet suggested that the body might be a gruesome sight. "We could go identify him later. I'll go with you." She took Ruby's hand. "This is going to be traumatic for you. I just don't think you want to see him this way right now."

"But I have to know if it's him. I need to know now. Maybe my George isn't dead."

"I can assure you, he's gone," the coroner said. "We already got an ID from one of our medics, who was acquainted with the deceased."

"So he's been identified, but Ruby needs to see for herself," Alice said. "Dr. Jane, do you have a photo that Ruby could see? Something to help her know that George is truly . . . resting in peace?"

"I think we got that." Jane lifted her iPad and started scrolling through. "Where's Photoshop when you need it." She frowned, scrolled on, and then nodded. "Here we go. Here's your husband, Ruby."

Alice leaned closer to Ruby, hand on her shoulder, for a look at the screen.

And there was George Byrd. The image showed one side of his face, which, thank goodness, was not bloodied. Although his skin looked pale, his eyes were closed, almost peaceful.

Ruby seemed to melt beneath her palm, deflating. "That's my George."

For a moment, the room went silent. Even the forensic techs paused, respectful and somber.

"I'm sorry for your loss," Jane said.

"Oh, George," Ruby spoke softly. "What happened to you?" She glanced up at the coroner. "What happened to him?"

"That's what we're here to find out." Dr. Jane slipped her iPad into a fringed leather pouch she wore slung over one shoulder. "And now, you need to let me do my job. Miguel? Are we about done here?"

"Yes, Doc."

"Did he kill himself?" Ruby pressed her palms to her cheeks. "Oh, Lordy! The guilt drove him to kill himself! Maybe I was too hard on him."

"Well, even if you were, he didn't commit suicide. He suffered head trauma, and his wounds were not self-inflicted."

"Maybe he hit his head from falling off the exercise bike," Alice suggested. "An accident."

Jane shook her head. "This carpet would have had a softer impact than the wounds indicate, and a fall like that wouldn't affect this portion of his head. George suffered multiple contusions. Blunt force trauma to the back of the head."

Alice stared at the exercise bike, trying to imagine a scenario in which George would have hurt the back of his head. Even if he had fallen back and hit his head on the handlebars, he would have suffered one wound, not many.

"Dr. Jane, help us out here," Alice said, even as the answer came barreling toward her.

Blunt force trauma. Back of the head.

Her heart thudded at the realization, but she needed to hear it. "Ruby won't rest until she has a better idea of what happened to her husband."

"I need to do a thorough autopsy. Blood work. His lips are awfully blue." Jane squeezed one pearlized snap on her shirt, spelling it out slowly, clearly. "Most likely, he died of head trauma, and the wounds were not self-inflicted."

"What do you mean?" Ruby squinted, unable to comprehend.

"You're saying that he was murdered," Alice confirmed.

Dr. Jane gave a nod. "As of now, this is a homicide investigation."

# Chapter Three

Murder.

The idea of someone killing George—bumbling, fun-loving, thigh-slapping George—was difficult for Alice to grasp as she corralled Ruby downstairs and found her a seat at the kitchen table. The room seemed to be fairly safe from foraging investigators and fingerprint dust. Madison explained that the kitchen and dining room seemed to be untouched by last night's occupants and thus had been left alone.

Ruby had sobbed all the way down the stairs. Poor thing. Even with George's body sealed in the black bag, the reality of his death had become vivid in that room upstairs.

"I can't believe someone killed my George," Ruby said in a warbling voice. "He was a good man, always cheerful. Always trying to make people smile."

"Maybe it was an accident," Alice suggested as she sat on a white leather chair. Ruby's square-backed chairs matched perfectly with the gray-veined Carrera marble table, a look Alice could never pull off in her casual kitchen. Ruby possessed an exquisite sense of fashion and design. "Classy,"

Alice's mother Clara used to say in her brassy Queens accent.

At the center of the white marble sat a shiny black bowl of fragrant lemons, and a fat envelope with an old-time illustration. It took Alice a moment to recognize it as a dress pattern.

"What's this?" Alice asked. "A Simplicity pattern? Brings me right back to our youth." As a kid, Ruby had followed in the tracks of her seamstress mother and sewn many a dress on the trusty Singer. Lovely creations in colorful fabric and just the right amount of lace or satin trim. Alice, in her worn hand-me-down dresses, had envied her so. By high school, Ruby had taken Alice under her wing, instructing Alice on the purchase of Butterick patterns and fabric (lots of fabric) so that her friend could sew dresses that fit Alice's ever-growing beanpole figure.

That had been back in grade school, younger days, simpler times. They'd been neighbors back in Queens Village, New York. Best friends through their college years. After that, their paths had meandered, sometimes intersecting only once every few years. Distant but close, until Ruby's husband Darnell had passed away some ten years ago, and Alice had enticed her friend to get out of New York and move to Oregon. Ruby had taken a buyer's job with a West Coast retailer, which had led her to specialize in hats and accessories. Which had led her to the realization that there was a real need for a full-service retailer of wigs and hairpieces for women of color. And so Ruby's House of Wigs had been born. Hard work, experience, insight, and a little bit of luck had brought Ruby success.

"Would you look at that empire waist?" Glad for the distraction, Alice pointed to the sketch of the dress on the pattern. "Hard to find a dress that flattering in the frocks on the store racks these days."

"I got that for Ada," Ruby said, mentioning her oldest daughter. "You know she's pregnant again."

"She is? Congratulations. You're going to be a grand-mother yet again."

"My fourth. Ada was complaining that she couldn't find anything decent to wear to the wedding. I was going to whip that up for her, but she found something in the meantime."

"The wedding." Alice pressed a palm to her chest. "You can't possibly host after this."

"I'm not throwing the wedding. Just putting up some family is all. And hosting a small rehearsal dinner." Nothing was small in Rubyland, but Alice wasn't going to argue. Not with the crushed expression on her friend's face as she glanced at the two arched openings, one lead-ing to the dining room, where wedding gifts were neatly set on display, and the other showing a fraction of the ac-tivity in the living room. "Of course, no one will want to step foot in here after they find out. Forget about having pizza parties and kids sleeping on the floor. My little granddaughter was always fascinated by the exercise bike upstairs. And now I . . . I won't be able to let her go near it." She pressed a fist to her lips and shook her head. "What am I going to do?"

Alice took Ruby's hand in hers and looked into her doe-like brown eyes. "You're going to get through this, honey. One step at a time."

Ruby closed her eyes and let out a shaky breath. "Thank you for being here. You're a good friend."

"Of course, I'll be here." The promise reminded Alice that she was supposed to be in downtown West Hazel in the next hour, having breakfast with the mayor. She hated to cancel her fund-raising plea to Tansley Grand, but for now, this was where she needed to be.

A tapping noise behind Alice startled her to swing around. A head popped into view at the kitchen door, evoking dual gasps from Alice and Ruby.

Taylor.

"Let me in," she called.

"This girl is shaving years off my life," Alice muttered as she rose and unbolted the door. "Feeling better?"

Taylor splayed her palms and cautiously pushed through the air around her. "The energy is still unstable, but non-threatening."

"What a relief." Alice gestured toward the table. "Come, sit with Ruby. I need to make a call."

"Of course." Taylor sat down and showered Ruby with emotive pouts. "How you holding up, Ms. Rooblebee?" Taylor's silliness could be annoying at times, but it was genuine, and sometimes that was the perfect antidote.

"Been better, honey."

As they chatted quietly, Alice went into the belly of the beast, crossing through the living room to find the quiet of Ruby's office, a small room on the first floor. Relieved to find it in perfect order, she paced around the white faux fur rug and went to the window behind Ruby's glass desk, where her laptops lay closed. The room was neat as a pin.

Outside the window, the small expanse of green lawn filled her view as she called the mayor's office and suggested a late lunch instead of breakfast. Tansley couldn't take her call, but her assistant agreed to the change. "Her schedule is falling apart, but that should work," said Cassidy.

Alice hung up and called the library, checking in with

Beto, who managed the phones and checkout desk. "All good here," Beto reported. "Will we see you soon?"

"Not until after lunch," Alice said, thanking him before hanging up. At least her library was one place that wasn't in chaos this morning.

Remaining at the window for a beat, Alice noted that Ruby's backyard was smaller than she remembered, and from the pristine grass and patio furniture draped in customized covers, it seemed rarely used. The yard backed up to acres of public space, a city park with soccer fields and trails, which George had used when he wanted to go for a run outside. Sometimes he'd jogged past Alice when she was on one of her walks.

But she wouldn't be running into George anymore.

A thump from above made her scoff. George always had to have the last word. But of course, it was just the folks collecting evidence. She went upstairs to . . . well, honestly, she was curious and she knew Ruby was in Taylor's capable hands. In the primary bedroom, the cowgirl coroner was missing, probably on to her next job duty. The two remaining techs, thirtyish male and forty-something woman in a baggy jumpsuit, were deep in conversation.

"Actually, I thought the mask thing was kind of classy," the woman said. "Did you see the sparkle on her mask?"

"And what's with the wigs?" he asked.

"You can become anyone you want. Little Gretel in the woods, or Marie Antoinette." The gal held up the bag containing the rhinestone mask and declared: "Let them eat cake!"

"You know Marie Antoinette didn't exactly say that?" he said.

"It's part of the fantasy. You ever dress up for sex, Dombrowski?"

He shined a flashlight under the bed, then shot her a bland look. "I find the opposite state of dress is more effective for that."

She took a moment to think, then nodded. "Buck naked?"

He shined the light onto his face before cutting it off. "Eyes up here."

Alice looked away and smiled as the two technicians chuckled. They seemed unaware or unconcerned about her presence in the room, and she was happy to stay and observe.

Dombrowski's grin faded as he scanned the room. "What I don't see is a heavy, loose object that could have been used to clock him. They've got no free weights. No heavy lamps or chairs. Nothing you could grab on to and take a swing."

"Yeah, I don't see any possible weapons in sight. And we know the victim didn't smack his head on the exercise bike. Even if he was facing the other way, the angles are all wrong."

"Another unsolved mystery."

"You know," she said, "sometimes the perp takes the weapon home. Like a souvenir. Or if it belonged to them. Like the butt of a gun."

"That would've done it," Dombrowski agreed. "A dull, heavy object."

The coroner's words arose in Alice's mind as she scanned the landscape of the room: *"Blunt force trauma. Back of the head."*

The techs were correct. Ruby's aversion to clutter and love of clean lines left the room quite barren. What had been used to hit George?

Alice moved on to the room next door, which was set up

as an office. A very messy one, with scattered papers, sticky notes, take-out containers, and dirty coffee mugs covering most of the surfaces. The room reflected George's eclectic sense of organization. Alice had worked with him in his capacity as a city administrator, and she'd had a taste of his administrative dysfunction. "Good thing I'm a numbers guy," he would say, when someone complained about a missed meeting or an unanswered e-mail.

Back in the kitchen, Ruby was still talking with Taylor, with no sign of the detective yet. Alice noticed the sun beaming in the dining room window and stepped in for a bit of a lift. She was immediately reminded of the upcoming wedding of Ruby's daughter Celeste to Jamal Carter. Ruby had mentioned setting up a display of the wedding gifts for guests to peruse during the rehearsal dinner held here. A dinner that Alice, with her cooking expertise, had agreed to cater.

Alice looked toward the kitchen, muttering, "That'll be creepy."

In the dining room, the table and buffet and two card tables were festooned with linen tablecloths and covered with wedding gifts. Oversized or petite, shiny or burnished, outlandish or practical. The array of fine crystal, silver, china, and appliances had all the charm of a high-end shop.

Alice strolled from one exhibit to the next, as if touring a fine arts museum. She passed bone china with a star in the center, a cappuccino maker, a Waterford crystal vase, a set of black cutlery. There were photos of trips to wine country, and activities in Hawaii, where the happy couple planned to honeymoon.

"You know, Ruby," she called toward the kitchen, "you really outdid yourself with this display. Nordstrom needs you desperately."

"Funny, because George said it made him feel like he was living in a department store," Ruby called back.

"It's tastefully done."

At the base of each gift was a card indicating who provided it.

*Limoges place settings from Rhianna Nettles, Mr. and Mrs. Lionel Benjamin, and Corey Jefferson.*

*Crystal vase from Tansley Grand.* The cut grooves in the crystal caught the light from the windows. A lovely gift from their town mayor.

*Marble cake stand from Darnetta Green.* Celeste did enjoy baking.

*Brass candlestick holders from DeeDee D'oria.*

"I hope they have a sizable fireplace." Where else would you put such a large piece? The candlestick holder was enormous, maybe two feet tall, but the warm brass was decorated with green rings—marble, perhaps.

Grotesquely large, but Alice sort of liked it. Had Celeste and Jamal actually chosen this for their bridal registry? Alice picked it up with a grunt. It was heavy, all right, and sort of odd that there was only one.

She replaced it on the table and looked back at the card.

"Candlestick holders," she said aloud as Madison appeared in the doorway.

"Gran, Detective Bedrosian is here, and—"

"That's it." Alice picked up the bronze piece and handed it to her granddaughter. "It's got heft, it's a blunt object, and its mate is missing."

Madison eyed the object in confusion. "What are you talking about?"

"I think the killer used the missing candlestick holder to hit George. You're holding a copy of the murder weapon."

# Chapter Four

"This thing must weigh ten pounds." Madison's eyes opened wide as she tested the bronze piece in her hands, giving it a slight swing. "And the mate is missing?"

"I don't see it in this room," Alice said.

"Let's ask Ruby." Madison was already ducking into the kitchen.

Alice gave a nod as she folded her arms in satisfaction. Madison would perform due diligence, but as far as Alice was concerned, this was it. She just had a feeling, not unlike that tingle when you land on your feet a bit too hard. The missing mate had been the weapon.

It didn't take Madison long to confirm that the candlestick holders had arrived as a matching set. The techs thought the size and weight might be a match, based on preliminary measurements.

"It's the right size," said Dombrowski, who had come down to the kitchen with his cohort, Gina. "I just wish we could find the other one, which is bound to have traces of blood or hair if it was used in the battery."

"Good chance the attacker took it with him," said Gina. "We've gone through the trash, the house, the yard, the bushes, and whatnot. Nothing. No cast-off heavy objects."

"Did you check the garage, too?" Bedrosian asked. The shirt-and-tie detective with salt-and-pepper hair and dark eyes had arrived abruptly and jumped into the situation without introduction. A bit rude by Alice's standards. "Maybe a tool."

"The garage was clean," Dombrowski said. "I couldn't even find a screwdriver."

"My George was not a handyman," said Ruby, filling a glass with water from the fridge dispenser.

"What are you doing?" the detective demanded of Ruby.

She held up the glass, emphasizing the obvious. "This is my home."

"But it's a crime scene." Lines creased his forehead as he barked at Madison. "Didn't you explain it to her?"

"She's mindful of the investigation," Madison said. "But she does live here."

Detective Bedrosian let out a groan as he raked back his hair. "This is not a good day."

"No kidding," Alice said. When she stepped up to the detective, she towered over him. Not something she usually enjoyed, but in moments like this it worked for her. "So maybe we should start over. This is Ruby Milliner, owner of this home, and wife to the recently deceased. So far, this has been a very bad day for Ruby. But despite her loss, she has waited here patiently to speak with you because she wants to help your investigation."

Bedrosian squared his jaw, looking from Ruby to Alice. "And who are you?"

"Alice Pepper." She extended her hand, shaming him into a handshake. "Ruby's good friend and neighbor."

"And she's the director of the West Hazel Library," Taylor offered. "And she figured out the missing candlestick thingy, which could be important to your case, right?"

As if on cue, Dombrowski held up the candlestick holder, and all eyes turned toward the detective, who seemed hard-pressed to emit a response from his tight lips.

"It could be a clue," Madison said. "We're sending it to the morgue for further analysis."

"There's your answer," Bedrosian said. "Looks like Officer Denham has the situation in hand."

Alice didn't miss the sarcasm in his tone. She'd had no idea that Madison worked under such a sourpuss detective.

Still, relief suffused the air. Taylor gave her sister a grin, a rare moment of cooperation between sisters. The two technicians packed up the last of their evidence and started to load the vehicle. Ruby got to sip her water. Small victories.

"All right, ladies. Let's talk now." Bedrosian leaned against the kitchen counter. As if he were going to whip up a meal for them. His questions were simple at first. Alice had to stop herself from jumping in and answering for her friend, who was still reeling from the shock. Ruby was asked about a home security system (which they didn't have) and the whereabouts of George's phone, which was missing.

When they started discussing the previous night, Ruby became more animated.

"So when you walked in to discover your husband engaged in an affair, you were angry," the detective said.

"Of course! Wouldn't you be?"

"Did you confront him?" Bedrosian asked. "Did you two argue?"

"Well, sure, if you could call it that. I screamed something at Blondie and she went running up the stairs. George told me I was home early, like it was my fault. I told him to pack a bag and get out. But he was all, 'I'm the man' and 'This is my house, too.' And all the time we were yelling, Blondie was upstairs wailing like a baby. Drove us both nuts. So I got in my car and hightailed it out of here."

Madison was taking notes in a black memo book. "What time was that, and where did you go?"

"She came over to my house sometime after ten, and she stayed through the night." Alice rubbed Ruby's shoulder as she volunteered the information. She didn't like the way the detective was pressing Ruby. "I'm your alibi, honey. Not that you need one. Madison's just doing her job."

"Gran, please." Madison tipped her head toward the boss. "Officer Denham."

"Sorry, Officer." Alice didn't want to undermine her granddaughter's authority.

"I'd like to hear more about the argument," Bedrosian said. "Were threats made?"

"No. He only threatened to keep the house if I divorced him."

"I meant did you threaten him?" asked Bedrosian. "Did you strike him? Slap him?"

"No, Detective. George and I, we didn't have an abusive relationship."

"But there were threats," Madison interrupted. "You were threatening to kill him."

"That was nothing." Ruby gave a wave of dismissal. "I wanted to get even, wanted to hurt him the way he'd hurt me."

"Which is a normal response in your situation," Alice

said, trying to protect her friend. Ruby was saying too much, giving information the police could misconstrue.

"I know what you're thinking, but I didn't hurt him." Tears gleamed in Ruby's brown eyes. "You can't blame me."

*They can, and they will.* Alice squeezed Ruby's shoulder.

"When I left, that blond floozy was still here." Ruby swiped at her cheeks. "She's the one you want to talk to. She's the one who killed my George."

"We're not accusing you, Ruby," Madison said gently. "We're just trying to understand what happened."

"We're almost done here," Bedrosian said. "Tell me, Ruby, who else saw this mystery woman? The one wearing your wigs and nighty?"

Alice didn't like the way he said "nighty," as if it were some lurid sin to possess a sexy nightgown.

"Nobody else was here," Ruby said indignantly. "And believe me, she was no mystery."

"Maybe one of the neighbors saw this woman entering the house," Alice suggested.

"We can canvass the neighborhood," Madison said. "Check and see who has doorbell cameras."

Bedrosian nodded. "These days, very few things go unseen." He turned to Ruby. "In the meantime, do you have someplace to stay until we complete the crime scene analysis? We like to maintain the scene for forty-eight hours, but the real point is, you don't want to be here, alone, at this time."

It was one of the first human statements the man had made.

"She can stay with me," Alice offered. "I have an extra guest room." Actually, Alice had five en suite rooms in the large house that had been renovated and furnished to hold a small tech company fleeing Silicon Valley in 2008. Her ex, Jeff, called the house a white elephant, and never ceased to point out how impractical it was for a woman flying solo. Still, Alice loved the place.

Ruby was nodding. "I'll go with Alice."

"Good." The detective went over to the kitchen window, peered outside, and then gave a nod. "We'll be in touch. Don't leave town."

As he left the kitchen, Alice turned her annoyance on Madison. "Don't leave town? He's got to be kidding. Ruby hasn't broken any laws."

"It's cautionary," Madison said. "Just don't leave Portland, okay?"

"How can I leave when I'm hosting a bridal party and family next week?" Ruby rose from the table and pulled on the cuffs of her jacket, looking crisp and professional once again. "And don't tell me I have to cancel the wedding."

"That's up to the bride and groom," Alice said.

"But nobody's going to want to be hanging out here." Taylor rubbed her arms, as if to ward off stray spirits.

Alice wasn't big on woo-woo, but she had to agree. A murder scene did not make a festive home. "We'll talk about it later," Alice said as the group began to file out of the kitchen and through a living room altered by crime scene markers and dust.

An odd sense of disorientation plagued Alice as she followed the other women and paused at the dark cherry-wood newel post layered in white powder.

Had a murder really happened?

Not here in West Hazel. Not George, the man who loved to laugh. People liked him.

Well, most people. Alice herself had gone toe to toe with him a few times over budget disputes. Library funding was not high on George's list of fiscal priorities. But just because the guy kept a tight hold on the town's treasury didn't mean he deserved to die.

And if he had been killed, who would the most likely suspect be?

The wife, of course. Her good friend Ruby.

# Chapter Five

"I confess, I'm a bit rattled," Mayor Tansley Grand said as the server headed off with their orders.

"Same here," Alice admitted. Amid the turmoil of the morning, it was hard to appreciate their quiet table in the umbrellaed shade of the outdoor veranda at Andre's Bistro. Lunch seemed like a frivolous pleasure when her friend needed her support. Still, she was here on a mission. Her library, the budget cut, her appeal to the mayor. Alice had met with the library board last night, and the members had agreed that she should make this appeal. "Alice," the board president, Will Chen, had told her, "you are our only line of defense."

No pressure. At least the mayor was a reasonable person.

With her gold-highlighted brown hair swept back and her lipstick gleaming, this confident woman was a far cry from young Tammy, the shy tween who'd spent her lunch hour in the school library years ago when Alice had brought the bookmobile to the junior high. But today, Tansley's usual brightness was dulled down to a low setting. "Thanks for bumping our appointment back a bit. Have you heard the bad news? About George Byrd?"

"I have. His wife, Ruby, is a friend, my best friend. I just left her at my house. She's calling her kids and George's family to let them know."

"His wife . . . of course. I didn't connect the dots that you knew Ruby. How's she doing?"

"As you'd expect. We're all in shock."

"Please, give Ruby my sympathies. I only got the news in an official capacity. Chief Cushman called to let me know there'd been a suspicious death. Then when I learned it was someone in the city administration, well, you can imagine the mad security speculations that went on."

"Does the chief think this is an attack on our town leaders?" Alice hadn't considered widespread ramifications.

"It doesn't seem that way. Unfortunately, the chief just left for a month-long vacation. And our crime squad is lacking in experience and . . ." The mayor's voice dropped off, and she opened her purse.

"Bad timing for our meeting, I know."

Tansley frowned down at her phone. "I'm so sorry. My office is calling." She put the phone to her ear and gave an agitated sigh. "You know I'm in a meeting."

Alice had no choice but to listen. But as the bad news seemed to trickle in, Alice felt that her time to plead for her library was trickling away. Her library, her people, her community . . . the whole ball of wax was in jeopardy.

But the mayor was in a pickle at the moment. A sudden death. A possible security threat. Snowballing from one emergency to the next, Tansley wouldn't have time to hear about a pesky matter like library funding.

"They *what*? Does the chief know?" She put a hand over her eyes. "All right, tell the police I'll be there in ten minutes."

Alice's heart sank. Their lunch was over. Her window was closing.

"Wait, what? I can't talk to the police here. It will create a public spectacle." Tansley put her napkin on the silver charger.

Under the table, Alice squeezed the hem of the linen tablecloth, willing the mayor to stay.

"Call them off," Tansley said, her voice taut with stress. "Tell them that I—"

"It's too late," Alice interrupted. At the steps to the veranda stood two figures in dark police uniforms. "They're here."

"Never mind." Tansley ended the call and cast a glance at the cops. "The optics of this are so bad. Half the people in this restaurant will think I'm being arrested, while the other half will want to run for their lives."

Alice was already on her feet, straightening her dress. "I've got this. Just don't turn away my Almond Chicken Salad."

Trying to exude poise and ease, Alice wove through the outdoor tables and made her way to the two cops standing at the entrance. As she drew closer, she recognized one officer to be her granddaughter, and the other to be Adam Lang, a doughy, thirtyish man who, in her estimation, really just counted as half a cop. He'd earned his lazy, irresponsible reputation the day she'd seen a patrol car knock over a large pot of plants at the curb in front of Tatiana's Flower Shop. When the car had started to drive away, Alice had dashed into the street and created such a commotion, the driver had to stop.

The driver, Officer Adam Lang, had claimed he hadn't seen the flowerpot. Didn't have his glasses on.

"Well, then it's a miracle you didn't run over a child," Alice had scolded him. She'd insisted he set the heavy pot upright, apologize to the folks in the flower shop, and borrow a broom to sweep up. Officer Lang hadn't been pleased, but he wasn't foolish enough to cross her.

Now, he had a stern frown on his face as he saw her approach. Madison, who was talking with the hostess, seemed surprised.

"Gran, I thought you'd be home with Ruby. We're—"

"You're here to interview the mayor, I know, but a public venue is no place for a sensitive investigation." Alice turned to the hostess, a smiley moppet who never seemed to have a care in the world. "Courtney, can we use the small upstairs room for a half hour or so?" Without waiting for an answer, Alice added, "If you want to escort these officers up there, Mayor Grand and I will meet you momentarily."

"Well, sure," Courtney agreed.

Back at the table, Tansley could barely believe the plan. "You headed off the cavalry!"

Alice nodded. "Cut them off at the pass."

"I'm eternally grateful," Tansley said, gathering her things. "What about our food?"

"You go on upstairs. I'll have it brought up for us." Alice moved quickly, not wanting to miss a minute of the interview. It wasn't often that a person could get an inside view of this sort of thing. And an inside scoop might help her better understand the circumstances of George's death.

By the time Alice got upstairs, Madison was just setting up her phone to record the interview. Taking a seat at a table a few yards back, Alice tried to give the vibe of supportive associate, rather than curious crime solver.

When asked to describe George Byrd's role in city government, Tansley painted George as an engaged city leader, a valued member of the team. Blah-blah, blah-blah. Nothing new there, but at least it gave Alice time to eat her lunch as she was starving, and Andre's chicken salad was divine, as usual. Listening to Tansley talk, Alice was reminded of how fortunate West Hazel was to have such a solid, thoughtful person serving their town. Alice liked their mayor, liked working with her, liked Tansley's backstory of a teacher and mother who reached the age of fifty, became fed up with PTA and local government, ran for office and won.

Speaking about George, Tansley went out of her way to give him credit for helping to crack a difficult case when the town had suffered a rash of home burglaries. When Tansley mentioned the Cola Bandits, Alice saw the officers nod.

Everyone in town was aware of the bandits who'd robbed the homes of wealthy residents, pilfering golf clubs, jewelry, and cash, and always leaving an empty can of cola at the scene. Cocky thieves, but not clever. When local detectives had struggled to identify the thieves, George, in his capacity as town comptroller, had released the funding to hire an outside consultant, a DNA-based forensic lab.

"George deserves much credit for finding the Cola Bandits," said Tansley. "The investigator he hired was able to match DNA from the cola can to one of the young perpetrators, who'd engaged in an ancestry search. We found our two thieves, thanks to George."

"And the DNA research firm," said Madison. "What was the name of it?"

"Something with the word 'eye' in it. As in eyeball. Eyedentify, I think."

"Yeah, well, we could've found the perps ourselves if we had that technical DNA equipment." Officer Lang sounded a bit resentful of the high-tech lab. He didn't seem to realize that small-town police departments did not possess high tech resources.

"Do you know of anyone who'd want to hurt George?" Madison asked. "Any professional threats?"

"Nothing that I can think of." The mayor smoothed down the lapel of her jacket. "You know, that's not how we roll in West Hazel."

"How about his financial stability?" asked Madison. "Do you know if George Byrd was in any financial trouble?"

The question hung in the air for a moment, capturing Alice's attention. Financial issues . . . an unpaid debt . . . maybe a gambling debt. Those were issues that could get a man killed. Had George been a gambler? A secret risk-taker?

"Nothing that I could speak of," the mayor finally said.

What a nonanswer.

This was something; Alice was sure of it.

# Chapter Six

By the time the questions petered out, both Alice and Tansley had to return to their respective places of work.

"I had your salad wrapped to go," Alice told Tansley. "Let me walk with you to city hall. I'm headed that way." True, the library was a few blocks from there, but Alice figured it would give her more time to plead her case.

The minutes of possible persuasion were ticking away.

Alice wasted no time, broaching the subject as soon as they descended the steps from Andre's patio. "Can we talk about the budget cuts, and how harmful it will be to our folks trying to use library services?" They passed the Sweet and Savory Ice Cream Shop, where a line had formed to sample the latest flavors mixing blueberries and sage, strawberry and bacon, or bourbon and buttered pecan into exotic ice creams. Alice waved to a few faces she recognized, a few senior citizens and a mother wrangling three kiddos. These were the people she served, the people who would suffer from budget cuts.

"It kills me to imagine what we might have to do," Alice confided in Tansley. "Cut down hours. Cancel community events. We'd have to let staff go, Tansley. Layoffs. Hurt people in their pocketbooks. Not to mention the programs that will be cut. We'll defund the knitting club or the geek group. Cut children's story hour, or one of the farm outreach programs. The children do love it when we have a goat or lamb visit."

"Alice, I'm sorry. I wasn't a fan of the budget, but I was overruled."

"It was George, wasn't it? I know the budget negotiations are closed door sessions—a product of the entire city council—but this budget is so anticrime heavy, it's got to be the baby of either George or Chief Cushman."

"Well, it wasn't the chief's brainchild," Tansley admitted.

They paused in front of the magnificent outdoor displays of Tatiana's Flower Shop. Tiered shelves of lilacs, yellow daffodils, red, orange, and purple tulips, and more exotic flowers formed bursts of glorious colors. Such a bright palette usually lifted Alice's spirits. Usually.

"Not to speak ill of the dead," Alice said, "but George really botched this budget."

"I think he was trying to recapture some of the glory of the heroic gesture of the Cola Bandits' arrest."

Alice shook her head. "He did have a hard time letting that go. You hire a firm to do DNA analysis, and suddenly you're a star."

"But it turned out to be a good idea in that case. A lot of folks felt menaced by the Cola Bandits, and George's intervention put an end to those thefts. That DNA firm was money well spent." Tansley nodded, as if trying to convince herself.

"But it's not the sort of crime-solving technology West Hazel needs on a regular basis," Alice said.

"I don't think it is. But George didn't agree. His new

budget diverted funds from essential services, like the library, and funneled money into law enforcement, all in the name of making our city safer."

"But West Hazel is a safe town," Alice said. "Our crime stats are low." They had reached city hall, and as they approached the tinted glass of the main floor, the automatic doors swept open for them. Inside the cool interior sat a burnished maple reception desk in the center of a waiting area with chairs and tables. Alice knew this entrance was brighter and newer than the rabbit warren of offices that occupied the two floors of city hall. The old building had gotten a bit of a facelift a few years ago, giving a more modern feel to a stodgy office building. They paused inside the entrance, where a few people were chatting in the common area.

"It's the perception of crime that scares people," Tansley said in a lowered voice. "So the crime-fighting vote won broad support on the city council. There was just one problem. At the time of the preliminary vote, folks didn't realize George's budget would extract funds from most city agencies."

"Who else will be hurt by the new budget?" Alice asked.

Tansley nodded toward the people chatting by the windows. "Most every agency on the council. There's Ed Nohito's department, responsible for municipal service including water, sewer, and streets. Last year Ed's team has successfully installed storm sewers in ten percent of our old city streets, but his department is looking at a ten percent cut."

Alice glanced at Ed, who nodded as he listened to a dark-haired woman speak.

"And you know Devon Martinez, head of social services. And that's Amelia Giordano, the school board chair.

These are hardworking leaders managing essential services."

"Like the library," Alice said.

"Exactly. Everyone is facing budget cuts, Alice. To be blunt, it really sucks."

Alice nodded across the room to Devon and Amelia, then lowered her voice. "So you're telling me that everyone is knocking on your door now, to plead their case?"

"Just like you," Tansley said. "Our leaders care; they're fighting to protect community services."

"I don't know how George managed to look these people in the eye," Alice muttered. Come to think of it, he'd had some nerve pretending to be her friend when he'd been secretly pushing a budget to squeeze the life out of her livelihood. That stinker.

"George hasn't been so popular around here lately," Tansley said.

"And you didn't think to mention this to the police?"

"I—I guess I should have." Tansley frowned. "As a rule, I don't like to air the dirty laundry of city hall to the police or media."

"Well. The way I see it, George's budget needs to go." Alice had little patience for bureaucracy. "Can't you take a revote? Amend the budget?"

"Maybe we could." Tansley's eyes narrowed as she considered the possibilities. "I can bring it up in today's meeting. The city comptroller has the power to veto any amendments, but then, with George gone, we have no comptroller. . . ."

Was this a silver lining in George's death? Alice hoped so. No disrespect for the dead intended, but now that she knew George had been the butcher hacking away at city programs, the list of his enemies was expanding.

As Alice headed out of the building, she couldn't help but wonder if one of George's colleagues had seen his death as the only way to kill the budget. The notion seemed far-fetched. Over the top.

But the truth remained. Someone had murdered George. Had the killing been a means of removing him from city government?

# Chapter Seven

D istress and worry faded as Alice ducked out of the hot
sun and stepped into the cool air of the library.

Her library. The sense of pride was strong, but the library wasn't really hers. She'd worked hard to make the place, the people, and the energy in this building a second home that welcomed everyone in the community.

The small flurry of activity near the self-checkout stations appeared to be business as usual on a hot July afternoon. In summer the library was a bit more quiet than usual, except for the times when summer camp groups and vans full of kids came to visit.

At the tall, cherrywood reference desk, a fiftyish, graying, black man held court, speaking with a wild-haired man who sported a colorful tie-dyed T-shirt. Their reference librarian Charles Wayland was a recent hire. A retired cop and veteran with a calm demeanor and a cool sense of humor, Charles had been a plum hire for Alice.

Beto stood behind the checkout desk, chatting with a customer about overdue fees. In many ways, Beto, with his dark, short-cropped hair and brown eyes, magnified a bit by his black-framed glasses, was the face of the library. That first person you saw when you walked in. He was a friendly greeter, and a great helper to all. Today he wore a crisp white shirt and black pants that made him look far more professional than necessary in the library. "Don't worry," he told the patron, "you can pay the fines when you have the money."

"I don't know how I forgot about those books." The woman wrangled a toddler dangling from her skirt. "They're sitting right on the kitchen counter."

"That happens to me all the time," Beto said, handing the woman her books and telling her to take care.

"How we doing?" Alice asked, stepping past the check-out desk toward the back room.

"Fine and dandy."

"All good. Thank you."

As the office door closed behind her, Alice pushed her bag into a cubby and surveyed the room. Two of the part-time high school kids were working on filing returns and labeling requested books to send to other branches.

Perfect.

She gave them a smile and headed over to join the library manager, Julia Abe, who was intently clicking and scrolling and typing on one of the PCs.

"Sorry my morning got dashed away," Alice said. "And I may have to leave early. There's been a death among one of my close friends."

"Oh, no! Alice, I'm so sorry for your loss." That brought Julia's gaze away from the monitor. "What happened?"

"My friend Ruby lost her husband."

"And it was sudden?"

"It was. Unexpected. I'll tell you more later. I just want to do a sweep of the building." It was Alice's custom to do a walk-through twice a day, just to keep an eye on things. No one said a librarian needed to be chained to her desk.

"Okay, and then I need you. Time to sign off on the September and October calendars."

"Already?" Alice headed toward the door. "Time does fly."

"And we've got to talk more about those new budget cuts. Ten percent—it's killing me. The only way we can cut that much is to cut hours and let some staff go."

"It's a deep cut, I know. But I don't want to move on anything yet. I was just talking to the mayor, trying to get the city to adjust the budget."

"That would be wonderful." Julia looked out toward the library. "I'd hate to lose anyone on our staff. We need to move forward, not backward."

"Agreed." Maybe it was crazy to hope for such a huge reprieve, but Alice couldn't stop trying. "I'll keep you posted," she said, heading out of the office.

She did a quick walk through the old wing, the "Quiet" room that still held many of the features of the old library, built in the 1920s, including the stodgy odors of floor wax, sweet nostalgia, and yellowing pages of history. A wispy, white-haired man was collapsed in a chair behind the stacks, but he was snoring softly, simply sleeping, so all was well. She went up the old worn staircase to the glassed-in meeting rooms. One was occupied by a handful of kids with graphic novels spread on the table. Summer fun.

She checked that the door to the tower was locked. The legendary haunted tower had become a West Hazel landmark, though it did little to enhance the community experience here in the library. Once every two months visitors were allowed to climb the narrow stairs for a supervised visit to the tiny windows, though the novelty seemed to have worn off once the forbidden territory had become accessible.

Back in the new wing, she appreciated the smooth run of the carpet and the natural sunlight from the building's high windows. Colorful display books lined the hallway as she dipped down to the first floor to the children's section. There, she found only a handful of children perusing the carousels and shelves. But in the meeting area—a carpeted pit leading to a low stage—bubbles floated in the air over the babies.

Infant story time—how she loved it.

Small blankets had been spread on the carpet, picnic style, for caretakers to sit with their babies for the short session of songs, reading, and bubbles floating through the air. One of the children's librarians was playing a ukelele and singing a fun little ditty about three curious little fish who defiantly swam away from their mother.

"And they swam, and they swam, all over the dam!" Nancy Savino sang merrily.

Down on the floor, most of the adults joined in on the chorus as they waved props or helped baby clap hands or otherwise tried to engage the child. No criers today, at least not yet. With a deep breath, Alice took one last look, a snapshot of hope. Here was joy and love and growth among the youngest in their community.

All good.

Moving along quickly, she returned to the office and went over the calendar with Julia. All of the regular groups, from the Needle Knockers Yarn Club to the Poetry in Motion poets to the Roots Genealogy Explorers, had their monthly meetings on the schedule. Last year they had added a monthly craft night with the chance to make tote bags and posters without any fee, and that had proven popular. The Kids Lego Club was so popular that they now scheduled it every week. One of the small meeting rooms was set aside for Puzzlers; anyone could drop in and work on ongoing jigsaw puzzles.

Weekly story times for infants, toddlers, and preschoolers. There were two guest authors, and two featured speakers. And First Tuesday concerts in the library.

"It's a very full calendar," Alice said.

"Something for everyone?" said Julia.

"I sure hope so. If there are any lonely hearts out there, we offer a few chances to make personal connections."

They were discussing possible alterations to the schedule when a teen staffer, Fiona Pearson, came in and motioned to Alice. "There's a man outside who's asking for you. Says his name is Stone Donahue. Is that really a name? I mean, I've heard of Rocky, but Stone?"

"That's what people call him," Alice said, looking down at her patterned jacket and black dress. Well, at least she'd worn something decent today, though she sensed that she didn't look her best. Not enough sleep, too much stress, too much rushing.

"Would you send him this way, please?"

Fiona squinted. "Send him in here?" The girl was full of questions. "I mean, is that okay? I thought the office was for staff only."

"True, it's not a public space, but I think Stone can be trusted not to divulge the secrets of the Dewey decimal system."

Fiona cocked her head to one side. "That was a joke, right?"

The girl's sincerity was quite endearing. "It was. Thanks for your help, Fiona."

Alice spent the intervening minute trying to assume a cool facade despite the flurry of expectation at the thought of seeing Stone. Ridiculous. Juvenile. Yet undeniable. She picked up an empty clipboard from one of the desks and held it to her chest. A prop to make her look busy? Well, she really was busy. Torn in a million directions but . . .

"Alice, it's good to see you." Stone's gravelly voice summoned her attention from the doorway, which seemed to frame his tall, spare, cowboy physique.

Cowboy? What was she thinking? As if he'd just walked right out of a western novel, which he could have with his worn jeans, crisp black shirt, and worn leather belt.

"Always a pleasure." The words gushed out as she hugged the clipboard to her chest.

"We haven't seen you or your Silver Puzzle Gals at the senior center lately." Stone was the activities director of the West Hazel Senior Center, and he kept a table reserved for an ongoing jigsaw puzzle. In fact, he had named Alice and her friends the Silver Puzzle Gals, and kept acting like it was a senior citizen's club, despite Alice's frequent objection that she preferred to work puzzles at home.

"Well, we've all been busy, but I've got the upcoming lasagna night on my calendar. Aunt Gildy loves her nights out."

"Glad to hear it." Stone frowned and lowered his voice. "The real reason I'm here is George. I was sorry to hear we lost him. How's Ruby doing?"

The concern in his hazel eyes made her want to cry. He seemed to know how she was feeling before she even did. "Ruby's hanging in there. She's shocked, of course."

"As we all are." He shook his head. "George Byrd was quite a character, wasn't he? That man knew how to push a person's buttons, but at the end of the day, you couldn't help but like him. He loved to laugh."

Stone was right. "George was one of a kind."

"I was hoping to talk to Ruby. Went by the house, but

the media had surrounded the place. They're all over the story. News trucks and antennas jacked up from the street. You can't get near it."

Alice let out a groan. "Thank God she isn't there. She's staying with me until things settle down."

"I figured you'd know how to reach her. I'm working on a piece for the senior center newsletter and possibly the *Gazette*. Sort of an homage to George. But I was hoping to take it a step further, talk about the support we need to draw on when we lose someone. I want to use you and Ruby and the other Silver Puzzle Gals as an example."

"You know, we don't have a club, and I'm not a fan of being labeled." Alice replaced the clipboard on the desk, feeling a bit more relaxed. "You don't need to be old to enjoy puzzles. My granddaughters partake."

"I never meant any offense. Just thought the name had a nice ring to it."

"It's cute, but not necessary. Friends are friends. And you don't need permission to write about getting the love and support we need after a death. As for an ode to George, you'll need to ask Ruby."

"I was kind of hoping you'd do that for me." He smiled down at her, this impossibly sexy man with a gravelly voice and a solid chest you wanted to burrow into for the night.

She couldn't say no to him.

"I'll talk to Ruby about your column."

"Thanks," he said, with a wink that was more sexy than condescending.

Alice smiled, and then stiffened when she looked beyond him and noticed Julia watching them in curiosity. Probably shocked that her sixty-five-year-old boss had enough vitality left to have a crush.

"And when you have a chance, we could use a new puzzle," she said. "Something colorful but soothing would be perfect with everything that's going on." Due to their habit of devouring puzzles, Alice and her friends often traded with the puzzlers at the senior center. Stone had made himself the unofficial messenger, toting puzzles back and forth.

"You got it. I'll drop something by your place soon." He gave her one last look, and she was sure she saw a light twinkle in his eyes. "You take care now."

She considered trying a seductive wink, but knew she would look like a dolt with a lash stuck in her eye. Instead, she just raised her hand in a pathetic little wave and watched him go.

# Chapter Eight

Alice tied an apron over her T-shirt and yoga pants, covered the chicken breasts with freezer paper, lifted the mallet, and gave the first fillet a whack. Nothing like tenderizing chicken to release the tensions of the day.

Working with the chicken, onions, spices, and a few herbs that were growing in pots on the balcony, Alice started to pull together a lovely Chicken Francaise, one of her signature dishes. She chopped and sautéed almonds and zucchini and turned on the gas under a pot of water for jasmine rice. She squeezed a lemon, taking a moment to savor the fragrance. Cooking for loved ones could be therapeutic. Once she started to sauté the battered chicken, Ruby appeared, looking a bit weary as she peered at the stove.

"Smells delicious. I know something good is happening when you're in the kitchen, Alice," Ruby said.

"You must be starving. I'm making a nice dinner for all of us. Violet should be home soon. Come. Sit. Want some lemon ice tea?"

"I'll get it." Ruby opened the fridge and took out the pitcher. "My head's still a little foggy. I fell asleep. Woke up still clutching my phone, but I think I finished all the calls I needed to make. I managed to reach all the kids and the wedding is still on . . . for now."

"I suppose it's good to stick with the plan," Alice said, flipping a cutlet. The bits of Parmesan melted into the breading like slivers of gold.

"Well, if the cops drag me into jail, I guess you'll have to give Celeste away."

"I'll do you one better," Alice said. "We'll break you out of jail."

"Oh, but I'd look so chalky walking my girl down the aisle in that orange prison suit."

They both chuckled over that as Ruby brought her tea to the table and sat down with a sigh. "I hope it's the right choice, going ahead with the wedding."

"Maybe you'll have some resolution by then," Alice said, chopping some fresh oregano. "And the media should be off your case by then. I drove by on my way home and they're camped in front of your house. Vans and trucks blocking the road. It was like a summer street fair, only without the funnel cakes and caramel corn."

Ruby pressed her palms to her cheeks and shook her head. "They've been calling the office, those reporters. Imani has been fending them off. I'm so grateful to be here with you."

"Of course, honey. That guest room is yours for as long as you need it." Alice's Palace had space for everyone.

As Alice whisked butter with olive oil, she remembered her talk with Stone. "I had a visitor at the library today." She told Ruby about her conversation with Stone, and his notion to honor George in his next column for the senior newsletter. "I told Stone I'd run his idea by you."

"Well, if anyone's going to write the story, I'd rather it

be Stone." Ruby was occupying herself by clearing away the Banksy puzzle from that morning. "I'm fine with that. And see if he can bring by a new puzzle. I'm about to bust open one of these old ones. Maybe the mandalas? It's just three hundred fifty pieces, but it's so colorful."

"We'll make quick work of that one. I'll text Stone now." Alice put down the whisk to shoot off a quick text to Stone. She finished the text with a little jab: **And where's my new puzzle?**

"I feel kind of bad about George's brothers." Ruby was searching through the open box for border pieces. "I talked with both of them, one in St. Louis, and the other somewhere in Idaho. They both said they couldn't make it for a funeral or whatnot. I know they weren't close, but they were the only family he had. Personally, I never met them. It makes me feel bad for George."

The mayor's comment about George's lack of popularity came to mind, leading Alice to wonder who would turn up for George's funeral. A bit of a concern, but this was no time to add to Ruby's burdens. "At least George knew he was loved," Alice said.

"By me *and* Blondie."

"I didn't mean it that way. I was talking about community."

"I know. I'm just feeling bitter and sorry for myself."

"You're grieving, honey. You have every right." Alice removed two nicely browned cutlets from the pan, popped them into a low oven, and started to sauté two more. "You're going to be okay, Ruby. You'll get through this. Not to pry, but do you anticipate any fiscal issues?"

"My business is in the clear. We drew up a prenup to protect my business since Ruby's House of Wigs was established and turning a profit before I even met George.

We kept our money separate. He had his salary from the city. I gave him a little allowance, mostly because I enjoyed paying for his little pleasures. Cigars and nice suits."

"And the big pleasures like the Maserati?" Alice had clutched her chest when she'd learned the price of that fancy car, a vehicle so low to the ground that you nearly had to squat to wedge yourself inside.

"The Maserati was a wedding gift," Ruby said as she sorted through puzzle pieces. "And boy, did he love that car. I can feel the disapproval, Alice."

"I'm just cooking chicken, minding my business."

"Granted, it was an expensive car, but it made him so happy. It brought out the fun side of George, and you know how animated he could be when he was in the moment. You know how he tried to make people happy. 'I'm just here to make your dreams come true!' He said that all the time, to so many people, and he really wished the best for folks."

"I did know that side of George." Alice had gotten a major dose of Joyful George when he'd brought a party of ten to her restaurant opening and run up a high tab of wine, appetizers, entrées, and desserts. He'd made everyone from the waitstaff to the chef feel appreciated. Joyful George had an easy smile and a need to get others aboard the happy train alongside him.

Ruby picked up a puzzle piece with fuchsia beads on it and considered it as if it were a valentine. "When George was in the moment, he made me feel like the world was a playground for the two of us. Just the two of us."

*Romantic love*, Alice thought. She'd been in that sumptuous orchard once, and it had been a lovely interlude, until the fruit had rotted and fallen to the ground.

The sound of the garage door alerted Alice that her sister was home. A moment later Violet walked into the kitchen with all the authority of a vice principal. Throughout the day Alice had texted her updates on Ruby's situation. From Violet's crisp, short answers, it had been clear that she'd been consumed with the visiting parents.

"Hello, gals. What a day! Parents love to talk about their little darlings. I couldn't tear myself away, Ruby, but tonight I'm all yours." She put her briefcase on a chair and leaned down to put an arm around Ruby's shoulders. "I'm so sorry to hear about George. How are you doing?"

"Awful. Trying to distract myself with this puzzle."

Violet tipped up the puzzle box revealing the photo of bejeweled mandalas in various color schemes. "The mandalas—a complex representation of the different facets of the universe. Such a perfect choice for this moment."

"And here I just thought they were colorful," Ruby said.

Violet pressed a palm to her chest. "The mind knows what the heart needs."

"Right now I think she needs a lovely dinner, and this will be ready as soon as I get the sauce to a boil. Why don't you go change and wash up for dinner."

"It's a plan," Violet said. "And I'm going to bring out my tarot cards to do a reading for you. And tea leaves, too. They can guide us toward what might have caused George to exit this world so suddenly."

"We have some answers on that front," Alice said. "The coroner thinks it was homicide. And they haven't ruled Ruby out as a suspect."

"What? That's awful!" Violet rose up, as if lifted on a clothesline. "In that case, we must do a reading. A few readings. And a ritual. We'll do something in the backyard under the moonlight, a bit of white magic."

"That's not necessary," said Ruby. "I don't need magic, Vi. Just time, and some answers from the police."

"But the readings will help you navigate your future," Violet pointed out.

Alice could see that Ruby wasn't much comforted by Violet's woo-woo. "I think Ruby is better off having a quiet night."

"No." Taylor emerged from the basement door. Her face was pale, and Alice could see that her hands were trembling. "We have to do something."

"Are you okay, honey?" asked Alice.

"No. I'm freaked out about George. I keep trying to get it out of my head, but that's the closest I've been to a dead body, and I'm afraid his spirit is lingering on us. He's settled over us like . . . like a bad spray tan."

"That's ridiculous," Alice said, tapping her wooden spoon against the pan a few times for emphasis.

But Violet was waving her hands, as if wafting air toward her body. "I'm feeling some vibrations here. You might be right, Taylor."

"Oh, no! You mean he's here?" Taylor shrieked.

"He means no harm," Violet proclaimed.

"Because he's not here." Alice took Taylor's arm to steady her. "George is dead."

"Taylor, honey, please calm down," Ruby said. "Trust me when I say you have nothing to worry about from George."

Taylor winced, then let out a breath. "If you say so."

"But the vibrations are strong," Violet insisted. "Tonight will be the perfect time to chase the dark spirits off and send George gently on his way."

"Where?" asked Ruby. "Where is George supposed to go when he's already dead?"

But Violet was already making plans. "We'll do a circle of herbs, and candles, of course. I have sage to burn in the firepit. Strong protection and . . . and we must all wear white as color vibrations distract the energy."

So much for Ruby's quiet night. As Alice stirred the sauce, she plotted ways to talk the ladies out of this fandango.

# Chapter Nine

Tensions were eased by the delicious repast enjoyed at the small table on the balcony. In the post meal haze, Alice folded her napkin and suggested that a ritual wasn't really necessary. Ruby jumped in to wholeheartedly agree.

"You can't ignore the dead," Violet insisted. "Taylor and I won't be able to sleep a wink until we put George to rest. Right, honey?"

Taylor nodded nervously as she pushed a crescent of zucchini around on her plate. "Is it going to be scary, Aunt Violet?"

Thoughtful, Violet folded her arms. "I find that spirits are quite similar to people. If you treat them with respect, they return the courtesy." She rose from the table with her plate and glass. Heading into the kitchen, she called back, "Now, remember to wear something white. I'll set up things in the backyard so we can start as soon as it gets dark."

Taylor gathered the other plates, then followed Violet in, saying, "I'll do the cleanup, Gran. You did all the cooking."

"Wonders never cease," Alice said, pleased that her granddaughter had stepped up to help. Most nights she simply disappeared into the basement and slipped out to meet friends.

"She's been scared into politeness," Ruby said. "I suppose death is a lot for a person her age, and maybe Violet's little ceremony will help her."

"Are you okay with the ritual?"

"I'm on board with anything that will help people feel better about what's happened to George. Might be nice to light some candles and honor George. It'll give me a chance to say my own little prayer. With the investigation going on, and the wedding, I don't know when we're going to be able to do a real funeral."

"All right then," Alice said, patting her friend's shoulder. "I'm off to find something white."

All white was not flattering on a tall, solid woman, and the T-shirt and Bermuda shorts made Alice feel like a giant from some mythical cloud kingdom. She longed to wear her loose, black cotton dress, but she knew it would bring out the vice principal in her sister, who would send her back to her room to change. So she emerged from her room looking like an unfashionable masseuse.

In the backyard she came upon Taylor, who was collecting pots of herbs from the balcony and placing them near the table in the yard.

"Gran!" Taylor exclaimed. "Oh, my gosh, you look like a tourist in the Bahamas."

"This dress code offends my aesthetic sensibilities."

Taylor wore a flimsy white T-shirt dress that revealed the lacy bra underneath and was barely long enough to cover her hoo-hoo. In fact, when Taylor bent down to move a pot of basil . . .

Alice had to look away, and the decorated picnic table

caught her eye. White votive candles lined the edge of the table, some in glass, some sitting on saucers. "My saucers," Alice said, picking up a candle. "My blackout candles, too." Someone had gotten into her stash, but she had to admit, when lit, the candles would make an impressive arrangement. At the center of the table was a string of green ivy that encircled a shiny brass bowl, along with large chunks of crystal. The spiky formations in blue, white, and amethyst usually resided in Violet's room, where Violet used them for healing, meditation, protection, and strength. Alice had never felt any magic holding a crystal in her hand, but if it helped her sister manage her life, more power to her.

According to the weather app on her phone, sunset would be at 8:44 p.m. on this late July night. Alice glanced up at the perimeters of the yard, which mostly faced the mountains to the northeast. Along the western fence line on her left, the sun had already set, leaving swaths of rose, orange, and indigo light in the sky over the twinkling lights of Portland. Although the yard was completely fenced, the terrain dropped down the hill at the rear of the lot, affording them a vista overlooking rooftops and trees.

How she loved this house. Thank goodness she had stood her ground when Jeff had pressured her to sell it during the divorce.

"Go ahead and light the candles, Taylor," said a voice behind Alice. She turned to see Violet emerge from the dusky shadows in a soft white confection of a gown. She cradled something in her arm. A dinner plate.

As she drew closer, Alice saw that it was tonight's leftovers. "My Chicken Francaise!"

"It's for George," Violet explained, placing it on the table in the center of the ivy. "A feast for the dead."

Alice shook her head. "If George doesn't eat it, it's

going back in the fridge. I'm not wasting perfectly good leftovers."

Violet didn't seem to hear. "I'm going to light this sage in the firepit. But where's Ruby?"

"Here I am!" A bundle of white came running out, her footsteps slowing when her white stiletto heels hit the soft lawn. Ruby was wrapped in the plush terry cloth robe from the guest room. On her ears, white rhinestone earrings glimmered in the falling light. She hurried over to join Alice. "I didn't have a thing to wear."

"You're fine," Violet said, fanning smoke from the firepit and wafting it toward herself as if she were bathing in a waterfall. She gave a happy shudder, then turned to the other women and welcomed them to the ritual.

"You can sit in those chairs there." She gestured to three wooden folding chairs that had been set off to the side of the table. "We don't want anyone too close to the flames."

"Lest we spontaneously combust," Alice muttered. The picnic table seemed ablaze from the candles, the flames oddly exciting against the falling blue veil of night.

When the women were seated, Violet stood before them, the moon rising behind her through the branches of a tall fir tree in the distance. And what a moon! A silver-pocked ball of cheese, familiar, icy bright, fascinating.

"What a terrific backdrop," Alice said. Had Violet known it would appear that way for their ceremony?

Violet explained that she had consulted her tarot cards, and she thought it best to let the cards rest tonight and focus on this ritual.

"Well, that's good, since I could use the rest, too," Ruby announced.

"This won't take too long," Violet said, with a gentle

smile. "But then again, time is a subjective construct of our minds, is it not?"

"Say what?" Ruby squinted.

"Aunt Vi, you're blowing my mind," Taylor said.

Indeed, this otherworldly personality was a side of Violet that they'd not seen before. It did explain some of Violet's overnight trips to woodsy cabins with her friends, which Alice had assumed were hen parties.

"Let's begin." Violet pushed a few of the candles aside so that she could access the items on the table. She lifted the metal bowl up to the sky and ran a brush around its rim, creating a ringing sound. "We are gathered here tonight to turn the wheel of life for George Byrd, ushering him into the world of the dead."

Glancing to her right, Alice saw that Ruby and Taylor were enraptured in the spectacle.

"We have gathered in white as it indicates rebirth into a purer light form." Violet raised her hands to the moon and smiled. Violet was in her groove, truly in her element.

Alice watched with a mixture of fascination and alarm. She'd never been a fan of magic tricks, and this ceremony gave her that hocus-pocus feeling. As if a George hologram might appear beside Violet.

"George, George, George. We are here for you, George. Here to send you off into the light." Violet chose a chunk of crystals from the table and held it up to the sky. "We use these crystals to block the dark spirits and create a filter that lets through only our friend George."

"Only George," Ruby called out. "Don't let any strangers through."

"No creepers," Taylor agreed.

Now Violet was swaying and humming and waving two long scarves through the air. Her tall, lithe body moved gracefully, reminding Alice of the years of ballet Violet had taken as a kid. And then Violet was singing a song as she swayed and twirled, red and purple scarves flowing in the air around her. Wait, was that a Fleetwood Mac song?

Violet's voice twanged with emotion. "Listen at the window! Dandelions! Dandelions!"

The song changed to a chant about transforming into light. "Look to the Goddess of the moon," Violet told George, over and over again.

Her focus waning, Alice suddenly wondered if the neighbors could hear them. The yard was well-fenced. No one could see them, but the neighbors might certainly hear Violet warbling.

Finally, the song ended and Violet somberly lifted her hands to the sky.

"And now, I am opening the gates to the Land of Death. I am calling on the Goddess to carry messages from the living to the dead." Violet gestured to the seated women. "Okay, Ruby, this is your chance to speak to George."

"That's okay." Ruby gave a little wave. "Truth be told, I don't believe in this stuff."

Violet extended her hands to Ruby. "You don't have anything to tell him?"

Ruby sighed. "Only that I'm going to miss him. And I'm not mad at him anymore. And . . . and I'm sorry his brothers won't be coming to his funeral. That's not right. Family should be there for him."

"Did you hear that, George?" Violet said, speaking to the moon. "She's going to miss you."

"But I'm not going to be stuck in denial," Ruby said, tears in her eyes. "So, George, you have a good eternity in the great beyond, and don't worry about me down here. I'll be fine. But I do want to know why. Why the affair,

George? We had a good thing going. And why'd you have to go and die when I was so mad at you? Why, George?"

The tears were streaming down her face now, and Alice wished she had a box of tissues at hand.

Ruby swiped at her face with the sleeves of her robe. "You know, George, if you could just answer or give me a sign. Any sign to let me know you're okay." She sobbed. "I'm such a fool for even asking, but . . . just a simple answer. . . ."

"Hello?"

A voice . . . a man's voice!

From out of nowhere.

Taylor and Alice exchanged a glance of terror. Who the hell was that?

Ruby pressed a hand to her heart. "Oh, my Lord, it's George."

# Chapter Ten

R uby grabbed Alice's arm and gave it a shake. "He's here! Violet summoned the dead."

Alice looked to her younger sister in amazement. "I'm afraid I underestimated your gifts."

Looking a bit off-guard, Violet pressed her hands in prayer position against her chest and turned back to face the moon. "A few more words, George. Please. Speak to us again?"

"Are you back there?" he asked.

That time the voice seemed more human. Earthly. When it was followed by the rattling of the side gate, Alice realized that someone was trying to get into the yard. Hopes fell back down to earth quickly as Alice crossed the yard and approached the gate.

"Who's there?" she called.

"Detective Bedrosian."

Alice looked back to the other gals with a shrug. "Maybe a noise complaint?" She opened the gate to see the detective, a fireplug of a man, standing there beside Madison. Alice tugged on her white shirt, wishing it were looser and more flattering. "We weren't expecting you, Detective."

"We rang the doorbell, but no one answered," he said, moving past her into the yard. "And your granddaughter, here, said it looked like you were home, so we persisted."

"Traitor," Alice muttered under her breath. No one heard. The police had already trudged past her into the yard.

"Sorry to bother you, but we have a few more questions for Ruby, and the sooner we get answers, the faster our investigation moves." Bedrosian scanned the yard, then stared at the picnic table. "That's a lot of candles. One of you gals having a birthday?"

"Something like that," Alice said. She blew a few out, then motioned to Taylor to finish the job. Violet stood still and stern, as if ready to officiate a wedding. Alice sensed that she didn't want the otherworldly side of her in the public view. The optics of rituals and seances weren't great for a school administrator.

"And look at that dinner." Bedrosian's eyes lit on the plate of chicken. "That looks delicious. Is that Chicken Piccata? It's one of my favorites."

"Chicken Francaise." Alice picked up the plate. "Just as delicious."

"I'll bet."

"Shall we go inside to talk?" Alice looked to her friend, who was adjusting the lapels of her robe, trying to compose herself. The poor thing had been in tears just a minute ago. Talk about through the wringer. "You up for another chat with the police, Ruby?"

"Might as well get it over with."

Alice secured the plate in one arm and went to Ruby. "I'll go inside with you."

"We'll clean up out here," Violet said. "Make sure the *gate* is *closed*, and all that."

"Thank you for *all that*," Ruby said, taking a moment to touch Violet's cheek tenderly before heading inside.

Madison paused by her twin sister to ask: "What the hell are you wearing?"

"It's wizard garb. Symbolizing purity and positive vibrations," Taylor said. "Jealous?"

"Just don't bend over while anyone else is around," Madison advised before heading in.

As they climbed the steps to the back deck and entered through the kitchen, Bedrosian made noises about how good the chicken smelled. Alice pretended not to hear. She usually loved feeding people, but this rude man was not currently on her list of deserving people.

They sat on the upholstered furniture in the living room. Alice grabbed a turquoise pillow from the sofa and held it in her lap to block the unflattering binding of her shorts. Ruby sat with her legs crossed, a glamorous look with her bare brown legs and white high heels. The woman had great gams.

Bedrosian seemed quite comfortable in the apricot velvet Queen Anne chair, and he got right to the point. "We want to go over the timeline from last night. Like when your flight arrived at PDX. What time you got home, and how long did you stay?"

"She already went through this with Mad—Officer Denham," Alice insisted.

"No," Madison corrected her, looking through her notebook. "You told me Ruby was here around ten or eleven, after her flight from Vegas had arrived, and she'd had an altercation with her husband at home. But, Ruby, Ms. Milliner, hasn't given an exact timeline."

"I . . . well . . ." Ruby outlined her right ear with one fingertip, a gesture that drew attention to her glittering earrings. "It was all in that order."

"But what time did you arrive at your home on Cherry Crest?" Madison asked. "Your best guess?"

"Umm . . ." Ruby squirmed. "Maybe seven . . . seven thirty?"

"No, honey, it was later," Alice said automatically, but Ruby shot her a worried look.

The detective nodded at Madison, as if he were omniscient. "Not as Alice stated."

"No, it was earlier," said Ruby. "My flight from Las Vegas was scheduled to arrive around six, and it was on time."

"An on-time arrival at six ten p.m.," Madison said.

"How do you know these things?" Alice demanded.

"I checked with the airlines," Madison explained. At least she wasn't so smug about it. "It was the only flight from Las Vegas to PDX last night."

"So, Ruby, that puts you at home around seven p.m." The detective leaned forward in the big chair. "Is that correct?"

"I had to collect my luggage, so more like seven thirty."

"Okay." Bedrosian sounded patient now. Alice didn't trust it. "So you were home to catch your husband with this woman around seven thirty. And you didn't get to Alice's house until much later. So you're unaccounted for during the time when your husband was killed."

Alice's throat went dry as she looked from the detective to her friend, unable to believe this new twist.

"The question is, Ruby, where were you in the hours between seven thirty and ten?"

All eyes were on Ruby as she recrossed her legs and shrugged uncomfortably. "Shopping?"

# Chapter Eleven

Alice didn't like this line of questioning at all. No one here was going to get her leftover chicken. Most of all, she didn't like the feeling that she was losing her connection with her friend.

"Ruby, what did you need from the store that night?" Alice asked.

"It's so embarrassing, but I was revenge shopping." Ruby slipped off her shoes, folded her legs under her, and sank back onto the sofa. "You're going to think I'm so petty and immature. Maybe I am. But I was furious with George. So I took some cash from him and blew it on clothes."

"You took his money?" Bedrosian asked.

"His money, my money, ours. It's not like it would hurt him financially, but I knew it would piss him off."

Madison looked up from her notebook. "How did you get the money?"

"I saw his wallet in the little cubby off the kitchen. We were arguing downstairs, and Blondie was upstairs, hiding in our bedroom, howling like a baby. George went upstairs to console her, which infuriated me all the more. I spotted his wallet, took a peek inside, and found over a thousand dollars in nice crisp hundred-dollar bills. Well, I was going to hit him where it hurt. So I lammed out of there, took the Benjamins, and went shopping."

"What stores did you go to?" Madison asked.

"I drove straight to the mall. Looked at expensive jewelry first, but then I went to the row of boutiques and tried on my favorite things—jackets. Purchased a sharp blazer in a houndstooth pattern. A black velvet bolero with sequins and seed pearls on the shoulders. A buttery red leather bomber, and a flowing duster in a brilliant shade of blue."

Alice nodded. Ruby loved her jackets.

Detective Bedrosian unwrapped a stick of gum and gave it a good chew. "Don't the mall stores close by nine?"

"They do." Ruby toyed with one of her earrings. "And when they closed, I drove back to the house to show George the jackets. I was determined to enjoy the feeling of spite. I pulled into the garage and texted him. I wanted him to come down so I could throw the jackets in his face, show him what he'd paid for. I did not want to go in there and encounter Blondie again. I assumed she'd had the decency to leave, but you never know."

"Was George angry about the jackets?" asked Bedrosian. "Did you argue again?"

"He didn't answer my text messages or my phone calls."

"So you went inside to find him?" asked Madison.

"Nope. I was so fed up that I peeled out of there and drove off around nine. Maybe a few minutes after."

Madison nodded. "That actually matches our video evidence. We canvassed the neighborhood and got the doorbell video from one of your neighbors, a Mr. Garrett."

"Tiger . . ." Ruby sat up straighter.

Alice recalled that Ruby had gotten a text from Tiger. She'd probably been too busy to call him back.

"I knew he had some security set up," Ruby said. "What could you see?"

"His camera captures activity in your driveway." Madison leafed through her notebook, searching for the right page. "It shows your white Cadillac pulling into the garage at nine twenty-one p.m., and then exiting and driving away at nine thirty-two."

"Well, you could have told me you knew that already," Ruby said. "What else did you see?"

Bedrosian waved his hands, casting a scowl on Madison. "We don't need to get into the weeds of our investigation, Officer Denham. Let's just stick to yesterday's timeline."

"But I want to know," Ruby insisted. "My husband was murdered, and I want to know who could've done such a thing."

"Believe me, when we have a suspect, we'll let you know." Bedrosian chewed his gum with annoyance.

A testy one, that detective. "Let me just remind you, Detective, that you're speaking with the wife of a homicide victim," Alice said. "A little compassion, please?"

Bedrosian instantly soured. "I'm here to do a job, and if that—"

"Detective." Madison interrupted him. "I think she's right. Ruby's been cooperating with us, and we can keep this pleasant and mannerly."

*That's my granddaughter.* Alice was impressed that she'd used the word *mannerly*.

"All right. Fine. Yes! I'm sorry." He folded his arms. "My sympathies, of course. Let's get back to the mall excursion. Do you have the purchases to show us?"

Ruby frowned. "Actually, I don't."

"You don't have the jackets?" Madison asked.

"What happened to them?" Alice asked. "I mean, you seemed to love them all."

"I got rid of them," Ruby said. "When George refused to answer me, I drove around, not sure what to do. I was so tired, I just wanted to go home, but I was not going to deal with George until he was contrite and on his knees. Instead, he had the nerve to ignore my calls. I couldn't go home to that."

"Of course not," Alice said sympathetically.

"I was so angry and fed up that I did something crazy. I stopped at the 7-Eleven and went around back. I gathered up the shopping bags and tossed my new purchases into the dumpster right then and there. I knew it would really steam George's clams to know his money went right into the trash."

Alice nodded encouragement, though it was hard to imagine Ruby within ten feet of a dumpster.

"And then I was thirsty, so I got a Slurpee and drove off and played my music as I drove around. I took State Street out of town and ended up on that twisty road by the horse farms. When I came to those ramshackle little houses at the edge of the freeway, I felt a stab of guilt, throwing away clothes when some folks didn't have the means to clothe themselves or their children."

"I felt so spoiled," Ruby lamented.

"So I went back to 7-Eleven and pulled those clothes out of the dumpster. Not as disgusting as I expected. I mean, they were still in the big shopping bags. I put the bags in my trunk, went inside to wash up, and bought a bag of pretzels. Then I drove to the women's shelter and left the jackets on the edge of their front porch. They hate it when folks leave donations there, but I couldn't stand to have the jackets with me for one more minute.

"Spite jackets.

"And still, I'd gotten no word from George. Not a single text. In four years of marriage we never went that long without making up after a fight. But then, I'd never caught him with a woman. I was hurt and tired, so I came here. I knew Alice would take me in."

Alice reached over and squeezed Ruby's arm. "You're always welcome here."

"So all the new jackets were donated. Out of your possession." Bedrosian drummed his fingers on the armchair. "Well, at least you can show us the receipts."

"Actually, I don't have them. I left the receipts with the jackets. In case any of the women wanted to exchange for a different size or color? When a jacket is that expensive, you should get exactly what you want."

The detective pressed two fingers to his temple. "All right, then, we can look at your credit card statements to verify the purchases."

"Haven't you been listening?" Annoyance crackled in Ruby's voice. "I purchased them with cash—the cash I got from George's wallet. A vengeance purchase? Is this ringing any bells?"

"I know I've been listening to a fantastic story." Bedrosian was stern. "Lots of twists and turns. Not a good alibi, but a great story."

"Alibi?" Ruby lifted her chin. "Are you insinuating that I had something to do with George's death?"

"Whoa, whoa, whoa." Madison held up one hand. "There are other ways to confirm your activity that night. We can get security footage from the 7-Eleven, as well as the mall stores. At least for starters."

"We can get those images from the stores," the detective agreed. "But I wonder, Ruby, do you think we'll see you in the footage, or maybe you were wearing your invisibility cloak!"

"Detective Bedrosian." Alice gasped. "This petty streak does not become you. If you consider the big picture—it's terrifying! Don't you realize the danger Ruby was in? Chances are, when she pulled into the garage, the killer was at work in the bedroom above her. Thank goodness Ruby didn't go inside. She might have encountered a killer wielding a brass candlestick—or worse." Alice took her friend's hand and fixed a cold stare on the detective. "That was a frightfully close call."

"Maybe," said Bedrosian. "Or maybe the killer had already struck and departed. Or maybe you whacked him, grabbed his cell phone, and hightailed it out of there. The camera showed us the driveway, but there's no telling what was going on inside the home. Honestly? Right now, anyone with any access to the home is a suspect."

Alice didn't like what he was implying. Of course, she understood the logic of his thought process, and the need to take a hard look at every person who'd had access to George last night. From the steely set of his jaw, she knew what he was thinking.

That it was Ruby who had struck the final blow.

# Chapter Twelve

R uby drew the lapels of the robe in closer and lifted her chin. "Think what you want, Detective. I did not kill my husband, and I have been completely honest with you this evening. My conscience is clear."

"And I can vouch for the good character of my friend," Alice said. "When you get to the bottom of this, Ruby's name will be cleared of any wrongdoing."

Ruby and Bedrosian were deadlocked, still staring at each other, when his cell phone buzzed and he pulled it out. "Sorry, I gotta take this." When he went out to the balcony, the heaviness in the room lifted.

"We all needed a break, anyway." Madison stood up. "Gran, okay if I get a cup of tea?"

"Of course. I'll make it for you." Alice headed toward the kitchen. "Did you get dinner?"

"No, but I can't eat on duty."

"I've got chicken here. I'll wrap it for you to go." It was a relief to step into her kitchen, to let her guard down as she moved through familiar spaces, preparing tea, dishing food into a container, washing the confrontation from her hands, and dabbing her face with a damp paper towel. Water on the face had a way of clearing the mind.

While the kettle was heating she peeked into the living room and saw that the detective was still outside. It gave her a chance to dash up to her room and peel off the uncomfortable white shorts. "I can't take you for one second longer," she said as she wrestled them off over her ankles. Free at last, she slipped on some gray joggers and a green Portland State sweatshirt and hurried back down to the kitchen.

As she prepared a tea tray, Alice searched her mind for a way to prove to the detective that Ruby was no killer. When you had been friends with someone for fifty-plus years, you knew her true character.

Alice still recalled the day they'd met. A summer day in Queens Village, New York, when a giant moving truck pulled up two doors away from Alice's house. Captain Montel Simone had been transferred to Fort Hamilton, in Brooklyn, and he and his wife, Denise, had chosen the house in Queens for their sprawling family.

From her window twelve-year-old Alice had seen them emerging from a VW van, six children, squealing and shouting as they'd sailed in loops around the yard and bounded up the porch steps into the house.

"Six kids!" she had told Violet breathlessly as she ran out of the house, barefoot. Her ten-year-old sister had followed dutifully, though not as enthusiastically as Alice, who embraced the event, welcoming the new kids. Alice had enjoyed witnessing their thrilling discovery of their new house. They were putting up a backyard pool! They had a cubby closet under the stairs! Four whole bedrooms! And their dad had built a fort for the kids to hang out. While waiting for his wife and children to make the drive from Michigan, Montel had drilled wooden footholds into a tree next to the flat-roofed garage. Now, every neighbor kid was trying to climb up and stake his or her claim in the shade on the roof.

Twelve-year-old Alice didn't like the fort. The climb up was bad enough. The climb down was a guessing game of finding a prong in the abyss below her feet.

Fortunately, the new girl her age wasn't into it, either. At age eleven, Ruby had already differentiated herself from the younger kids. She was a queen bee, the informal boss of her siblings.

Unlike Alice, who had lived various lives through books she'd read, Ruby had already lived in four different states *and* Panama. She was grounded in the real world. This was a girl who knew who she was.

That summer Alice felt honored when Ruby whisked her into the screened-in porch for lemonade, teen magazines, and a few rounds of the game Trouble. She showed her the sewing machine she used to make clothes and promised to help Alice turn her boring jeans into bell-bottom hip-huggers. Alice promised to show her around the junior high and take her to the pizza place.

The friendship born that summer had lasted all these years. There'd been long absences when they lived in different states, and periods when they were each preoccupied with the business of life: a husband, a family, a career. Still, their friendship was a given.

So . . . how well did Alice know Ruby? Inside and out. Of course, everyone had secrets, and as best friends, they tried not to pry. But did Ruby possess the mettle and bitterness and cruelty to kill George? Absolutely not. And Alice was ready to spend every waking hour defending her friend.

Alice set the tray down and began pouring hot water. Ruby and Madison were happy to choose their own tea, herbal blends for both women.

Detective Bedrosian stepped in from the balcony, still awash in bad humor. "That was Dr. Jane. Turns out you were right about the weapon, Alice. The candlestick holder seems to be the right size and weight for the wounds on George's head. But, of course, there were no traces of blood or hair on the candlestick you found."

"So the murder weapon is still missing," Alice said. "Perhaps the killer took it with him." It felt good to put some of the pieces in place and move ahead with the investigation. After all, she was expert at finding the right puzzle pieces.

"It's possible he—or she—removed the weapon from the scene," Bedrosian agreed. "As of now the cause of death was blunt force trauma, but that could change when we get the toxicology report on George's blood, which usually takes four to six weeks."

"Four to six weeks?" Ruby lowered her teacup. "The killer could knock off a zillion other people during that time."

"You're right," Madison agreed. "But that's the standard time for testing. I know it's almost instantaneous on crime shows, but real life is different."

"We're going to accelerate some results, considering something the coroner noted. His lips were quite blue, not consistent with head trauma. And she found a red mark on George's neck, near the spine, that's consistent with an injection." Bedrosian frowned, shifting from one foot to another. "Honestly, I don't usually divulge information like this to family members, not so soon, but maybe you can help us. Did George have a medical procedure recently? Like a steroid injection to the spine, something like that?"

"Not that he mentioned," Ruby said. "And he would

have definitely told me if he had. George hated needles. Would pass out at the sight of them."

Bedrosian nodded. "Good to know."

"So we're looking at head trauma as the cause of death," Alice said, thinking out loud. "Would that require exceptional force? I mean, could a woman strike a blow that hard?"

Bedrosian mulled the question over, then turned to Madison.

"I'd say that's a good question for Dr. Jane," Madison said, making a note.

Hearing a sniffling sound, Alice turned to Ruby, who let out a sob. A fresh round of tears had begun.

"I'm sorry, honey," Alice said, realizing how cold the discussion must seem to Ruby.

"I can't believe somebody killed him," said Ruby. "Who would do that to George?"

"In homicide cases, we start by looking at the victim's inner circle. The people who are closest to him." Bedrosian's gaze was locked on Ruby.

"Stop looking at me!" Ruby protested. "I loved my husband."

"Even after you found out he was cheating?"

"I was mad, but not crazy enough to kill him." Ruby's grief was now galvanized to fury. "You want a crazy woman? Then you find out who was in my house last night, wearing my nightie and my wig along with some creepy getup from a masquerade party."

Bedrosian and Madison exchanged a look, and Alice sensed that they had information they were not disclosing.

"Ruby's right," Alice said. "Who is this blond floozy, and what does she have to say about George's state of mind last night?"

"We don't have an ID on her just yet," Madison admitted, causing Bedrosian to tighten up.

"So instead you're here, badgering the widow?" Alice shook her head. "You must have information about Blondie's comings and goings. Isn't she on the doorbell cam that you scrutinized?"

"We can't discuss all the details of an open investigation," Bedrosian said.

"But the victim is my husband, my George!"

"Exactly. This is a criminal investigation, not a family affair." Clearly annoyed, Bedrosian nodded at Madison. "We should go. We got enough for now."

"Wait, just one minute." Alice confronted Bedrosian, stepping between him and the door. "Are you penalizing Madison—Officer Denham—because she has a personal relationship with Ruby?"

"Gran . . ." Madison held up a hand to stop her. "Please . . ."

"I demand professionalism of all my officers," Bedrosian said evenly.

Hands on her hips, Alice kept her voice low, maintaining control. "I should hope so. And I hope you remember that professionals can still be decent human beings."

"Just let us do our job," he said, heading out the door.

Alice searched her mind for a stinging retort, but Madison stopped her with a glare and a warning to "Let it go." Watching them leave, Alice hoped her granddaughter was standing up to that cranky man. Alice did not like having to deal with that royal pain in the tush.

# Chapter Thirteen

"At last, the coppers vamoosed!" Taylor said, holding a pen as if it were an elegant cigarette holder. "I thought they were gonna shut this gin joint down."

Alice squinted at her. "You've inherited your mother's flair for drama," she said, regretting the words as they came out. She tried to avoid discussion of she-who-should-not-be-named. Her only daughter. Her greatest heartbreak.

"I thought they would never leave." Ruby picked up her high heels and headed toward her room. "So many questions. I didn't know that detective would try to flip me from the frying pan into the fire."

"Ruby, wait," Taylor called. "There's news coverage about George on TV, and I figured you'd want to see it. I froze the screen so you could see it all."

"I'm afraid to look," Alice said. She disliked the sensational spin that local news stations tried to put on current events.

Ruby and Alice settled into the comfy sectional sofa in the den while Taylor took the remote and reversed back to the beginning of the Breaking News report. Keisha Brandon, a thirtyish black woman with thoughtful, bright eyes and beaded, braided hair, stood on Cherry Crest Lane, in front of Ruby's house. It felt odd to see Ruby's porch and that round window up by the roofline right behind Portland's Action News logo.

"Your house looks like a movie set," Alice told Ruby.

"I'm glad Keisha is covering the story," said Ruby. "She's a straight shooter."

Above a chyron that stated: WEST HAZEL CITY LEADER FOUND DEAD, Keisha spoke about the shock of a suspected homicide in the quiet Portland suburb of West Hazel. "The death of George Byrd, a prominent member of the city council here, has been deemed a homicide, and investigators are still scrambling to piece together information that will help them apprehend his killer."

Photos of a younger, smiling George, sans glasses and with thicker hair, appeared on the screen. Alice figured the pictures for five or ten years old, but Ruby liked them.

"He was a handsome man," Ruby said sadly.

The reporter went on. "Police say it was an anonymous tip that sent them on a welfare check of Byrd in the early hours of the morning."

An anonymous tip? From whom? Alice hadn't thought to ask about why the cops had come to the house, and the police hadn't mentioned the tip to Ruby. Had Blondie called the cops after a few hours of remorse? Alice mulled it over, determined to get more information about it.

"Viewers may remember the victim, George Byrd, for the key role he played in solving the string of West Hazel burglaries known as the Cola Bandits case. In that case, the only clue left by thieves who'd robbed more than a dozen homes was an empty cola can. One of the bandits made it known that cola-flavored soft drinks were his beverage of choice." Keisha said this last bit with a slight smile, a nod to the quirk of the previous crime.

"George Byrd was the city leader who hired a genealogical firm that cross-checked DNA from the crime scenes with ancestry records. The results ultimately led to two high school seniors who had much of the stolen property stored in their garages."

"Why is she talking about all this?" Taylor said. "George is the story."

"While the police warn it's too early to speculate, some people are wondering if Byrd's death might be related to his role in that high profile case. One of the young men who was indicted, Tony Preston, vowed that he would take revenge on the people who unjustly accused him of his crime," Keisha said, speaking with convincing earnestness.

"No, no, no, you've got it all wrong, Keisha," Ruby said, talking to the TV. "That Tony kid was full of baloney! It was the floozy who did it! Find out who she is and you've got your killer."

"Honey, Keisha Brandon doesn't even know there's a floozy involved," Alice pointed out.

"Well, she should," Ruby insisted. "I have half a mind to call the information in to Keisha myself. If the cops can't figure out that woman's identity, the media will find her."

Keisha gestured toward Ruby's house with sadness and concern. "At this point, the police think this might be a random killing, a possibility that has residents of this quiet suburb on edge tonight."

"A rando?" Taylor shuddered. "I didn't even think of

that." She raked back her long, red-tinged hair in agony. "I'll never sleep tonight."

"Police want the shaken community to know that they are actively investigating the case and are asking that anyone with information contact the West Hazel PD."

"Well, bully for them," said Violet, having joined them to watch.

"Are we all really on edge about a killer on the loose?" Alice touched her chin. "I didn't get a strong sense of that when I was out and about today."

"The media is stirring the pot," Violet said, "as they are apt to do on occasion."

"They've got me scared," Taylor said.

"You watch too many horror films for someone who lives in the basement," Violet told Taylor, snuggling in next to her on the couch.

"All I know is that George would have liked the way he was portrayed," Ruby said wistfully. "A bit of a hero, and with some flattering photos."

"I'm so sorry you lost him, Ruby," said Violet. "And sorry the police interrupted our ritual. I made sure the portal was closed, but we can try again tomorrow night."

"Might be best to let George rest," Ruby said. "We'll see what tomorrow brings."

"We will see," Violet agreed.

"But I do appreciate your help, Violet. The way you pulled that ceremony together, quick as can be. I appreciate all of you. Where would I be without you gals?"

"We love you, Ruby," Taylor said.

The innocent fervor in her granddaughter's voice made Alice choke up a bit. Taylor's failure to launch was a huge annoyance at times, but in moments like this, when her human response was so spot on . . . Alice couldn't be prouder.

"I feel like we should start a new puzzle," Violet said. "The gang's all here."

Alice shifted on the sofa, and the cushion beneath her adjusted, supporting her, wooing her. "My heart says yes, but my weary body says, 'Are you kidding me?'"

Ruby snuggled into a pillow. "Let's just hang out here and watch something light and fluffy."

"That sounds glorious," said Violet. "See if you can find the show about those wacky friends who live in New York. What's it called?"

"Um, *Friends*?" Taylor picked up the remote and took control.

Alice hugged a cushion and took her phone from her pocket. Her mind was too preoccupied to fall into a TV show. She looked at the news coverage of George's death on the other two major networks, then saw that she had a text from Stone.

**I hope this provides more help than harm,** he wrote, along with a link to his online article for the *Hazel Tidings*. She felt too tired to read it, but she couldn't resist a peek. Once she started, there was no stopping.

> *A wise man once said that the key to greater happiness lies in helping others. Having known George Byrd as a colleague, I have to say that this is something George knew. In his role as city comptroller, a fancy word for the treasurer who proposes budgets and often tells leaders their agency can't have money, George kept a tight fist around city finances. Because he was the man who said no, George was not always well-liked.*
>
> *I know this on a personal level, as George Byrd once refused additional funding for the West Linn*

*Senior Center, where I serve as the director. When George said no, I was not pleased. I had a few choice words for the man who chose to deny funding for the service that shuttles our seniors around town. "Calloused. Indifferent. Ageist." Those are just the words I can publish here. But I was wrong about George. He did care. After the meeting, he came to me and offered to look over our budget with me. In the end, he found a way to keep the shuttle services running by making a few modifications to the weekly schedule.*

*Since George's death, I've encountered a handful of city leaders who had similar experiences. George took on the unpopular job of saying no to folks, but then took the time to work with them to design a financial program that delivered necessary services. With a negotiator like George at the helm, most folks felt that they got a fair deal. Rest in peace, you fiscal wizard.*

*George is survived by his wife, Ruby, who is also a personal acquaintance. During this difficult time, I'm relieved to know that Ruby has the support of a few amazing women, some of whom she has known since they were knocking around as girls in a New York City neighborhood. These gals have a small puzzle club that trades with the seniors to keep new puzzles circulating. Jigsaw, anyone? That these women are still friends and now neighbors here on the left coast more than five decades later is a testament to the power of friendship.*

*A recent study found that loneliness is an epidemic. I'm here to let you know that friendship is the only cure.*

Alice tried to dab her tears away with the cuff of her sweatshirt before anyone noticed. It seemed wrong to blubber about friendship after Ruby had suffered such a loss.

Alice was especially touched by the way he'd mentioned how she and Ruby had met as kids. She was sure she'd told that story at some senior center activity, but she'd never expected anyone to pay much attention. Stone had listened; it was a novelty for a woman in her sixties to be heard, but he had paid attention.

"Ladies, I'm sending you Stone's article, so look for the link on your phone," she told the gals. "It's lovely."

"Great, thanks," said Violet.

There was no answer from Taylor and Ruby, who had both dozed off. Sweet.

And the power of suggestion was strong. Sleep was just what Alice needed. She said good night and went upstairs to her bedroom, her comfortable retreat. It took no time to wash up, change into soft, stretchy pajamas, and lodge herself amid the comforter and pillows in her vast bed. Heaven on earth.

She opened her bedside novel to the bookmarked page, then paused.

"Good-bye, George," she said, more for herself than for any lingering spirit.

Good-bye to George, and hello, Stone. After that article her opinion of Stone Donahue was in flux. He wasn't just a handsome pseudo cowboy, fit for a Marlboro ad. There was a kind person there, a good heart.

Not to obsess on that. He was just a man. But a good heart was so hard to find.

She dropped off to sleep imagining Stone on a horse. A

palomino? She didn't know horses, but that sounded grand and majestic. Stone was dressed in rugged, worn cowboy gear and riding off into the red, orange, and pink horizon of a western sunset.

Such a good heart.

No, she wasn't obsessing at all. . . .

# Chapter Fourteen

The next morning Alice felt refreshed when she threw back the covers, stepped out onto her bedroom balcony, and breathed in the vista that spread out around her. "I'm so grateful," she told the nearby rooftops and towering fir trees, the rolling, green Willamette Valley, the shiny cluster of downtown Portland, and the whitecapped mountains beyond.

As a kid, she'd barely believed that volcanoes were real, and now here she was, standing on an Oregon balcony peering into a volcano in Washington. Mount Saint Helens's flat top testified to its most devastating eruption in May 1980, an explosion that had killed fifty-seven people and caused major damage to homes, roads, and bridges. Alice had been in Oregon then, but she'd missed most of the action as she'd been south in Corvallis, preparing to graduate from college. Oh, those senior year memories with Ruby as a housemate! They'd had their fair share of college shenanigans, while pulling each other forward to graduation.

Looking to the right, she saw Mount Adams, also in Washington, and then, so much closer, the looming peak of Mount Hood, a majestic giant that seemed to reign just miles away on the horizon. Even now, after all these years in Oregon, the sight of these mountains could take her breath away. When it wasn't raining, affirmation by the mountains was a part of her morning ritual.

These views were one of the reasons she couldn't leave this house.

*"Sell it, and we can save the restaurant,"* Jeff had told her, when she'd realized that the restaurant had already been lost to her.

*"Sell it, and we can travel the world,"* Jeff had said.

And give up her home?

*"Sell it, and you can retire."* He'd seemed giddy with the idea. "We'll buy a little camper and blow out of this popsicle stand." But Alice liked her job. The steady flow of people through the library was her lifeblood. This town was home, these people her neighbors, her beautiful home.

Thank God she had finally stopped Jeff.

Breathing in the sunshine, she reminded herself that life was good and stepped inside to start her day.

Downstairs in the kitchen, Alice had just stolen half a cup from the dripping coffee when Madison stopped by.

"I've got a box of pastries fresh from Dolly's Bakery, and what appears to be a puzzle." Madison put the white pastry box on the counter and held up a plastic bag full of puzzle pieces. "I found this on the doorstep."

"It's probably from Stone." Alice took the bag and checked for a note. "No note, no box. I'm surprised he didn't ring the bell. But you know Stone Donohue, director of the senior center? We trade puzzles all the time."

"Seems like a nice man."

*A good heart.* Alice fetched the kitchen scissors to cut

the string on the box. "What have we here? Apology pastries?"

"They are sort of a peace offering." Madison turned away to grab a mug and pour herself some coffee. The girl was a master at masking her emotions.

"Peace pastries from Bedrosian? Because he's the one who should be apologizing." Alice lifted the lid, releasing the magnificent aroma of fresh-baked deliciousness. "You know, I try to stick to high fiber cereal in the morning, but a turnover doesn't count against my diet if I'm not involved in its purchase."

"An interesting diet plan." Madison added milk to her coffee.

"Who's on a diet so early in the morning? I always figure the best time to start a diet is tomorrow." In her black tunic and flowing pants, Ruby seemed to float into the room. Today she wore a maroon-tinged A-line wig with bangs and a slight wave that came just below her chin.

"That's a smart look for you, honey." Alice turned the box toward her. "Have a fresh apology pastry, courtesy of Detective Bedrosian."

"Only they're not from the detective," Madison said. "Not really. He doesn't even know I'm here."

"Well, apology or not, I love a good scone. This one looks like raspberry." Ruby picked a scone out, and Alice handed her a small plate.

"Let's sit at the table, like civilized human beings," Alice said, plating a cherry turnover for herself and refilling her coffee.

When they were seated at the table, Madison put down her mug and finally faced them. "Ruby, I have to apologize for last night. I feel like Detective Bedrosian was lacking in respect and empathy, and he took it out on you."

"I can handle Bedrosian." Ruby seemed far more interested in the scone.

"The thing is, he's all jacked up about this investigation. It's his first homicide, and he's feeling the pressure."

"His first?" Alice shook her head. "The department put a newbie on a murder case?"

"West Hazel hasn't had a homicide in three years. It's not like he had a lot of chances to practice. Anyway, Bedrosian is supposed to be working under the chief's supervision, but unfortunately, Chief Cushman is on vacation in France. A river cruise."

"So Detective Bedrosian is driving solo, without a navigator," Alice said.

"I'm the navigator, I guess. I've been assigned to assist him. Otherwise, they wouldn't have put a rookie officer like me on a case like this."

"Honey, I'm so proud," Alice said.

"My point is, I'm grateful for the opportunity, but I get why Bedrosian is stressed. I talked to him about calming down. Using a more even tone with people."

"He's a moody one, all right," Ruby agreed. "But honestly, he's not my beef. What I want to know is, why aren't you out there looking for that blond tart? She was there with him. I'd say she's your prime suspect."

"Exactly." Alice nodded. "So tell us, Officer, what's the scoop on Blondie?"

"I'll tell you, but you've got to promise to keep it to yourselves until the official press release is out. We're planning to make a statement this afternoon to enlist the help of the public."

Ruby pushed her plate away. "My lips are sealed."

Madison leaned forward, as if she needed to keep a secret from the walls. "Turns out the woman wasn't blond after all, as she was wearing Ruby's wig. She has longish brown hair, pulled back in a ponytail in the video from the neighbor's security camera."

"I knew it!" Ruby gasped. "I'll never wear that wig again."

"Who had the security camera?" asked Alice. "That Tiger person?"

"Tiger Garrett. The footage isn't crystal clear, but it does cover activity in Ruby and George's driveway. We could see your Cadillac pull in at seven twenty-six and then leave around twenty minutes later. We believe the mystery woman arrived as a passenger in George's Jeep around six forty-five. The car drove right into the garage, so we can't confirm that it was her. But it looks like she was in the house with him until eight twenty p.m., when a woman in a ponytail can be seen leaving and getting into a car that seems to be an Uber or Lyft. She wore a feathered mask, which covered much of her face."

"Have you reached out to Uber or Lyft?" asked Alice.

"I'm on it, Gran. I've reached out to both car services to see if they can identify a driver and get me passenger records. Here's a still photo of her that we're going to release later today. Anyone you know?"

They peered at Madison's phone.

"It's so hazy," said Ruby. "And that mask is hideous."

"Not someone I recognize," Alice said. "Average height and weight."

"A woman in a ponytail . . ." Ruby opened the bag and poured out the puzzle pieces. "I need to get working on this. Helps free my mind. So basically, we need to find Ponytail Girl."

"Dark hair in a ponytail isn't a lot to go on." Alice grimaced as she began to help Ruby go through the puzzle pieces. "Come on, Madison. Help me find some border pieces."

"I've got to get to work. And don't you need to get to the library, Gran?"

"I took the morning off. I'm taking Ruby to a funeral home. She mentioned that you advised her to make arrangements for George."

"I'm glad you're on it." Madison nodded. "I don't know when they'll release the body, but you want to have someone lined up to take care of things."

"A morbid topic." Ruby didn't look up from the puzzle pieces, a welcome distraction. "What is this puzzle, anyway?"

"I'm not sure, since it came without a box. Something that Stone dropped off. But it'll come together quickly. My guess is it's only two hundred fifty pieces." As Alice slotted together two pieces of the border that seemed to form a royal-blue tree trunk, she wondered about the recording of Ruby's driveway. "So the driveway footage . . . does it show anyone else entering the house?"

"Just Ruby and the exiting mystery woman."

"So that narrows down your suspects." Alice collected two orange border pieces. "Ruby and the Mystery Woman."

"Great," Ruby groaned. "Guess I'm still in the hot seat."

"Actually, Ruby, you may be in the clear," Madison said.

"What?" There was hope in Ruby's voice. "How?"

"I've done some investigating, and you have some solid alibis." Madison smiled. "I haven't gotten the video from the mall yet, but the salesclerk at Nordstrom remembers you. Apparently, that sale made her day. I took the liberty of calling the shelter, and they confirmed that the jackets appeared on their doorstep that night, along with sales receipts. The manager at the 7-Eleven provided the store's security footage late last night. The video footage is perfect. It's time-stamped, and it shows your car in the parking lot. Shows you purchasing your Slurpee. And there are images of you at the dumpster. All confirming the timeline that you gave us." ·

"Please do not share the footage of me at the dumpster." Ruby pressed her fingertips to one temple. "You did a lot to prove I was just out shopping and riding around."

"It was important," Madison said, "because Dr. Jane has narrowed down the time of death. She thinks George was killed around eight or nine p.m."

"While Ruby was at the mall," Alice said. "So Ruby is no longer a suspect?"

"As it stands now, we're looking closely at the mystery woman, who left the premises between eight and nine."

"Hallelujah!" Ruby said. It was a huge source of relief for Ruby and Alice.

As Madison prepared to leave, Ruby had a breakthrough. "Superman. Ladies, we have the caped crusader in this puzzle."

"There are a few superheroes here," Alice said. "This is definitely Wonder Woman."

"I'm heading out," Madison said. "Is Taylor here?"

"Probably downstairs."

Madison gave a look of dismay. "Gran, I hope she's paying you rent. You know, she thinks she doesn't have to pay because she's not using a bedroom? That's so lame."

"Leave the fiscal arrangements up to Taylor and me," Alice said.

"When is she going to get a job?" Madison was indignant. "She couldn't even hold on to that barista job. And now I have a feeling she's getting money from Mom."

"Okay, I definitely don't want to hear this." Alice pretended to plug her ears with her fingers. "But how does she-who-shall-not-be-named have enough resources to loan out money?" she asked, then waved Madison off. "No, don't tell me. I don't have the capacity to deal with her."

No room in her heart.

Not enough time in this life to worry over someone who refused to be lifted onto her feet.

Not enough strength to endure the heartbreak and disappointment.

"Thank you for the apology pastries, Madison," Alice said. "You're doing a great job, honey. Shoot me a text when you've found the killer."

"Oh, Gran." Madison sighed and headed out.

# Chapter Fifteen

"We just can't do a funeral right now," Ruby told the aloof but very soft-spoken gentleman who'd ushered them into the Green Acres Funeral Home. "First of all, the police may not release his body for another week or so. And even then, I have a family wedding to put on. The funeral needs to wait for two or three months. Maybe then George's brothers can schedule a trip, and all the talk of murder will settle down."

"I'm sorry for your loss." Peter Hatten gave a grim nod. "But I would advise having a brief ceremony this week, a chance for people to remember and grieve. I'd be happy to put that together for you."

"Nope," Ruby said firmly. "Not doing anything that might get in the way of the wedding."

Twenty minutes later, as Alice was driving them home, Ruby had second thoughts.

"Honestly, I thought the undertaker was playing me for the money, but now I'm having second thoughts. I mean, what's the right thing to do to honor the death of a cheating husband?"

The question gave Alice pause. "There's no established

etiquette for it. I think you need to do what feels right to you."

"Then we should do our own little memorial for George. It might give some closure to have a short ceremony. Something respectful. Let the minister say a prayer. I think it would give me a chance to move on and enjoy the wedding." Ruby let out a sigh. "Yes, that feels right. I can have people gather in my backyard, and . . ."

"Just yards from the crime scene?" Alice said. "That would be too creepy. You should use my yard."

"Would you mind?"

"Not at all. In fact, I'll cater it for you."

"That would be a weight off my shoulders. I'll pay for everything, of course. But we'll keep it simple. Work associates, neighbors, and friends, only. Which should make it small, since George didn't have many friends." Ruby frowned. "Come to think of it, I can't think of a single friend of his to invite. Is that weird?"

Alice thought it was a little odd, but she shrugged it off and focused on the road.

When Alice arrived at the library, the pre-K story hour was just about to end. Alice went down to the children's section to do a little meet and greet with the children and their caretakers. She was surprised to see that only three children had attended.

"I know I'm late, but where is everybody?" Alice hugged Charity, one of the moms who, along with her daughter Penny, was a regular at the library.

"Everyone's a little tense about leaving their homes," Charity said, watching as her daughter toddled over to a teddy bear on a low shelf. "Our afternoon playdate at the town pool was canceled. People are nervous that there's a murderer on the loose."

"I'm no crime expert, but I think it's safe to take a dip in the kiddy pool. It's not like he struck in broad daylight at a public place," Alice said.

"Fear isn't always rational." Charity squeezed her hand. "I'm being extra careful, but I think we still need to live our lives."

"Absolutely," Alice agreed. For her, the thought of staying at home and hiding behind locked doors seemed far more frightening than being out in the sunshine, around other people.

In her informal patrol of the rest of the library, the topic of the homicide came up in a few other conversations. Everyone was uneasy that a killer was on the loose. Back in the office, Alice phoned the mayor.

"It's a problem," Tansley admitted. "Folks are still in shock. The police were here at city hall today, going through George's office. It's all so upsetting."

"It's a lot to handle," Alice agreed. "Ruby has maintained her sense of humor, but there are moments when it doesn't seem real."

"And then the cops comb through his office, and you know it's over. They copied his e-mails and hard drive, but George wasn't a big computer person. Now there are just a few boxes left behind. Which probably should go to Ruby. Do you think she'll want his personal property?"

"What does it entail?"

"There's a pair of bowling shoes and some plaques. Not sure what else."

"I'll ask Ruby, but I suspect she'll be interested." In Alice's experience, part of the grieving process involved sorting through the possessions of the person you loved and taking a moment to remember them in their element. She had savored the smell and luster of her father's old pipes, and remarked upon the light in her mother's watercolors before packing them away.

"Before I let you go," Alice said, "I have to ask again about the budget. I was just talking with Julia, and it's hard to set up our future calendar without knowing how deep the cuts will be."

"I'm sorry, Alice, but we haven't straightened that out yet."

"I would say take your time, but honestly, George left us in a pickle. I admit, not all thoughts of him are fond right now."

"Same." Tansley sighed. "I promise you, we'll get to the bottom of it, but from what I've seen so far, it appears that George involved the city in some expensive contracts that might be difficult to terminate."

"What sort of contracts?"

"It's complicated," Tansley said. "Trust me, we're looking into it, doing our best to straighten it all out."

"Madame Mayor, you sound like a politician."

"You got me there," Tansley said.

"Sorry to bother you at work, honey, but I have a question about the case." Alice was in the library office, speaking in lowered tones as she watched the activity in the main room through the tinted glass. "I've been wondering about the call for the welfare check."

"Groaaaan." Madison grumped. "Not sure we should be talking like this."

"Nonsense. I'm your grandmother. Now it was reported

that the request for a welfare check on George came from an anonymous caller. But earlier Ruby was saying that George really had no friends. So that means the call probably came from the mystery woman. She clocked him, and maybe had a guilt pang and sent the police to revive him."

"That's our theory right now."

"So what was the source of the call?" Alice asked.

"An anonymous tip. Just as reported."

"But, honey, when a call comes into the nine-eleven dispatcher, the police station has caller ID." At least, they did in mystery novels.

"So. It probably identified as 'anonymous.' "

"Usually there's more information. The number might come up, even if it's not identified. And it's all computerized, so there'd be a record." From the silence, Alice sensed that Madison was interested. "Can you check into it? Get more information?"

"I can try."

"Wonderful! Talk to you later, dear."

Wednesday evening was dinner night at the senior center, and normally Alice and the puzzle gals attended for the camaraderie, an easy dinner, and free wine.

On this night Ruby declined. "I really need to start going over George's finances. I'm a little scared that he might have maxed out his credit cards, big spender that he was. And I wouldn't mind some quiet time. But give Aunt Gildy a big hug for me."

Dinner night also gave Alice and Violet a chance to visit with their aunt, ninety-year-old Gilda Pepper, who took the shuttle bus here from her assisted living facility. They sat on either side of her at the family-style table, making sure she got bread to go with her salad and lasagna. Top-ping off her wine. The food at the senior center was tasty enough, and Aunt Gildy could still pack it in. As per her usual habit, Gildy abandoned conversation to methodically devour the food, while other senior diners delivered monologues about when the grandchildren visited, who married a doctor, and what was on the menu for next week's dinner.

Alice and Violet asked the other diners polite questions as they ate their lasagna. They knew that once Gildy had finished eating, she'd perk up.

After the meal most folks headed over to the jigsaw tables, where the distraction of the puzzle allowed for free-flowing jokes and conversation. Alice glanced over at the puzzle corner, where there were two jigsaw puzzles going, one nearly complete, one with borders done and many pieces sorted by color into flat plastic boxes.

Not to be a snob, but Alice liked to work puzzles at home, in her own kitchen, where there was a peaceful rhythm among her friends. Sometimes the folks here got a little prissy, hoarding puzzle pieces because they wanted to work a certain section on their own.

Her plate clean, Gildy wiped her face thoroughly and sighed. "That was delicious."

"Shall we move over to the puzzle corner?" Violet suggested. "I'll grab your walker for you."

"Not tonight. Tonight, I want to warn these folks about the news. Not for nothing, but our lives could be in jeopardy."

Alice and Violet exchanged a curious look.

"Is there a new disease going around?" asked Violet.

"Haven't you heard? There's a killer on the loose." Gildy had a low Lauren Bacall voice with a lingering New

York accent, a novelty that Violet and Alice often discussed.

"Here comes the accent," Violet said under her breath so that Gildy couldn't hear. Not that it mattered. Gildy was hot on the gossip about the local homicide.

"It's the intonation that makes her sound like a mob boss," Alice argued. "I could listen to her for hours."

"I think she's pouring on the accent for attention," Violet maintained. "Mom and Dad never talked that way. The 'deeze, dems, and doze.' It's too much."

"True, but Mom and Dad went to college. Gildy was a secretary at the steelworker's union in Queens. She's a tough broad."

"I *am* a tough broad," Gildy agreed, though Alice couldn't imagine how she'd caught that comment. "I can protect myself, and I'll tell you how. Last night I found my candlestick holders in the closet—that set that your mother used to have. I think they're marble, but they might be faux. Hard to tell. Anyway, I removed the candles, and then put one candlestick in the shower, the other under my pillow. I figure if this wise guy killer breaks in and tries to off me in my sleep, I'll give him a good whack."

"It's a wonder she didn't 'whack' the nursing aide," Alice muttered to Violet.

"It's a miracle," Violet agreed.

"I heard about that," said a woman with whimsical rhinestone-studded glasses.

"A guy gets killed in his own home," a man said. "I tell you, the world's in a sad state."

Alice touched Gildy's arm. "Aunt Gildy, did you know that Ruby's husband is the man who was killed?"

"The bee's bunion?" Gildy said in a loud voice. "What are you saying?"

Violet pointed to her own ear, mouthing, "Hearing aids."

"You remember our friend Ruby?" Alice enunciated, facing Gildy so she could lip-read. "She usually comes here to dinner with us? Well, it was her husband, George, who was killed."

"That's terrible news," Gildy lamented. "Terrible. Where's Ruby now? Is she all right?"

"She'll be fine. She's grieving, of course."

"So you knew the man who was murdered?" asked the woman with the rhinestone glasses.

"We knew George," Violet said. "It's very sad for us."

"But aren't you terrified?" asked rhinestone glasses. "You were *that close* to the killer. Aren't you afraid you could be next?"

"I don't really look at the situation that way," Violet said.

"We all need to be careful," Alice said, trying to sound authoritative. "But I think it's important that we continue to live our lives."

"I'm not going to get a moment's rest until they catch that killer," said one woman.

"Don't go out alone after dark," a man said.

"Of course. Be careful." Alice wanted to reassure them. She wanted to argue this wasn't the work of some random killer who attacked people while they were at home on an exercise bike. On the other hand, she couldn't prove that it was not a rando, as Taylor would put it.

"There's a killer on the loose in West Hazel!" Gildy exclaimed. "We have to save ourselves."

"We do!"

"Where are the police when we need them?"

Alice stared at the rabble-rousers as tensions began to simmer.

"Aunt Gildy started quite a commotion," Violet whispered.

"I'm afraid so. And here we are without torches and pitchforks."

# Chapter Sixteen

"It's getting a little loud over at this end." The low, steady voice of Stone Donahue immediately eased the tension. "What's going on now, Ellen? Didn't you get enough lasagna? There's plenty more garlic bread if anyone wants it. Someone overordered and we've got enough to open an Italian restaurant."

"We're talking about the murder," Gildy reported.

"A homicide, right here in West Hazel," said Ellen, the lady with the snazzy rhinestone glasses.

"You're talking about my friend George Byrd?" Stone folded his arms as he looked down at the diners. "A sad thing. I hope you all read my homage to George in the *West Hazel Tidings*." He scanned the people at the table. "Please tell me someone is reading my weekly column."

"I read it, Stone," said one man.

"I follow your column every week," said someone else, as if it were a competition.

"I thank you," Stone said with a nod.

Somehow, his easy intervention had diffused the tension, and Alice was grateful for that.

"Now, as to safety, I share your concern, Ellen, Gildy,

Todd." He acknowledged them one by one, and they seemed to feel heard. "Make sure you lock your doors, and use the buddy system. Go places with a friend if you can, but don't let this tragedy steal your freedom. I agree with what Alice was saying. Don't be afraid to live."

"And on that note"—Alice arose—"I'm going to clear away some of these plates. I understand there's ice cream for dessert." That news evoked some positive comments, and Alice set to work stacking paper plates. Stone started clearing at the other end of the table. They met at the garbage can.

"Thank you for being the voice of calm," Alice said. "Gildy leans toward the dramatic."

"She's worried. It's a bad situation."

"You have a gift for smoothing things over. Also demonstrated by your column. I expected something trite, but it turned out to be a tribute to friendship."

"Thank you, Alice. That means a lot coming from you." He looked off for a moment, then winced. "You think I'm trite?"

They both laughed, stepping back to let a server bearing a tray of ice cream pass by.

"Now that I have your ear, I have a bone to pick with you," Alice said. "I have to ask, what's with the Justice League puzzle? It was a little dark and, well, superhero-ish. Dark and bold. Not the sort of thing I asked for to cheer Ruby up."

Stone shook his head. "I didn't drop off a puzzle at your house recently. But that reminds me, I've got something set aside for your group. A beach scene that has a sixties surf shop vibe. It's right over here."

He took a puzzle from a shelf and handed the box to Alice.

The splashes of bright color brought a smile to her face. The surf shop in the sand was chockful of summer items: surfboards, beach chairs, flags, banners, flowers, palm trees, beach buggies, towels, flip-flops.

"Delightful. This will lift our spirits. But I can't stop wondering who dropped off the Justice League puzzle."

"Clark Kent?" Stone suggested.

Alice smiled, though the mystery bugged her. "I guess it will sort itself out over time." She declined the ice cream cup offered by the server, and looked up at the clock. Approaching six p.m. The social would go on for another hour or so, but the events of the past two days had worn her out. "I think I'm going to call it a day," she told Stone.

She went over to check in with Violet, who was happy to stay and help their aunt onto the shuttle. "You take the car," Alice told Violet. "It's still light out, and it's an easy walk home."

"And I'm going to walk with her," Stone said from beside her, dipping into the conversation.

Alice declined, but he insisted, and Violet pointed out that it was the safe thing to do.

"There's a killer out there," Aunt Gildy reminded them.

Alice kissed her aunt good-bye, handed Stone the puzzle, and headed out.

A golden tint of late sun bathed every lawn, flower, and field. Oregon summers could be so green and sunny. Glorious! But this evening was far from perfect. Walking alongside Stone to the meandering path, Alice realized the tension of the folks at the senior center was quite real. Like a burr in your shoe, the worry persisted. A killer was out there.

"Thanks for seeing me home," she said. "It's best to be careful."

"Looks like we're just in time for a kickin' sunset." He gestured toward the treetops that fell away to the west, revealing clouds of rising color in pink and apricot.

"Beautiful," she agreed.

"Not everyone gets a light show like that every day. I've seen some amazing sunsets in my travels. Cambodia, Greece. There's a spot near the ocean in New Zealand where you get this incredible sense of the earth when the sun sets over the boulders on the beach. Spectacular. But in my mind, there's nothing like the sunsets we have here in the summer and fall."

"We need these sunsets to make up for the rest of the year, when the gray drizzle makes people go batty," she teased.

"It all balances out."

Stone had lived in various places and held so many different jobs that he could hold his own on just about any topic. The conversation flowed easily with him. She asked him about interesting foods he'd encountered in different spots of the world, and they chatted on about cooking and books and baseball.

"I used to have a goal to visit every stadium in Major League Baseball," Alice said. "So far I've visited eleven, but I'm probably not going to hit them all."

"There's still time. You're too young to give up on your bucket list."

"I'm not so sure it's on the list anymore. Baseball was more my ex-husband's passion. And the idea of that much travel seems tedious. Lately I've realized how much I love my home, my work, this town. I'm afraid I've become quite provincial."

"Nothing wrong with that. It's a good thing to find

your happy place. You know, contentment is an attractive quality."

"Aw, shucks," she teased. "Am I blushing?"

"Maybe it's the sunset glow. I'd like to talk more about that bucket list. Let's have dinner sometime. We could check out a new food cart on Hawthorne where I hear they make amazing empanadas."

"You're too kind, but I'm afraid I have to decline."

Looking back at her, he rubbed his forehead with two fingertips, looking genuinely perplexed. "What am I doing wrong here, Alice? What do I have to do to court you properly . . . to win your heart?"

"You're doing everything right. Hitting all the right buttons." Alice pressed a hand to her chest, as if it could prevent her heartbeat from leaping in excitement. "I'm afraid the problem is in my court."

"Not that old pearl."

"What?"

"That worn-out excuse: *It's not you, it's me.* Can't you come up with something more creative?"

"But it's true. I'm not of the mind to be courted right now." A relationship with Stone tempted her. No doubt it would be nice. But she was still in the rebuilding phase of her life, trying to repair her finances, her heart, her soul. The divorce was amicable, a fine word for all appearances. People on the outside couldn't see the rocky spires of ice beneath the surface of an iceberg.

She let her gaze lift beyond the trees and rooftops to Mount Hood in the distance, the sun setting orange and pink around the mountain's giant grooves of ice and rock. The mountain made her feel grounded, inspired, honest. "This confident, pleasant facade is just an appearance, you know. In truth, I'm a has-been chef, a woman nearing retirement age who's still struggling to get on solid financial footing and take care of herself."

"You're no has-been. Some of us are late bloomers. That means the best is yet to come."

"I wish I could believe that. I'm sorry, Stone. I do like you. I hope we can stay friends."

"Friends." The word came out as a grumbled complaint in that gravelly rumble that was so oddly appealing. How easy it would be to fall for him.

But no more. The last fall had broken her, and she was still in the middle of repairs.

No more.

# Chapter Seventeen

"Good morning. It's just your grandmother, checking in to see if you've found George's killer yet," Alice said, phone to her ear on Thursday morning.

"Gran, this is not normal." Madison sighed. "You're supposed to call and invite me over to dinner or tell me you're baking cookies. Or ask for help planting your azalea bushes."

"What's the harm in a little homicide update?"

"Why can't you be like a normal grandmother?"

"Normal is boring."

"That you'll never be. Sorry to disappoint you, but the case is not solved yet."

"That is a shame. People are so worried about this killer being loose. But I know you're doing your best. Tell me, did you find out who placed that phone call requesting a welfare check on George?"

"Not exactly. But I did get more information. I actually visited the dispatch center, which is over in Tigard. Do you know we share a dispatch hub with five other towns?"

"Makes sense. What did you find out?"

"I went through the actual call log, and you were right.

The caller identified as anonymous. But there was a phone number of origin—the general services number for West Hazel City Hall."

"The call came from city hall? What time?"

"At five thirty-three a.m." Madison's voice was pitched with excitement.

"Well, that's something. So it must be someone who works at city hall, to be able to get into the building so early."

"That seems likely," said Madison.

"This is perfect timing. I'm going to George's office at city hall today to help Ruby pick up George's personal possessions. I'll keep my eyes open, see what I can learn."

"Gran, we already swept the place. We interviewed people there. It's all sewn up."

"We'll see," Alice said. "I'll keep you posted."

It had taken a bit of finagling for Alice to clear her morning schedule yet again to help Ruby. There were standing meetings that happened once a week with staff, with the library council, with the Friends of the Library. Also meetings with educators, community leaders, and charitable groups. Planning meetings. Budget meetings. List development meetings to discuss new acquisitions.

Meetings and lists, and lists and meetings! Alice knew this pattern so well, she could dance a jig to it. Still, it required her presence. With Julia's help, she'd managed to push some meetings to the afternoons and cancel some of the others.

"I'd like to make this a quick stop, and then to the bank," Ruby said as they approached city hall. "As I mentioned last night, I can't escape the awkward feeling that everyone knows my husband was cheating."

The previous night, as they'd cracked open a three-hundred-fifty-piece puzzle of colorful candies—one of their favorites that they enjoyed doing over and over again—Ruby had shared her embarrassment over her personal life going public. The release of the police photo of the mystery woman had made the cold hard facts quite obvious to the general public.

"I feel like my associates and neighbors are peeking in and judging me," Ruby had said.

"But you didn't do anything wrong, honey. This one's all on George."

"Still. I was the fool." Ruby had shuddered. "It feels crummy."

Now, as they entered the building, Alice felt protective of her friend. "We'll keep the small talk to a minimum," Alice agreed, though that was unlikely. Ruby was not prone to short conversations.

Ruby's heels clicked on the polished floor as they passed through the lobby. Dressed in a black linen skirt, a black blouse with chiffon sleeves, topped by a linen duster, Ruby could certainly dress the part of the fashionable widow.

Alice would have felt drab by comparison in her black smock dress and comfortable sandals if she hadn't grabbed her blue and black pajama-weight jacket at the last minute. She liked to think that the short-waisted jacket, which fit her to a T, had the magical powers of making her appear supremely professional. Yes, she believed in magic.

Alice ushered Ruby over to the mayor's office, where Tansley had her assistant Cassidy lead them in.

Tansley rose from her desk and came over to greet them. She wore a gray pantsuit with a teal shell that brought out the blue of her eyes. "Ruby, how are you?"

"Hanging in there."

Tansley gave Ruby a warm hug. "I'm sorry to see you under these circumstances. So tragic about George. We're all in shock."

Ruby nodded. "There seems to be a lot of that going around. I still can't believe it."

Tansley shook her head sadly. "I hope the police solve the case quickly. I spoke with the chief last night. He's thinking of cutting short his vacation—a European river cruise. I didn't know what to tell him. But the investigation is certainly going on in his absence."

"Oh, yes." Ruby gave a coy look, a lock of hair curling against her chin. "I've seen Detective Bedrosian in action."

"Let's get you those files. Cassidy?"

A bright-eyed woman in her mid-twenties appeared at the door. Cassidy Pearson, the mayor's assistant, had always struck Alice as carefree and unflappable.

"George's office is all packed up?" asked Tansley.

"I can check with Nicole," said Cassidy.

Tansley looked at her watch. "I have a minute before my next meeting. I'll show you the way."

The mayor led them past a roomful of cubbies, where people were talking on the phone and typing on keyboards. "Excuse me, Nicole?" Tansley leaned into one of the cubicles. "George's wife is here to pick up his things." She turned to Ruby. "Have you two met? Nicole has managed to take over the accounting and bookkeeping. George trained her well."

When a thirty-something woman arose tentatively from her desk, Ruby gasped.

"Come here, you!" Ruby went to her immediately, embracing her in a hug.

"I'll leave you all to it." Tansley headed back to her office.

George's assistant seemed a little stiff, but Alice knew that not everyone was a hugger like Ruby. And perhaps Nicole was grieving and doing her utmost to hold herself together. After all, her boss had just been murdered.

"I can't believe we lost him," Ruby said.

Nicole said quietly, "How've you been holding up, Ms. Milliner?"

"Call me Ruby, please." Ruby stepped back from her embrace. "It's been hard. Especially with the circumstances of his death. I just can't fathom what might make someone do that to him."

Such an honest assessment. Alice was proud of her friend for sharing her feelings.

"It's so scary," said Cassidy.

"What are the police telling you?" asked Nicole. "Do they have suspects?"

"Nicole . . ." Cassidy reprimanded her.

"It's okay. They're looking at one or two suspects. They turned my house into a crime scene, but my daughter still wants to come and have her wedding here next weekend."

Cassidy pointed out that a wedding seemed like a very positive thing at a time like this. It could be a blessing.

Two other women emerged from their cubicles to agree. They were introduced as Asia and Linda. And then the conversation went off-track to wedding details that made Alice's thoughts glaze over. As she watched the women talk, she tried to imagine that someone in this room was the mystery woman. Anyone here could have come into this office early in the morning and called to request a welfare check on George.

What else did they know about the woman? Brown hair swept back in a ponytail.

Both Cassidy and Nicole had long, dark hair. Cassidy's

was pulled back, while Nicole's was twisted atop her head. Come to think of it, the mayor had sandy brownish hair, too.

Alice took a little stroll around the room and the suspect list expanded . . . three, four, five women in the cubbies. That made a total of eight women working with George, eight women who might have been having an affair with him. Not to mention the other women in leadership positions who had private offices here in city hall.

*It would help if we could narrow this down a bit.*

A lanky, nervous summer intern named Kevin strolled into the large office pool. Kevin! Finally, one employee who wasn't on the suspect list.

Cassidy pressed prayer hands to her chest. "I've got a meeting coming up but, Kevin, would you please help Ms. Milliner move things out of her husband's office. You know, George's office?"

"Sure." Kevin led them to a small window office that already exuded a vacant spell. He flicked on the light and looked around. "This is it. These five boxes. I'll go get the cart."

Ruby frowned at the boxes. "Anticlimactic."

Alice sat at the desk and systematically opened every drawer. "All empty. At least someone here did their job."

Ruby picked up a pair of bowling shoes from a cardboard box. "Is this it? The only souvenirs of George's time working for the city? His only legacy?"

Alice could think of a few people who currently had some choice words about George's legacy, herself included, but she didn't want to drag her friend into the budget fiasco that George had left behind.

"Let's see. Looks like two boxes contain files, and three contain personal items," Alice said. "Workout clothes, plaques, a coffeemaker . . ."

"George loved his coffee."

"I do wonder about the paperwork." She sifted through some of the files. Personal papers would belong to George, but the folders contained budget reports, invoices. "It looks like these are supposed to stay here. Maybe go to storage?"

Ruby shrugged. "The kid said we should take 'em. I'll take 'em and dump 'em if I don't need them."

"I wouldn't mind taking a look at these, when I have more time," Alice admitted. Especially the budget files.

"So take them," Ruby said.

"Here we go," Kevin said, wheeling the cart in.

"Thanks for your help, Kevin." Alice stood back as he loaded the boxes. "I'm just wondering, have the police been here? Did they take any of Mr. Byrd's files?"

"Yeah, the police came by and photocopied a few things. And Nicole helped them get some electronic copies of records."

"Very good." Alice smiled at the intern. Since no one seemed to care about the files, Alice was happy to wheel them out of the building and load them up in Ruby's trunk.

It wasn't likely that the files would lead her to George's killer; but she had a shot at learning more about George's severe budget cuts for West Hazel. Maybe she would find some expenses that could be cut so that Alice and her colleagues providing city services could breathe easy again.

Later, she would dig in and exercise one of a librarian's superpowers: research.

# Chapter Eighteen

With the boxes loaded in the trunk, they stopped at the bank to begin the process of closing George's bank accounts. Alice had gone through this when her father died, and she recalled feeling frustration with the cantankerous rules and regulations.

The wide-eyed teller, who looked like she was still in high school, fluttered a bit when she heard that Ruby's husband had recently passed. "Can you just hold on one second?" she asked. "If you wait here, I'll get my manager."

They waited patiently as the girl disappeared into the back. "Just pointing out that our teller has long, brown hair, too," Alice said, "but she's too young to fall for George."

"Let's hope so," Ruby said. "If I find out he was messing around with a kid that age, I'll find a way to kill him again."

The manager, Simon Seltzer, was a fiftyish man with a kind voice and a comb-over that looked a bit greasy. He ushered them over to a desk at the back of the bank, listened to Ruby's story, and confirmed that George had two accounts at the bank. "Let's see who the beneficiary is," he said, as if a big surprise was in store.

Ruby's eyes popped in annoyance as Seltzer clicked and typed at the terminal. She didn't have the patience for his showmanship, and Alice didn't blame her.

"Well, lo and behold. The beneficiary is one Ruby Milliner."

"Told you." Ruby slid her ID over to him. "I was his wife, you know. Tell me what his balance is, please."

"I'm not really authorized to do that." The manager winced, adjusting the knot of his necktie. "The thing is, we'll have to fill out some paperwork and get a copy of the death certificate before you can withdraw money from Mr. Byrd's account. There's a claims process that will take time and—"

"Mr. Seltzer, I assure you, I just want to know the balance so I can prepare to settle his debts. Knowing my husband, I assume that he's drawn on his credit line."

"Well, that would still be confidential information."

Alice watched Ruby draw in a breath, preparing to pounce.

"But I am his widowed wife. His beneficiary. And I have the money to pay off his debt. I'm the sole owner of Ruby's House of Wigs and Hairpieces, a successful business. And by the way, it's not just wigs for women. We do carry some discreet hair pieces for men, Mr. Seltzer, if you happen to be interested. But the point is, I don't need George's money. I'm probably not even liable for his personal debts, but I will clean up his messes. That's just the kind of person I am. Just tell me, how bad is the damage?"

Flustered, Simon seemed to soften. "Maybe . . . I suppose I could give you a look at his account status."

"A look?"

"Nothing in writing," he said quickly.

"Fine." Ruby fixed a stern gaze on him. "Just tell me how bad the damage is."

He gave a nervous little cough and looked around, as if he were about to get caught committing a crime. "Here's his current account status," Seltzer said, turning the monitor toward Ruby.

Alice leaned in to get a gander. But something looked wrong.

George didn't owe the bank money.

There was more than a hundred thousand dollars posted in his account. To be exact, $112,313.28.

"A hundred grand!" Ruby gasped. "What, did he rob a bank?"

Seltzer frowned. "We don't joke about things like that here."

Ruby was floored, and Alice shared her surprise. Where did George get that kind of money?

# Chapter Nineteen

"I must be the first widow in the history of the world to be upset to learn her husband had money," Ruby said as Alice drove home from the bank. "Where do you suppose he got it from?"

"Maybe he tucked it away, a thousand from every paycheck?"

"George was never a saver. Whenever the Maserati needed something, he always leaned into me." She winced. "And to think he had the money to buy his own sports car. That stinker."

"What can you do? I mean, you need to find out where the money came from."

"I'll call my lawyer to start working on the estate. Then I'm going to call the mayor, see if George got any bonuses from the city."

"From the city?" Alice was skeptical. "I doubt that."

"My big worry is that the money came from something illegal. But how am I supposed to find that out?"

"That is a good question."

Once Alice arrived at the library, the day was chockful of demands. First, she attended a standing meeting with the Friends of the Library, a charitable organization that ran fund-raisers and special programs to help draw community members into the library. Their annual West Hazel Reads program was hugely popular. Every year in February, the Friends distributed free copies of the chosen book for that year. Then in March and April the library sponsored activities that tied in with the theme of the book.

At today's meeting, the Friends had a proposal that lifted Alice's spirits.

"You know that nook on the second floor of the old wing?" said Patrick Hastings, the Friends chairman. "The one near what used to be the staff kitchen?"

"I know it well," Alice said. "Sort of an awkward space, too big for a display table, too small for significant shelving."

Patrick nodded. "The Friends would like to turn it into a coffee bar for library patrons. There would be a charge, of course. Coffees and pastries, maybe sandwiches. We've talked to a few local vendors who would mentor a new business here. It would be an opportunity for an entrepreneur to launch a coffee shop that, after a year or two, could move to a food cart or brick and mortar store."

Alice felt a smile rising from her core. "Wonderful. And after the vendor is somewhat established, a year or two, we would bring in a new entrepreneur?"

"Exactly," said Stacy Tillman, one of the Friends. "A way to serve our patrons and promote entrepreneurship."

"I like it," Alice said. "I'll need to get board approval, but I don't see that being a problem if the program is funded. How soon can you have it up and running?"

The Friends meeting was followed by a Collection Development meeting, in which all the librarians discussed the list of books slated to be ordered that week. As many high-profile books were released from June to August, the eight "adult" librarians in the meeting were chomping at the bit to order the latest hot summer reads. Alice approved every purchase. The librarians on her staff were constantly perusing book reviews. They read advanced copies and studied data on which books in the collection had been checked out the most. These folks knew how to shop for books.

As the meeting broke up, a gaggle of women passed around a wrinkled paper, scoffed, and held it up beside their faces.

"Could be me," said Nancy Savino, one of the kids' librarians.

"Or me. It's my alter ego." Julia held the murky gray photo up to her face and gave a murderous look.

"What's that?" Alice asked them.

"The police photo of the person of interest in the homicide." Charles looked on with a dry expression. "We were just remarking how it looks like nearly every woman."

"With this photo as a clue, half of the women in West Hazel could be arrested," Nancy said.

Alice nodded. "Not a very effective tool for the investigation, I'm afraid."

"Ah, but there is one silver lining," said Charles. "The photo looks nothing like me."

The hours went quickly, filled with a multitude of tasks to catch up on. It was late, after six, and Alice was about to head home when she overheard a discussion at the checkout desk between Beto and a cheerful, middle-aged woman who was tapping her library card on the checkout desk with a concerned frown.

"Are you sure there's no other way?" The woman's

brow was creased with the concern of a caretaker—a mother or a teacher. A woman who looked after the people around her. "I'd like to do this legitimately. The thing is, I need all three machines now, but I'll only need them for the duration of the class, the next three weeks."

"I'm sorry, Ms. Lauridsen. When you check out an item from the Library of Things, you can only take one item at a time."

"You can call me Lory." She propped her elbows on the counter and rested her chin on her hands. The posture made the dimples in her round face more apparent. "And you are Beto, I see from your name tag. So here's the thing, Beto. If I go home and grab my husband and my daughter and they return with me, they'll be able to check out the other two sewing machines?"

"That would work." Beto cocked his head to one side, frowning. "I'm sorry it's inconvenient. But I can't change the rules."

"Sorry to butt in." Alice joined them at the counter and introduced herself. "I couldn't help overhearing. What do you need the machines for?"

"I'm teaching a summer course, adult education at a community center in Portland, and I need as many sewing machines as I can get my hands on. The students are immigrants from many different countries, and I've seen them make amazing creations on the one machine we have. Flowing pants and gowns and dresses. Aprons and hijabs. I'd like to give them a chance to practice a skill they feel confident with while we practice speaking English."

"Of course. And you want to check out all of our sewing machines until when?"

"The class ends in three weeks."

"This is exactly the sort of use these machines are intended for." Alice nodded. "We'll find a way help you."

"That would be awesome." There were those dimples again. Warm and cozy came to mind when Alice saw them.

Alice glanced over at Beto. "We're going to have to figure out a way to do an end-run around the system. But we appreciate what you're doing, Lory, and our purpose is to supply the resources you need. You can use my library card number to check one out, and let me see if our facilities manager is still here."

"Um." Beto shifted awkwardly. "Lory, do you want to check one out on my library card?"

"That's so kind of you," Lory said, "but I don't want to get you into any trouble."

"Beto can't be in trouble around here," Alice said. "He's our chief ambassador. Now, Beto will get you a cart, and we'll get you all checked out with three sewing machines."

"Thank you so much." Lory smiled. "You've made my day . . . my week! And the summer class will be that much better for these students."

Walking back to pick up the machines, Alice felt grateful for the little things that could make a difference.

# Chapter Twenty

When Alice got home from work, she found Ruby working a puzzle in the windowed kitchen nook.

"You look like you could use a good friend and a challenging puzzle." Ruby tapped the chair beside her and motioned for Alice to sit. "Take a load off and tell me about your afternoon."

Alice hung her bag on the back of the chair and sat down with a sigh. "We may be installing a coffee bar in the library."

"Yay. I'd go there."

"But my budget cut still hasn't been straightened out."

"Boo."

"I shouldn't complain. Life is good. I get to work around people and books." She picked up two puzzle pieces and tried to fit them into the border.

"Well, I spent the afternoon going through the stuff from the office, and there's plenty of budget stuff you might be interested in. But nothing that shows me where George got his money. So next I need to look through George's checkbook and the stacks of papers that he always had covering his desk."

"Sounds like a plan."

"Good. Because you're going over to the house with me to fetch the stuff."

Alice's mouth puckered in a sour expression as she looked up from the puzzle.

"Come on," Ruby said. "The house still feels a little spooky for me to go alone, and we'll just be a few minutes."

"Isn't it an active crime scene?" Alice asked.

"Last time we drove by, all the yellow tape was gone. Besides, I'm not going anywhere near the crime scene. I'm just going to dip into George's office, and then grab a few things from my office, too. I need my laptop and notebooks so I can work more efficiently from here." Ruby was already on her feet, her keys jangling from the ring looped through her fingers. "I'll drive, so we can use my garage clicker."

During the short ride to Ruby's house, Alice extracted a promise that they'd be in and out in mere minutes.

Ruby pulled her Cadillac into the garage and closed the door behind them. "The fewer people who see us, the better," Ruby said. She paused to take a breath, and then pulled open the door to the house, which put them in a little vestibule behind the stairs. Ruby proceeded through the hall to her first-floor office. "I need to pack up that laptop, and all the notebooks on the bottom shelf. That's how I do my record-keeping for the company." She started to cross the room, then paused on the white fur rug. "And this rug, too. It's one of my favorite things."

"Really, honey? Fur?"

"It's a fake. Fooled you, though." Ruby kicked off her high-heeled mules and let her feet sink into the sumptuousness. "Divine."

"Stay on track," Alice said. "Laptop. Notebooks. Rug. What did you want from upstairs?"

Ruby pointed a finger toward the ceiling. "Upstairs. George's checkbook or any bank statements."

Alice nodded. "Let's see what we can find."

The stairway wall and banister were still covered in smudges and dust spots from the attempts to dust for fingerprints. Alice kept her hands to herself all the way up. At the top of the stairs she noticed that Ruby avoided looking toward the primary bedroom, the place where the police had found the body.

George's office was still a mess of dirty dishes, wrinkled papers, and coffee mugs.

"Pretty much the way it was when I peeked in the morning after the murder," Alice said. "The police didn't disturb much of this in their search." Alice looked around the room. There was a one-drawer computer desk, a recliner, and floor-to-ceiling bookshelves. "No file cabinets? Are they in the closet?"

"Nope. George didn't believe in them." Ruby pointed to the disheveled piles of papers and newspaper clippings on the desk. "This was George's filing technique."

"Pretty sloppy for a comptroller."

"Probably because his assistant did all the accounting." Ruby frowned. "George was great with PR, but he was not a detail man."

"Okay, then." Alice started to gather up papers. "This is going to be messy."

"You can use this." Ruby found a canvas "PBS nerd" tote bag on the floor and handed it to Alice.

"Well, at least he supported quality television," Alice said as she stuffed wrinkled papers inside.

"Here's his checkbook." Ruby waved the blue vinyl cover in the air and closed the desk drawer. "Let's see what he was up to."

"No, no, no. You can go through it later." Alice took it from her and shoved it into the bag.

"What about the puzzles up here? I have some stashed in his closet. Should I grab them?"

"First things first. I'll finish here. You go downstairs and grab those things from your office. I'll meet you at the car."

"Yes, ma'am, Sergeant Pepper."

Although the tote bag was a generous size, Alice had to work to jam all the odd clippings and notes inside. She took a moment to stack the empty food containers in one spot, beside the stained coffee mugs. Better, but still a mess.

Still trying to avoid touching the dusted surfaces, she descended the stairs and entered the garage. Ruby's laptop was already stowed in the open trunk, along with a few notebooks. Good. Almost there.

Alice shot a look at the elephant in the room, George's Maserati, which was parked in the space beside Ruby's car. Low and long and shiny royal blue. She walked alongside the car to the back of the garage so that she could see the front of it—the metallic grillwork mouth and headlight eyes. No, it wasn't a living creature, but it had nearly consumed George. She would never understand men and their cars. She'd taken a few spins with her ex-husband, Jeff. A sleek, fast hunk of metal brought fleeting happiness.

She turned and moved past the rear window, pausing to look out. From here she could see across the back lawn to the wooden fence. The day had grown overcast and gray, and with the long shadows from the tall trees in the park, it seemed like dusk was closing in over Ruby's house.

She'd forgotten about the yard.

It backed up to a West Hazel common area known as Jasmine Park, which included a community path and a common area of ball fields and wooded trails. Ruby's yard was fenced off from the park, but there were a few low points where a person could hop the fence. George used to do it all the time when he went for a run.

Had the police considered the backyard as a point of access when they canvassed the neighborhood? Alice doubted there were cameras back there. Leaning closer to the dusty window, she noticed that it was unlocked.

A blatant security violation for George's Maserati.

And where was the screen? Missing.

She pushed the window up, peered out, and saw a metal frame wedged between the outdoor wall and the hedge. The screen. Someone had pried it off and stowed it there.

Someone had used this window to gain access.

Could the intruder still be inside?

Probably not. But just in case . . .

She needed to get Ruby out of here and scram.

She pushed the window shut, sidled around the car, and flew back inside, calling Ruby's name. "Ruby!"

There was no answer.

She paused a moment, trying to hear past the thumping of her heart in her chest. Could Ruby be upstairs? No. She wouldn't go up there alone. Right now, Alice herself didn't have the nerve to brave those stairs. She hurried past the empty living room, past the staircase, to Ruby's office.

No Ruby. Only a stack of notebooks and the rug, rolled up and ready to go.

"Ruby!" Alice strode through the dining room, forged into the kitchen. "We need to get out of here." She didn't want to panic, but that unlocked window had given her a bad feeling. A tight, piercing hold she couldn't shake.

"Ruby, tell me where you are *now.*"

"Give me a minute!" came a muted voice from the room off the dining room. Ruby was in the bathroom, thank goodness.

Alice moved in that direction. "Honey, we need to go," Alice said, trying to keep the trepidation from her voice. "Let's hurry it up."

"I'm indisposed. I'll just be one minute!"

"Seriously." Alice wrapped on the door gently. "Pull yourself together and let's go. We'll be at my house in two minutes."

"Be right there."

Alice leaned against the wall by the bathroom door, standing guard, but wishing there were a guard here to protect her.

What were those creaking noises and where were they coming from? She held absolutely still and listened. A bristling noise. A stirring. It was as if the house was groaning, settling around her. Or were the floorboards of the stairs moaning under someone's footsteps? She didn't see anyone, but she couldn't see the shadowed steps at the top.

Maybe it was just her imagination, but she really wanted to get out of here. She edged along the wall of the hallway and stepped into the kitchen. It was so gray, the shadows of the yard bearing down on the back of the house. The light from the microwave clock lit the way as she went to the back door and looked out.

The yard was empty, of course.

Back through the kitchen, she paused at the arched opening to the dining room. In the gray gloom, the shadowed gifts looked mocking and tawdry, an odd ode to capitalism.

She stepped across the threshold and something crashed into her . . . a dark figure.

"Whaaaat?"

Something hard as rock and covered in dark fabric pummeled Alice's rib cage and pushed her back, back into the kitchen. The impact knocked the wind from Alice's lungs, and her legs stumbled beneath her. She couldn't make out the bundle in black—a person?—trying to tackle her. Back, back, back . . . she was propelled until she slammed against the fridge.

The pain, the shock, the fear . . . it was all too much.

She was going down.

# Chapter Twenty-one

Alice felt herself sliding to the floor, all the while knowing that if she went down, she'd be defenseless against her attacker. Heart pounding in her ears, she braced herself and sucked in a painful breath.

Defend yourself! Pull yourself together!

She leaned back and managed to regain her footing. Recovering against the stainless-steel surface, she stood her ground, held up her arms for defense, and pushed back.

The assailant gasped, probably more surprised than hurt. Alice shoved again, and this time she grabbed onto a soft hoody and the edge of a round breast. A woman!

A grunt, and the woman shoved at her, then heaved a heavy object in her direction. The weight hit Alice's hip and fell down, landing on Alice's sandaled left foot with a thud.

"Whahhhh!" The searing pain forced her to crouch and clamber in an awkward dance on the kitchen floor.

As she was coping with the agony she realized the woman was backing away from her into the dining room and running off. Groaning, Alice hobbled over to a kitchen chair as Ruby appeared, her black polka dot blouse partly stuck in the waistband of her pants.

"What's going on?" Ruby asked. "Who was that?"

"Did you see her? It's a woman."

"The woman who killed George?" Ruby turned. "The floozy?"

"I think so! She's trying to get away," Alice said, but Ruby was already running after her, toward the front door.

As Alice took her cell out of a pocket and elevated her leg, she saw the heavy object that had smashed the base of her toe.

"A cake stand." The marble cake stand sat on its side on the floor, unharmed. Her foot had not fared so well. The hard stone had hit the top of her foot near the spot of a previously broken bone, an area that had become arthritic.

And now it throbbed over the adrenaline kick that was beginning to ebb.

"Those stinking wedding gifts." She tapped the screen of her phone and called 911.

# Chapter Twenty-two

"I thought I was going down, but your Frigidaire kept me on my feet," she told Ruby.

"You know, I have always believed in quality appliances." Ruby underscored the comment by taking a bag of peas from the freezer and handing it to Alice. "This might help that swelling."

Seated in a white kitchen chair, her injured foot propped on another chair, Alice applied the frozen peas to the swelling knob and sat back with a sigh. She felt safe here in Ruby's kitchen, attended to by Madison, Bedrosian, and numerous cops. Red and blue lights from police vehicles on the street strobed in through the kitchen window every few seconds. West Hazel's finest had responded in a jiffy.

But this safe conclusion didn't negate the edgy anxiety she felt at the thought of her assailant. Some woman had attacked her—used brute force. It was such a violation.

Bad karma. It undermined Alice's usual good feeling about the world.

"Okay, Alice." Bedrosian placed a chair across from Alice, sat down, and gave an awkward smile that seemed to be his attempt at sympathy. "If you're feeling up to it, we need to get your account of how it happened."

"Well, it started when I was in the garage loading up the car. I noticed that one of the windows was unlatched, the screen missing. It seemed that someone had tampered with it, and I knew it was a way to gain access to the house without being seen from the street. And that discovery made me—"

"Hold on." Bedrosian stopped her and shot a scowl at Madison. "Did we know about this? A rear entrance to the house?"

Madison looked up from her notebook. "We knew there was a park behind the yard. Jasmine Park. But there's no access to it from the yard, which is all fenced in, so—"

"Except for the low points of the fence," Ruby said. "George used to hop over it all the time and go for a jog. The fence is more for privacy than security."

Detective Bedrosian pointed at one of the uniformed cops. "Go to the garage and check out the window. See if it's an access point. Take pictures with your cell phone." He nodded at a second officer, a pale, dark-eyed boy who seemed barely old enough to drive. "You, go check out the back fence and the park behind it. And while you're at it, see if any of the neighbors have noticed anyone hopping the fence back there."

"You want me to canvass the neighborhood, Detective?" the young cop asked, imitating a cop on *Law and Order* in the most adorable way.

"Yeah, do that." Bedrosian turned back to Alice as the officers headed out. "As you were saying? You noticed the garage window was unlocked."

"Right. It gave me a bad feeling as I realized someone

else might be in the house with us. But actually, there's no telling how long that window was unlocked."

"There's no way of knowing." Bedrosian gave Madison a hard look. "Unless there's a note in the initial homicide report."

"I'll take a look," Madison said.

"Anyway . . ." Alice tried to draw the negative attention away from Madison, who was, after all, doing a great job. "I realized the killer might have climbed in through the window, escaping detection by security cameras. And I also realized there might be someone in the house, hiding. That may seem far-fetched, but I just had a feeling of alarm. When I came in to fetch Ruby and get out, that feeling of apprehension was even stronger. I heard noises, movements, I guess."

"But you didn't leave?" asked Madison.

"I was in the ladies' room," Ruby said.

"And then, I was in the kitchen, looking toward the dining room when something just bowled me over." Alice described the attack, the few details of the woman she'd been able to see. "She was wearing a dark hoodie. Ruby chased her out the front door, and I called you."

Bedrosian nodded. "It could have been a burglar. Did we find a sack of objects ready to pilfer?"

Madison shook her head. "Nothing out of place besides the stone cake stand." She hugged her notebook to her chest. "I'm wondering if tonight's assailant was our mystery woman, returned to the scene of the crime."

"For what reason?" Bedrosian asked.

"I don't know. To retrieve something she left behind? Find something she knew was hidden in the house? She may have been here in the house, searching, when Ruby and Alice arrived."

"You think she was here all along?" Ruby cringed. "That's just spooky."

"I think you're right, Madison," Alice said. "I think the woman in the black hoodie is our mystery woman. She's probably freaking out because her photo, murky though it is, was released to the public. She feels like everyone is watching; everyone knows it's her. So she snuck in through the back, intending to stay away from the cameras. When I think of the way she was trying to get past me, I wonder if she was trying to get out the kitchen door to the yard. But the way I was dancing around in pain, there was no getting by me. She was forced to flee out the front door."

"I wish I'd gotten a better look at her as she dashed past me," Ruby said. "All I can really recall is the black hoodie, tied up tight around her face."

"Maybe your neighbor caught a better image of her on his security camera," Bedrosian suggested.

"You mean Tiger." Ruby nodded. "His cameras have come in handy."

"I'd like to have a word with this Tiger," Bedrosian said, taking out his cell phone. "Let's see if Zhao can locate him."

While he was on the phone, Madison came to the table and sat close to Alice and Ruby. "Gran, how're you holding up? Can I get you anything?"

"I'm okay. A little bruised. But mostly I'm glad to be in one piece. You know, it's traumatic, having someone come after you like that. I can still feel the adrenaline in my system."

"Are you sure you don't want an ambulance?" Madison's eyes were round, full of concern. "At least have your foot looked at by a doctor. It's so swollen. What if it's broken?"

"It's going to be fine," Alice insisted, ignoring the searing pain that seemed to get worse each time she moved her foot. It hurt like heckles, but right now she couldn't bear the ridiculous attention of an ambulance and team of medical techs.

"Do you think you're up for going over this?" Madison put her notebook on the table so that Alice could see her notes. "It's for the police report. I just want to make sure my account of tonight's events is correct."

"Of course, honey. Or, sorry, *Officer.*" Alice looked over the notes and clarified a few things for Madison. They were still recapping the narrative of the attack when one of the uniformed officers returned; this time the young, dark-haired cop was accompanied by a tall black man with a low-key presence that seemed to calm the room. The newcomer wore a Hawaiian print shirt and squarish sunglasses that accentuated his wide smile.

"Tiger, thank you for coming over." Ruby got up to give him a hug.

"Girl, I've been worried about you, and it only gets worse when I see your house surrounded by police vehicles a second time this week. You got to stay out of trouble."

"Don't I know it," Ruby agreed, smiling up at him. Probably thrilled to be called "girl" at the age of sixty-four, and by such a handsome man.

"Seriously, though, I was sorry to hear about George," Tiger said. "How're you holding up?"

"Hanging on. This is my friend, Alice. She was attacked right here in this kitchen."

"Hey, Alice." He leaned down to touch Alice's shoulder and removed his shades to look her in the eye. "The officer told me someone jumped you. Unbelievable. You okay?"

"On the mend," Alice said, immediately seeing why Ruby spoke so highly of Tiger Garrett. The man had genuine warmth.

"I came over to tell you, I think I might have run into

the woman who attacked you, Alice. Or, actually, she ran into me."

"You actually saw her?" Ruby held up her hands.

"I was out watering my roses like, thirty minutes ago, I guess, when a woman in a dark hoodie came running across the street. I'm pretty sure she ran up your driveway, but she was sure running like her hair was on fire. Tripped on my hose, and when I tried to help her up, she just gave me a nasty look and started running again."

"Do you know this woman, Mr. Garrett?" asked Madison.

"I recognized her, but I'm not sure of her name. Almost didn't recognize her in that hoodie and sweats. She was usually more put together when I saw her here with George. They worked together at city hall."

"Someone who works with George?" Ruby blinked.

A coworker, indeed. It made perfect sense to Alice. The affair had been with someone George saw often at work. And when that woman had felt regret about what happened that night at the house, she'd gone into work early to call for the police to check on him.

"Yeah, they came here to the house to finish up projects, maybe one or two nights a week."

"When I was conveniently absent, no doubt," Ruby muttered. She picked up her cell phone and began scrolling through it. "I've got some photos. Last month's office picnic." She held the phone up to Tiger, but he shook his head. She showed him another photo. "Is it her? Is it this one?"

"Come on, now." Tiger scowled. "That's Mayor Grand; I would've told you if it was her."

"You never know." Ruby swiped to another photo and showed him the screen.

He squinted a moment, and then nodded. "Yes, that's

her," Tiger said. "She was always coming around with George. Said they worked together."

Ruby looked back at the photo and frowned. "They sure did."

"Who is it?" Alice asked as all eyes were on Ruby.

"Nicole." Ruby turned the phone around to flash the photo at the others in the kitchen. "It's George's assistant, Nicole Bender."

# Chapter Twenty-three

Ruby went over to the back door. "Right under my nose. They stabbed me in the back, and I let it happen, here in my own house."

"But, honey, you didn't know," Alice said. "How could you know?"

"And just this morning that Nicole floozy gave me a hug, and looked me in the eye, and made all nice while she was stabbing me in the back." As she spoke, Ruby paced back across the kitchen to the kitchen sink, where she turned again.

Alice noticed Bedrosian and Tiger edging back, making sure to stay out of Ruby's way. They knew the power of a woman scorned.

"I wouldn't be so quick to make any assumptions," Madison said. "I mean, we don't know that Nicole is the mystery woman. Maybe Nicole and George really were working together here at the house. It could have been just a business association."

Tiger's eyes opened wide with a dubious look. Alice shared his skepticism.

"George was not one to work overtime or put himself out for a job." Ruby strode back to the door. "He was more focused on enjoying life. Mr. Easy Street." She shook her head. "He is so busted. But he's dead."

Madison turned to Detective Bedrosian. "What do you think? Is this enough to get a warrant? I mean, Tiger can ID her."

"A warrant for what?" he asked.

"Assault on Alice?" Madison posited.

"The neighbor saw her running down the street." Bedrosian shook his head. "It's hardly a declaration of breaking and entering, let alone a murder."

"Are you kidding me?" Ruby went behind Alice's chair and placed her hands on her friend's shoulders. "Nicole what's-her-name assaulted Alice, and yet she gets to walk free and go out and murder someone else's husband?"

Tiger rubbed his chin. "When you put it that way, there is a strange logic of cause and effect."

"You know, when I saw her today, she asked me about the police right away." Ruby wagged a finger in the air. "Most people ask how I'm doing. But Nicole was all like, 'Do the police have a suspect yet? Are they looking at me?'"

"Well, she didn't actually go that far," Alice said.

"You know what I'm saying," Ruby insisted. "That woman is guilty with a capital G."

"We can question her," the detective said. "We can put some weight on Tiger's identification of her, and I agree it was suspicious she was seen fleeing around the same time as the assault."

"And Tiger saw her here with George on more than one occasion," Alice pointed out. "At the very least, she might shed some light on some of George's activities and associates."

"You go talk to her," Ruby said. "I want that girl locked up tight for what she did to George."

"First things first," Bedrosian said. "Innocent until proven guilty. We might get hair samples and fingerprints from her that prove she's not connected to the homicide."

"She's in deep," Ruby said. "I can feel it now."

Was Ruby right? Alice tended to favor science and fact, though she did put some weight on instinct.

Madison took out her cell phone. "I'll need to track down Nicole's home address."

It was the signal to disperse. Tiger went off with Ruby to carry the white rug to her car, and the other officers returned to patrol.

Alice lowered her foot to the floor and braced herself as she stood up and applied pressure.

*Yeeowza!* Such a raw sensation. Her foot was a ball of pain.

"Gran." Madison was immediately at her side. "You need to go to the ER."

"I just need to get home and keep my feet up."

"Your entire foot is swelling."

"It makes my ankles look thinner, don't you think?"

"You're going to need X-rays. You may have broken bones."

"It can wait until morning. Spending the night waiting in the ER is not my idea of a good time."

Madison frowned, her disapproval apparent. "Okay, but promise me you'll see a doctor in the morning."

This granddaughter of hers was so bossy. Still, her motives were pure. "Fine," Alice said. "Your wish is my command."

Back at home, Taylor was at the stove pulling wilted basil leaves out of a primavera sauce, though she seemed embarrassed when Alice arrived and found her in the kitchen. "I'm sure it's not as good as yours."

"It smells divine." Alice limped past the stove, trying not to react to the shambles that once was her kitchen. Taylor had been roasting peppers over the gas flame, and then shaving off the black skin. That combined with olive oil and papery garlic skins . . . Alice looked away. "Do you have enough to feed us, too?" she asked. She was usually the cook, but didn't feel up to it tonight.

"Of course! I was making it for all of us," Taylor said. "Now that you're home, I'll put water on for pasta."

Alice looked longingly at the kitchen nook. "I could use some puzzle therapy, but I'm beat."

"Rest for now," Ruby said, helping Alice to the comfortable couch. "And get that foot elevated. I'm going to unload the car, then shower. Being in that house makes me feel so . . . sullied."

"I get that," Alice said, sinking into the soft cushions. Her eyes were closed before Ruby left the room.

"I've got something for you."

Alice awoke to see Violet bearing a cardboard box. She'd dozed off, but only for a few minutes. "What's that?"

"From Ruby's car. There's one more. She says they're a gift for you."

"A gift." Alice scoffed as she pushed herself upright on the couch. "In a way, I suppose that's true. Bring it right over here, please and thank you."

While Violet went to get the second box, Alice reached in for a few files. These were much neater records than the random papers in George's home office, and Alice suspected that his assistant Nicole had something to do with that.

In fact, the budget proposal was well organized, with a table of contents and an index, which helped Alice zero in

on her library budget. She was scowling over the 10 percent cut, shaking her head, when Violet arrived with the
second box.

"What's cooking, good lookin'?" Violet teased. "You
look a little down in the dumps."

"At the moment, I'm stewing over the way the city is
cutting our library budget." She explained the budget cut
George championed before his death. Then she went on to
tell the tale of her encounter with a violent assailant,
whom she believed to be George's assistant, Nicole.

"Wow! You've had quite a day. I can get you an ice pack
for your foot. And I'm happy to go over the budget with
you. I have a good head for numbers."

"You used to come home with the math star-pupil
badge pinned to your collar."

"I always liked algebra, where you make one side of an
equation equal the other," Violet mused. "And sometimes,
it feels the same with budgeting. You just have to make the
credits equal the debits. It can be like a game. Do you
know what I mean?"

Alice blinked at her. "The statement you just made? I
agree with none of that."

Violet chuckled. "But really, it can be fun."

"Let's agree to disagree and figure out where the money
is going." She handed Violet the budget report. "If George
cut ten percent to all of the essential services, there must be
a surplus somewhere. Who is getting that money?"

"Well, let's see. Schools took a cut. Transportation lost
ten percent. Streets . . . parks and rec . . . environmental . . .
library. That's you, of course. All lost ten percent. The
only place I see an increase is this special services. What's
that?"

"I have no idea." Alice leaned closer to look at the report. "There's an asterisk there, that says something about law enforcement affiliation. And a footnote. Where does that take us?"

"To the police department budget, apparently." Violet checked the table of contents. "Page twenty-three." She flipped through the pages. "Here we are. So. The police department did not get its budget cut. And the additional funding is going to an outside vendor that's working with the police. The vendor is called EYE-dentify." She squinted at Alice. "That sounds familiar."

"It does." Alice Googled them on her phone. "You remember that firm. They did the DNA testing that helped catch the Cola Bandits."

"Yes, that's right. They picked up the DNA from a cola can that was left behind and did a search with it. Lucky for them, it matched with a sample one of the thieves had sent in to a heritage search firm." Violet nodded. "Actually, it was a clever way to catch those thieves."

Alice nodded at the report. "How much is budgeted for the DNA folks?"

"Apparently someone in the city signed the firm on as a consultant, to the tune of one hundred thousand dollars per month." Violet's jaw dropped as she slapped the report shut. "This is the sound of my jaw hitting the floor. They're paying these guys more than a million dollars a year."

"That's it," Alice said. "We found the big-ticket item in the budget. EYE-dentify."

# Chapter Twenty-four

Friday morning Alice woke up in pain, her ankle feeling as if it had been pierced by a quiver of arrows. With each step to her balcony, she let out a little moan. "Ooh. Ooh. Ooch." Somehow, the pathetic expression made her feel better.

Looking out at the spires of dark green trees and the distant mountains, she was grateful to be here. Grateful for coffee and ibuprofen to get her through her day. Curious about what she might find out about Nicole Bender. She'd texted Madison twice without answer. Imagine that respectful girl ignoring her grandmother!

She hobbled downstairs in her robe and found Ruby and Taylor in the kitchen. "I took the day off to do prep for tomorrow's memorial," Alice said. "But I guess now I could call it a sick day."

"Oh, sugar," Ruby cooed, "I was hoping your foot would be better today, but I can tell it's not. Take a seat and I'll get you your coffee."

"Does it hurt, Gran?"

"It's tender," Alice admitted, propping her leg on a chair.

Taylor and Ruby exchanged a look, then began in unison, "You need to see—"

"A doctor, I know. I called Dr. Angelino's office, and they said I should come in." The scheduling person at the clinic had actually told Alice she'd need to see someone else because her doctor was booked up. The sad state of health care! But Alice knew how to weasel her way in.

"That's good," Ruby said, sliding a mug of coffee in front of Alice. "I have a nine-thirty meeting, but I could get Imani to cancel so I can drive you. Or maybe I could push back the warehouse inspection to noon."

"Don't cancel anything," Alice said, figuring it was better to have her friend distracted and back at work. "I'm thinking that Taylor might agree to drive me."

"Me?" Taylor turned from the open fridge. "I can drive your Audi, Gran?"

"Well, as long as I'm in it."

"I can do that. Totally. Yeah. Put me down as the driver. Do you want some eggs?"

"Scrambled would be lovely." Alice wasn't used to being waited on, but she was pleased to see Taylor rising to the occasion. She took a sip of coffee and scanned the puzzle pieces laid out on the table. "I see we have an advanced-level challenge this morning."

"All the background pieces are black," Taylor complained as she dropped a lob of butter into a sauté pan.

"It's a puzzle that makes you aware of the shapes of the pieces," Alice said, reaching for her reading glasses.

"I've started a pile of classic ladder shapes over here," Ruby said. "Each one has two keys and two locks."

"Very good." Alice took another sip of coffee, and then tried to piece one corner together.

They chatted as they worked, stopping only to eat the eggs and toast Taylor had whipped up.

"So creamy," Alice said. "Did you add half and half?"

"A touch of sour cream, and some chives from the herb garden."

"Delicious," Ruby said, clearing away the dishes. She was loading the dishwasher when Madison arrived.

"Where were you?" asked Alice. "I've been texting you."

"I know." Madison shook her head. "Technically, I'm at work, but I knew you were itching for an update on Nicole Bender."

"Absolutely." Ruby dried her hands on a towel. "Is she under arrest?"

"You're going to be disappointed to hear that she's not," Madison said. "We paid Nicole a visit last night. Bedrosian behaved himself. He actually seemed friendly. But Nicole was tight as a clam, and she denied any impropriety. She said she had a strictly professional relationship with George. Claimed that she's met Ruby, but she's never been to your house. When I told her someone saw her coming out of Ruby and George's house yesterday, she just shrugged it off. Said he must be mistaken."

"That's disappointing," Alice said.

"She's so guilty." Ruby scowled. "I can barely stand it."

"What was her alibi?" asked Alice.

"She doesn't have one. Says she was home all evening reading a book."

"Hurray for reading," Alice said. "But all her denials sound fishy to me. Did you believe her, Madison?"

"Not at all." Madison cocked her head to one side, considering. "She was cold, definitely guarded. The whole time we were trying to interview her, she kept looking down at her phone and tapping the screen. Serious avoidance."

Alice considered this as she held her coffee cup out for a refill from Ruby. "I think she's lying, and I wish I could talk to her. I think I could eke out the truth."

"Gran, no," Madison said. "Don't approach her."

"I mean, why won't she at least confess to having an affair with George? It's not a crime. And why did she go back to the house yesterday? Must have been something important. Will she try to go back again? If I didn't have errands to do today, I'd stake out Ruby's house . . . or drop by Nicole's place for an honest chat."

"Gran, remember your promise? You're going to see a doctor. And please, no stakeouts. Someone attacked you yesterday. Promise me you will not put yourself in danger today."

"I'd like to hear that promise, too," Ruby said. "Yesterday was such a fright. We can't let anything else happen to you, Alice."

"Ladies, I appreciate your concern, but I'm a librarian. It's a low-risk occupation."

"You know what we mean," said Madison.

"Fine." Alice straightened the lapels of her robe. "I will try to behave myself."

Madison paused at the door and gave her a stern look. "Try hard. Really hard."

# Chapter Twenty-five

"Alice Pepper to see Dr. Angelino." Alice stood at the reception desk smiling down with such magnitude she was sure the young man with the spiky hair couldn't help but be charmed.

"Pepper." He frowned. "I have you slated to see one of the physician's assistants, Heather."

"But I need to see Dr. Angelino. If you let her know I'm here, she'll squeeze me in."

"I'm sorry, Ms. Pepper, but—"

Alice was already limping toward a chair. She turned back to thank the young man, then sat down, as gracefully as one leg would let her, beside Taylor.

"I thought you had an appointment," Taylor muttered.

"I do. It just needs to be straightened out." Alice didn't mind seeing her doctor. Dr. Isabella Angelino was honest, smart, insightful—all the things you'd want in a physician. But she was so overbooked these days, that Alice was often palmed off on young associates. And that was not acceptable. So Alice had taken to pushing her way in to Dr. A.

"So while we're stuck here, I guess this is a good chance

to talk," Taylor said, looking down at the floor awkwardly.

"Your enthusiasm is blinding."

Taylor frowned. "Is that sarcasm?"

"Of course it is. What's up?"

"So you know I've been camping downstairs in your house. I'm not using up one of the bedrooms or anything—"

"But you know you could."

"Ugh. I hate adulting." Taylor sighed. "I don't have the money to pay you rent, Gran. I know I'm failing to launch. I'm old enough to support myself, like *Madison*, but the things I've tried haven't worked out for me."

A barista, a grocery checker, a waitress, a Christmas elf at the mall . . . Taylor had a knack for landing jobs. Keeping them was another story. "What would you like to do?" asked Alice.

"I'm thinking of taking the classes to become a paralegal. You know, it's pretty easy to get a job with a firm, and you could do house closings and stuff."

This from a girl who'd struggled to write papers in high school. "How would that be, proofreading contracts and editing clauses? Analyzing documents for compliance to laws?"

Taylor raked her hair from her eyes as she let her head roll back. "That would be so boring. But it pays pretty well."

"It's important to me that you find a way to support yourself in this world." Alice frowned. "That's what I care about. Your well-being. This journey you're on, well, the right path may not be apparent for a while." Alice didn't want to excuse Taylor's lack of direction. But the girl needed to find a worthwhile goal before she raced forward.

"Does this mean you're not going to kick me to the curb, like Madison said?"

Alice scowled. "Of course not. Why would she even say that?"

"She said I'd have to go move in with Mom."

Alice held up a hand as her muscles went stiff. "I can't go there."

"Madison says I'm going to be a failure, just like Mom."

"Stop." Alice let out a breath. "Why do you and your sister say such cruel things to each other?"

Taylor shrugged. "We're sisters."

"Stop bickering with your sister. Focus on moving ahead in a positive way. What would you enjoy doing?"

"I've been writing some songs, and my friend Max wants me to perform with him at a gig."

Songs and a gig. Hardly the career track Alice had hoped for. "Okay. That sounds like fun, but I was thinking of a skill that could earn you a living. What might that be?"

Taylor sighed. "My heart needs a world without fiscal parameters."

"How about we make a deal. If you help me with the shopping and cooking for tomorrow, I'll let you go rent free for another month."

"How about two months?" Taylor countered.

Alice put her hands on her hips, then gave a laugh. "Agreed. You know, I'm hep to your cooking abilities. The way you add complementary spices. The balance of sweet and sour, acid and salt."

"Yeah, that part makes sense to me, and I kind of enjoy cooking right now. But I'll stop as soon as it's not fun anymore. I've learned that everything in life has to be a game. In that way I'm like an otter, my spirit guide. I won't do anything if it's not fun."

Alice nodded. "Maybe I should have gotten more of that lesson at an early age. But still, otters don't have to renew their driver's license and pay the rent. They don't have to suffer through root canals. And swallow fat, chalky calcium supplements."

"Gross. I'll never do stuff like that."

"You'd be surprised." Alice smiled. "You still have much to learn, Grasshopper."

Taylor looked over at the receptionist. "Gran, sometimes I have no idea what you're talking about."

"Alice Pepper?" called a nurse. "Dr. Angelino will see you now."

Alice rose onto her healthy foot and smiled down at Taylor. "See? Persistence."

"No fractures," Dr. Angelino said. "But you must stay off this foot for the next two days at least. Do you hear me, Alice?"

"It's not broken." Alice slid off the exam table onto her feet. "That's great. Thank you."

"No, no, no. Sit down again." Dr. Angelino held up one hand. "You must stay off your injured foot and keep it elevated. I don't think you're quite up to crutches or a rollator, but I will get you a wheelchair to take you to your car."

Alice waved it off. "Not necessary. I can make it."

"A wheelchair," the doctor insisted. "And when you leave here, what are you going to do?"

"We're going to the grocery store," Taylor said. "And then home to start prepping and cooking for an event."

"And how will you get around the store, Alice?"

"I'll . . . wait in the car?"

"You could do that," Dr. Angelino said. "But I don't believe you will." She looked at Taylor. "Listen, Grand-daughter. This is serious. Don't let her walk for two days. At the store, she can use one of those motorized scooters."

"I wouldn't be caught dead," Alice said.

"Then you can't go into the store. And when you're cooking, make sure she's sitting."

"Got it," Taylor said. "Don't worry, Doc. I'll take good care of her."

Alice had wanted her granddaughter to be empowered, but this was ridiculous.

"I have to admit, I'm more than a little mortified," Alice said as she looked in the car children mirror to tie on her wide-brimmed, floppy sun hat. Stashed in the trunk, it hadn't seen the light of day since her trip to the coast last summer. She slipped on a pair of dark sunglasses to complete the disguise. "There. No one will know it's me."

"Maybe. But you're sure to frighten children and small animals."

Taylor pulled the car right up to the curb so that Alice could hobble into the store and engage one of the scooters. She adjusted her hat and glasses before taking off, but as she cruised down the produce aisle, her attitude softened. There was no pain as she whirred past a pyramid of green apples and paused to score a bag of lemons. No matter that the dark glasses diminished her vision and she accidentally bumped into a shopping cart near the parsley. Scootering was fun.

Taylor caught up with Alice by the dried apricots, which she was purchasing to use in a baked appetizer with brie and filo dough. "I've got the produce covered," Alice said. "You can take the list and work on it while I get my prescription filled."

Taylor held the list out, took a photo of it on her phone,

then handed it back. "Got it. If you need me, I'll be looking for three dozen parbaked rolls, whatever that is."

Alice motored to the back of the store, grazing a cart of avocado cartons along the way. "Sorry!" she called to the young man unloading the boxes. "First day with the new wheels."

As she cruised past meat and seafood cases, she came to terms with her prejudice against this little scooter. It wasn't that she couldn't accept growing old; she simply couldn't accept being stereotyped and dismissed. But riding a scooter in the store, at least for today, was allowing her accessibility to life. It was time to toss out her own biases.

In the pharmacy area Ruby parked the scooter by a display of power bars, made her way to the counter, and removed her glasses and hat. When she saw that her favorite pharmacist, Craig Grand, was on duty, she gave a little wave. A charming, gray-haired man, probably pushing seventy, Craig had married the mayor a few years ago. From Alice's perspective, Tansley and Craig were proof that love could come later in life, and she was happy for them both.

"Alice, how can I help you today?"

"A prescription was called in for a muscle relaxer?" she said. "That's not an opioid, right? Because you know I don't take those." She had seen firsthand the devastation those drugs could cause.

"Let me check what the doctor wrote." He warned her not to take the medication for more than three weeks, and suggested that she stick with ibuprofen if that provided enough relief. "How did you injure the foot?"

"Long story, but in a nutshell . . ." She gave him an abbreviated version of yesterday's adventure, leaving out Nicole's name.

"Wowza. You've really been through the ringer these

last few days. Tansley and I read that piece about George. How is Ruby holding up?"

"I suppose she's feeling better now that she's not the prime suspect in a murder. But we're pushing to figure out who killed George. I think it's the only way Ruby will have closure."

"Ruby's got a good friend in you, Alice. Hard to believe this is happening in our little town."

"Hard to believe." An assistant came over with her filled prescription, and Craig held it out for her.

"Any further instructions?"

"Medical advice aside, be careful. You don't want to mess around with a killer."

"Indeed." She thanked him and cruised off to see what ingredients Taylor had collected in the cart.

They met in the spice aisle, where they divvied up the last few items on the list and agreed to meet at the checkout counter. Alice checked two containers of eggs for her mini quiches, and then headed to the front of the store.

While backing up the scooter, she clipped a cardboard bread display, and ended up dragging it a foot or so until a nice teenager dislodged it. "Thank you," Alice told her. As she approached the checkout line, she misjudged the extended basket at the front of the scooter and bumped the tooshie of a woman in line.

"I am so, so sorry!" Alice exclaimed. She removed her shades as the woman wheeled around and caught her with searing blue eyes. "Are you okay?" Alice asked.

"Alice Pepper," the woman said, squinting. "This is what happens when they let you out of the library?"

# Chapter Twenty-six

Alice recognized Carrie Preston, a wealthy resident of West Hazel and a former patron of the library. For years Alice had worked with Carrie on a weekly basis when Friends of the Library had made Carrie the president of their organization. "Carrie, it's been a while. How are you? Aside from being nicked by a madwoman on a scooter."

"I've had better days. And I see you have, too."

"No broken bones, at least. I'll be fine in a few days," Alice said.

"You should see the other guy," Taylor said, joining them. "Gran has a mean left hook."

"Serves him right for tangling with a librarian," Carrie teased, then looked away. The awkwardness wasn't just Alice's imagination. Carrie held the plant she was purchasing up to her face, breathed in the scent, and sighed. "My indulgence. *Philadelphus*." She showed them the white petaled flowers with golden centers. "People call it mock orange, because of the citrus aroma. Something to brighten up my garden."

"They're lovely," Alice said, surprised by the woman's

candor, even more surprised that Carrie would shop for something herself. A woman of her means could have a florist come in every day and string flowers from the chandeliers. Then again, even wealthy people needed their privacy. Especially after your son was convicted of felony theft. Carrie's son Tony, one of the Cola Bandits, was still serving time in prison.

Although the community had been shocked to learn that one of the Cola Bandits had been a college-bound young man from a well-to-do family, Alice had always sensed that the surprise to his parents had been even more traumatic. Tony's father JB had retired from the family business soon after the trial, and the Prestons were rarely seen around town these days. When Carrie left the Friends of the Library organization, no one was sure of the reason. Alice sensed that she'd become too uncomfortable to appear in public. In any case, her joy and intelligence had been sorely missed.

"Carrie, it's so good to see you, truly," Alice said. "Please, let me buy the plant for you. As a token of apology for bumping into you."

"No, no, you don't have to do that." Carrie tucked the plant closer into the crook of her arm. "Apology accepted as long as you promise to pay attention to moving traffic."

"Deal. It's been ages since I've seen you at the library. Everyone misses you."

"I don't get out much anymore," Carrie said. "I use the library's download program and use my e-reader. Or if I'm feeling *really decadent*, I borrow an audio book and let someone else do the reading."

"Truly luxurious," Alice agreed, and she chuckled along with Carrie.

Taylor looked away as if they were kooks.

"Not sure if you're aware, but the new Anna Quindlen will be in next month," Alice said. "You might want to reserve a copy." Quindlen was a favorite author they'd shared years ago, when Carrie was a regular at the library.

"I'll get on that," Carrie said as she stepped up to the checker. "I wish she would publish more often."

"Right? If only she could write faster," Alice agreed. "But then, I guess life gets in the way."

"It sure does." Carrie put her credit card away and picked up her *Philadelphus*. "Take care, Alice."

"You too. Good to see you, Carrie." As Alice waved, she tamped down the regret over the way things had played out for Carrie Preston. Of course, one couldn't change the past. But she wished that Carrie still felt comfortable coming into the library. It seemed the shame of her son's misdeeds had not yet worn off.

Outside the store, Alice tied her hat back and reset her sunglasses. She was waiting in the scooter for Taylor to bring the car around when she heard someone call her name.

"Alice! Is that you?" The casual, gravelly voice could only belong to one man.

Stone Donahue.

The last person she wanted to see while riding a senior scooter. Careful not to look in his direction, she turned the scooter and headed down the sidewalk toward McDonald's. *Go away!* she thought. *Vamoose!* Maybe he'd figure he'd made a mistake. Or doggonit, maybe he would just give up.

Gritting her teeth, she goosed the throttle on the handlebar for maximum speed. Go, baby, go! She was moving down the sidewalk outside the store, but slowly. For all its convenience, the scooter lacked speed.

But she was moving, and he wasn't calling her name anymore. Maybe she'd lost him.

"Alice." Suddenly Stone was walking briskly alongside her. "I thought that was you. What's with the new ride?"

She laid off the throttle and the scooter halted. A slow halt, as it was barely moving anyway. Gazing up at his craggy but handsome face, she felt her pride melt. "Honestly, I'm embarrassed to be seen in this thing. It seems so . . . ridiculously infirm."

"That's crazy talk. When a person needs medicine or crutches, you use 'em." He hitched back his baseball cap and leaned down closer to her level. "So what's going on with you? Seems you were motoring just fine two days ago when we walked to your place."

"I wrestled with an intruder at Ruby's place. The woman attacked me, but I was too startled to get a good look at her. She was hooded, and it was dark. My foot was injured in the tussle."

"I'm duly impressed you stood your ground."

"If you could call it that."

"Why'd she attack you?"

"We think she came into the house in search of something, but that's just a theory. Actually . . ." She looked over her shoulder to the abandoned grocery cart at the front of the store. "I need to get back. I've abandoned the groceries, and it was my job to keep an eye on them while Taylor brought the car around."

"No worries," he said as she maneuvered a few turns to get the scooter back in the opposite direction. A grocery store scooter was not prized for its turning radius. "Let me give you gals a hand."

They chatted about the memorial service as Taylor pulled up in Alice's car.

"I got an e-mail invite from Ruby," he said. "Planning to attend."

"I'm supposed to cater it, but this damn foot is slowing me down. Taylor has graciously agreed to be my sous-chef."

"I'm giving it my best shot," Taylor said as she hoisted a canvas bag of groceries from the cart. "I don't have that much experience."

"I do." Stone lifted a carton of wine and slid it easily into the car. "Wait, did that sound cocky? I'm trying to say I'd be happy to help. A few years back I did a stint at a four-star restaurant in San Francisco. And while I was teaching English in Tokyo, I learned how to roll sushi."

"And you once worked on a horse ranch," Alice said. "And you were a lawyer. Plus you have some medical training. When did you find time to do all these careers?"

Stone let out a laugh. "I'm an old man."

"I appreciate your offer." Alice looked at Taylor. "What do you think? Another pair of hands in the kitchen might help."

"Yes, please!" Taylor gushed. "Stone, you've saved the day."

# Chapter Twenty-seven

Cooking with Taylor and Stone made the afternoon go quickly. Perched on a stool at the kitchen island, Alice was able to slice and dice and supervise. She had so much fun being the boss lady in the kitchen, sort of like old times when she'd started the restaurant, that she nearly forgot they were preparing to honor a dead man.

Since they ended up with plenty of extra ham and eggs, Alice rolled out two large pie crusts and prepared two full-sized quiches. "We'll have a family dinner," Alice said. "Taylor, can you put together a green salad? I'll call Madison and let her know. Stone, you'll stay, of course. Unless it's true that real men don't eat quiche?"

He grinned. "I love quiche, and so far no one's kicked me out of the man club."

When everyone sat down at the table, Ruby stood and lifted her glass of wine for a toast.

"I just want to thank you all for taking me in, supporting me, loving me. It's been a tough time, but it is wonderful to finish a day of work and be able to sit down for a homemade dinner with friends."

"I second that," Madison said. "Thanks for cooking, guys."

"It makes me enormously happy to have you all here," Alice said. "Now, sit down, honey, and let's dig in."

Looking at the faces around the table—the twins, Violet, Ruby, and Stone—Alice had to admit that she was a lucky woman, indeed. Her other problems—holding on to her house, her job, her beloved library—were secondary to this dear family and friends.

The quiche was delicious, cooked through but moist, the crust golden brown. There was a contented silence as everyone enjoyed the meal. After a few bites, curiosity got the better of Alice and she had to ask, "What's the latest on the case?"

"I've been looking into Nicole Bender's background," Madison said as she buttered a sourdough roll. "She looks like she's barely twenty, but she's actually thirty-seven, once divorced."

"I had no idea she was in her thirties," Ruby said. "She does look young."

"A high school graduate," Madison went on, "but no college when she moved here from Springfield and got hired by West Hazel. She took some accounting classes at community college and worked her way up through the hierarchy of city administration. Some of her colleagues in the office say she's pretty good with accounting programs and online spreadsheets, an area George was apparently weak on."

"He didn't even own a laptop," Ruby said as she speared some salad greens with her fork. "If it weren't for me, he wouldn't have even learned how to text. Technology was not George's friend."

Taylor and Madison nodded respectfully, but Alice sensed that they thought this was ludicrous. A person in their generation had little tolerance for someone who refused to navigate technology.

Stone asked what Nicole had been doing in Ruby's house. A very good question.

"Well, we're all assuming that she's the mystery woman, correct?" asked Violet.

"Yes, yes, and she's also the one who attacked Alice," Ruby said.

"That's a lot of assumptions," Madison pointed out.

"But probably true," said Alice.

"What I want to know is, what was she doing in Ruby's house yesterday?" Stone asked. "I mean, the night she was with George, we get that. But then to return to the scene of the crime? There must have been some pretty strong bait to lure her in, at the risk of getting caught."

Violet pressed a napkin to her lips. "I love the fish imagery."

Stone smiled at her, but went on. "Just saying, her motive must have been strong, if she was going to risk getting caught at the scene of the crime. And then to attack Alice and fight her way out of there?" Stone shook his head. "She was definitely after something."

"And if she didn't find it," Alice said, "is she going to come back?"

"That's why I can't rest!" Ruby slapped a palm against her chest. "That woman is coming back to my house. She's going to strike again. I can feel it. Maybe she already snuck in again?"

"No." Violet held up her hands. "She's waiting for the perfect opportunity. Tomorrow, the day of the service. I've read about that. Thieves look at the obits in the paper, and then strike the deceased's home while the family is at the memorial service."

"I didn't think of that!" Madison said.

"Well, Nicole is going to know the exact time of the service, because I e-mailed her an invitation," Ruby said. "That was before I knew what she was up to. Now I know she's going to be a no-show. She's going to break into my house again tomorrow, while we're doing George's memorial here."

"Let's not miss the fact that Ruby's home will be quite vulnerable," Alice said. "If funeral services are bait for thieves, the crooks might be lining up at the door tomorrow."

"What can I do?" Ruby wrung her napkin into a twist. "Hire a house sitter?"

"More like a fleet of armed guards," Taylor said. "You've got all those wedding gifts sitting in there. Easy merchandise."

"The gifts should be moved out of there," Stone said. "Put them in a locked storage area."

"Good idea," Alice said.

"We should do that ASAP," Violet said, the administrative side of her emerging.

"I'm going to get my assistant Imani on it," Ruby said, taking out her phone at the dinner table. "We have space in the office, and it's a secure location. Hello? Yes, Imani, I have something for you. . . ." As she spoke, Ruby left the table and paced to the windows overlooking the city and distant mountains.

"And I'm going to talk to Detective Bedrosian about assigning an officer at Ruby's place." Madison tapped the screen of her phone, texting as she spoke. "At least for tomorrow. We'll post a cop inside the house. Lure in the mouse."

"It would be nice if it were that simple." Alice buttered a last piece of roll and folded her napkin. "Cell phones have been unsheathed; I suppose dinner has ended."

Taylor and Violet started clearing dishes, but Stone

chuckled as he remained sitting at the table. "You do have a way with words, Alice."

She smiled after him as he took the salad bowl and water pitcher into the kitchen. It made her heart ache to keep him at arm's length. She didn't know how to navigate with this marvelous man whom she'd slotted as a *friend*. She would need to tread carefully.

"It feels weird leaving the dishes to other people," Alice shouted toward the kitchen.

"Yeah, and it feels weird for me to be doing the dishes," Taylor answered. "When are you going to be better?"

"Oh, my aching leg—I mean, foot!" Alice let out an exaggerated moan.

"No, no, Taylor," Violet said sternly, "wooden spoons do not go in the dishwasher."

The sliding door from the back deck opened, and Madison came in, ending her call. "That's settled. Bedrosian is going to put a uniformed cop inside Ruby's house tomorrow, starting at noon."

"Thank you," Ruby said. "And Imani is going to have a truck with two movers at the house first thing in the morning. We'll store Celeste's wedding gifts at the office for safekeeping."

"That's settled." Alice pushed her chair back, preparing to get up from the dining room table. "Shall we work on our puzzle?"

"In a little bit," Violet said, placing a bundle wrapped in a red and purple silk scarf on the table. "First, I want to do a short reading for Ruby." She opened the shiny fabric to reveal an oversized deck of cards.

"Ooh, tarot cards." Taylor took a seat at the table. "This'll blow a few wigs off."

"Take a seat, Ruby," Violet said, "and let's think of an open-ended question to ask the cards."

"Why don't you do it with someone else." Ruby waved her off. "I'm good."

"Okay if I sit in on this?" Stone asked, pulling out the chair beside Alice. "I have a cousin who reads tea leaves, but I don't know much about tarot cards."

"Of course," Violet said, "but you must not touch the cards. Another person's energy could alter the reading. All right, honey." She placed the deck on the table. "You shuffle the cards, and then turn over three of them. That's all. We're going to do a past, present, and future reading."

Ruby let out her breath in a huff, sat down, and picked up the card deck. "Fine."

"As Ruby shuffles, we need to ask the cards a question pertaining to her situation."

"Who killed George?" Taylor blurted out.

"Something less direct," Violet said, then closed her eyes, zoning out.

"Why did Nicole kill George?" Taylor asked.

"A lover scorned," Ruby said as she did a waterfall shuffle.

Alice considered the question. "In mystery novels, there are a few classic motives that you see over and over again. Unrequited love. Revenge. And the biggie, money or greed. For Nicole Bender, I had assumed it was the matter of a lover scorned. But for her to return to the scene of the crime, I think there's some money involved."

Ruby frowned. "Yeah, after our trip to the bank, George is good for it."

"What do you mean?" Madison asked.

"You know," Alice said, deflecting, "George has not been too popular among city leaders lately. A few people in the city administration were peeved with George for cutting their budgets. I confess, I was one of them. His cuts are going to damage my library."

"But you didn't kill him," Taylor said.

"No, I did not."

"So will the cards tell us who did kill George?" asked Taylor.

"Of course not." Madison shook her head. "Let me remind everyone that tarot cards do not count as evidence in a court of law."

Violet, who had seemed to be meditating with her hands in prayer position under her chin, opened her eyes and came alive. "All right, Ruby. You can stop shuffling and pick three cards from the deck. Three cards—past, present, and future. They will represent your past situation, the current problem, and your guide to facing the problem in the future."

Ruby put the deck on the table and lifted the top card. "This will be past." She turned a card over and let out a gasp when she saw the illustration on the card. A man was facedown on the floor with ten swords plunged into his body.

Alice felt her jaw drop at the graphic depiction of death. Gruesome.

"The ten of swords." Even Violet seemed a bit concerned.

Ruby stared at the card, wild-eyed. "Oh, my soul, it's my George dead on the floor!"

# Chapter Twenty-eight

"Ew." Taylor's nose wrinkled. "There's even a knife stuck in his ear!"

"Actually, it's not George," Violet insisted. "I'm sorry, honey. Although I know it looks like a dead man. The card is really about you. I mean, your situation."

Alice folded her arms, wondering how her sister was going to backpedal out of the terrible moment. So far, she seemed to be spinning the wheels in deeper.

"Yes, it does symbolize an emotional crisis, a terrible time in which you're overwhelmed by emotions. Struggling to find a way forward. Which you just went through when you learned of George's death."

Ruby frowned. "I don't think that's me."

"It's not as bad as it may seem," Violet said. "If the man would just lift his head up he would see that the waters on the horizon are calm, and the sun is rising."

"How can he lift his head when he's dead?" Taylor asked.

"Don't be so literal," Violet snapped. "Also, the ten card is the end of the cycle—the cards run one through ten—so good things await. Just ahead you'll find Aces and the Wheel of Fortune card."

"I do like *Wheel of Fortune*," Ruby admitted. "Though I miss Pat Sajak."

"Okay. Let's keep going," Violet instructed. "Turn over a card for the present."

"It can only get better, right?" Ruby said as she flipped a second card. "The Moon. A very annoyed moon, looking down at two barking dogs."

"The moon tells us that everything is not as it seems," Violet said. "There's an illusion in this situation. Hidden secrets. Maybe danger and secret enemies. But, Ruby, you know something is going on behind the curtain. Your instincts are right. Your feminine power will prevail."

"This card is so much more chill than the dead guy," Taylor said.

"Right," Violet agreed. "*Chill*. This card makes sense to me because there's an investigation going on. There are facts that are still unknown to you. But trust your instincts."

"Okay, then, last card." Ruby turned over a card called Strength.

"A woman petting a dog?" Alice said. "It's quite anticlimactic after the murder card."

"Geez, Alice, it's a lion," Violet said. "She's subduing a lion because she has strength. Physical and mental strength. This is a wonderful prescriptive card for the future, Ruby. It's your strength that will guide you through this difficult time."

Ruby flexed one arm and gave a mock smile over her biceps. "Look at me, a black Rosie the Riveter. Thank you, Violet. Aside from all the daggers in the one card, it was a very nice reading."

"I can't take credit or blame for the cards that turn up."

Violet gathered up the cards and straightened the stack. "The tarot speaks its own language. But I'm glad you found it helpful."

After Violet took the cards back to her bedroom, Alice faced Ruby and asked, "What did we learn from that?"

Ruby shrugged, but Taylor piped right up, saying, "Something is going on beneath the surface. Something dark and mysterious. And we need to find out what that is."

Alice nodded. "So find the killer."

Madison put up her hands. "I could've told you that." She got up from the table and kissed Alice on the cheek. "I'm outta here before you rook me into working on that ridiculous puzzle. It's too tedious. See you guys tomorrow."

"I'm heading out, too," Stone said. "I'll be here early tomorrow to get some last-minute prep done, and load the coolers."

"And train the neighborhood kids how to circulate appetizers," Taylor said.

Stone gave her a skeptical look. "Impossible."

Alice moved to the kitchen table where the black puzzle was in the works. "This one is truly a beast. So many pieces in black. Though you've made some progress." The black border was complete, with some corner pieces filled in. A pink, rose, and gold blob that seemed to be in the center was taking shape, along with a white illustration of a scrawny leg in a girl's shoe. "What is this pink thing?" asked Alice.

"An ice cream cone?" Ruby suggested.

"A platter of chewing gum," Violet said, prompting the others to chuckle.

"I can't do it," Taylor said. "I'll be in my lair."

"You know, you can move into one of the bedrooms," Alice called after her.

"She likes her tent," Ruby said, trying to interlock pieces with a smidge of orange gold on the edge.

Within the next hour, they had nearly assembled the pink blob in the center.

"I'm telling you, it's a big ham hock," Violet said. "Maybe the puzzle is an old advertisement for a butcher."

"Not very appetizing, if you ask me," Alice said. "Let's assemble the banner with the words in it."

"Two of those pieces are all blurred," Ruby said.

"I noticed that," Alice agreed, yawning. "Maybe a stain. It's getting late."

"But we can't give up now," Ruby said. "We have to finish."

"It's Friday night. Not a school night." Violet reached for a small pile of pink pieces. "So we can stay up a little later to get this sucker done."

"Who gave us this puzzle, anyway?" Alice asked.

"I don't know," Ruby said. "Taylor found it on the front porch."

"An anonymous puzzle? That's just gross." Violet dropped a few pieces back onto the table. "Why didn't you tell me? It could be dusted with arsenic . . . or worse. Anthrax!"

Alice began to laugh with a sip of water in her mouth, which made her choke and cough.

Violet's eyes opened wide as she pointed to her sister. "See? There's something toxic in the puzzle!"

"I choked on water," Alice said. "And while I doubt the theory of toxic chemicals, I do agree with the girls. This is a crappy puzzle."

"I don't care one way or the other," Ruby said. "I've been working this puzzle all day and my fingers haven't fallen off. I'm hooked, and I want to see what the banner says."

They rushed to assemble the words on the banner. Working together, they found that it read: *To Kill a Mockingbird.* " But with the revision inked on by what seemed to be sharpy, it read: *To Kill a Mockingbyrd.* "

"B-Y-R-D. Like the way George's last name is spelled," Ruby said. "Do you think this is supposed to be about George?"

"So George was a mockingbird?" asked Violet.

"It's a muddled message," Alice said, confused. "In Harper Lee's book, the mockingbird is an innocent songbird that brings joy to people. Its death is equated to a loss of innocence. Was George an innocent?"

"Oh, my George was a lot of things, but innocent was not one of them," Ruby said.

"So . . . just spitballing here. Does it mean that George was the opposite? That he killed someone's innocence?"

Violet frowned. "I don't like the sound of that. It opens the door to so much negative energy."

Taylor emerged from the basement and took a peek at the puzzle before heading to the fridge. "Aw. That's cuter than I expected. Scout in her ham costume."

"I should have figured that out," Alice said on a sigh. "But why did someone give us this puzzle, Taylor? Any ideas?"

Her granddaughter looked it over and frowned. "Maybe it means that George Byrd mocked someone, and that's why he was killed?"

"Who would want to tell us that?" Ruby asked.

"And the Justice League puzzle," Alice added. "What did that mean?"

"That's obvious," Taylor said. "It means that you ladies are the Justice League, working together to avenge evil and save the world. Alice Pepper's Lonely Hearts Puzzle Club is actually a group of silver-haired avengers."

Alice sighed again. She'd never liked Taylor's name for her group of friends. So trite. And she was dubious about the message of the puzzles. She would dismiss the puzzles as meaningless if this second puzzle didn't have the alteration pointing to George.

"Why would the killer drop puzzles off here?" Alice wondered aloud.

"Because you and Ruby were written up in the *West Hazel Gazette*, in Stone's column," Taylor pointed out. "Maybe the puzzles are from the killer, maybe not. But, Gran, someone is trying to give you and Ruby a message. And it has something to do with George."

"It's late. We've got the memorial tomorrow." Ruby arose from the table and stretched. "And I'm too tired to worry about any of this now."

"The one thing I know for sure is that I have to get a lousy doorbell camera and a security system to figure out who is leaving puzzles on my doorstep."

"Who could it be?" asked Violet.

"The killer," Ruby insisted. "Definitely the killer."

"Maybe. Maybe not." Taylor shrugged. "Why are we obsessing over these random puzzles?"

"Because the puzzles are sending us messages." Alice pressed a palm to her forehead. "Which I haven't been able to decipher."

"Could it be Nicole?" Taylor asked, leaning out of the fridge with a carrot in hand. "Is Nicole a fan of puzzles?"

"No! Yes? I don't know." Ruby covered a yawn. "Honestly, I have no idea."

"I'm off to bed," Alice said. "Turn off the lights when you're done. All of this will have clarity in the morning."

"If only wishing would make it so." Violet gave her a skeptical smile. "Good night."

# Chapter Twenty-nine

"Thank you so much for coming," Alice said, shaking the hand of a prune of a man who had oddly orange hair. She looked to Ruby for help, but she was engaged with a dumpling of a woman who served on West Hazel's city council.

Alice pressed a hand to her belly, realizing that hunger was making her compare people to food items. Not a good day to skip breakfast, but preparation had been hectic, with some last-minute chopping, plating, and avocado mashing to manage. Fortunately, Stone and Taylor made a great team. The three teenagers from the neighborhood who had been hired on to serve food and clean up had arrived right on time. Alice found them adorable, polite, and clueless, but Ruby insisted that the price was right.

Alice and Ruby had been standing here in the front yard for more than forty minutes, a receiving line of sorts, greeting most of the mourners and directing them down the side path to the backyard. Ruby had figured that a short meet-and-greet would forgo her having to circulate through the guests all afternoon, but neither she nor Alice had anticipated quite so many people attending the "intimate" memorial. Somehow, the word had spread so that anyone in town who'd ever heard of George Byrd seemed to be streaming down the block.

"And how did you know George?" Alice asked the orange prune, trying to move things along.

"I cut his hair. Phil Lantham, that's me. I have a booth in the barber shop on State Street, and George and I go back. For six years he's been coming in, sitting in my chair."

"So you're the reason George always looked so suave." Alice had to dig into the bottom of the barrel for that compliment, and she was getting tired of digging. But the barber seemed pleased. "If you go right down past the purple rhodies, you'll find the gate to the reception area, where there are some snacks and drinks."

Phil nodded and headed down the path, his red-streaked hair gleaming in the sun.

Beside her, Ruby was also wrapping it up, sending the councilwoman to the yard. Alice shifted from one leg to the other, testing her sore foot.

"How's your foot feeling?" Ruby asked.

"Still tender, but much better. But I'm grateful that Taylor and Stone jumped in to take over the food. It gave me a good chance to rest."

"Do we finally have a break here?" Ruby shielded her eyes with one hand to scope out the street. "I sent out twenty or so e-mails, and somehow we have like, three times as many guests."

"The rush is over for now," Alice said. "I say we go straight to the airport and hop a flight to Paris."

"Perfect." Ruby clasped her hands together in delight, the gemstones of her rings twinkling in the sun. "Or, we head into the backyard and finish with George's send-off."

Alice sighed. "When did you become the reasonable one?"

"I learned from the best." Ruby took Alice's hand. "Here we go. You lean on me, sugar, and I'll get you where we're going."

"Thanks, friend. Did you take note of the city hall gals, all moving as a group?"

"I sure did. They all came together, which is understandable. You want to know someone at a thing like this. But one person was conspicuously absent."

"Nicole Bender," Alice said as they approached the open gate. "I thought she might make an appearance to allay suspicion."

"So far, she's a no-show." Ruby's eyes squinted suspiciously. "Whatever that means."

They passed through the gate and were absorbed by a group of neighbors.

"Well, hello," came a greeting from a burly, bearded neighbor, Richard.

"Ruby, dear, give us a hug!" said Richard's wife, Bridie, a pleasant woman with a very sweet jasmine scent and peachy cheeks. Richard and Bridie Thompson were Brits who had come to Oregon for his work and decided to make the Northwest their home. "There's our brave girl." Bridie enveloped Ruby in her arms as other neighbors leaned in to repeat their condolences and words of sympathy.

Alice immediately stepped back from the group, summoned two floating servers, and snagged two pairs of mini quiches and baked brie and walnut tarts. Ah, sustenance! Now maybe she could stop equating people to foods she craved.

As Alice dipped back into the group, one neighbor was joking about how much George loved that Maserati.

"Sometimes I would see him in the driveway walking around it with a shammy cloth, buffing it out for an hour or more. It made him happy, I think."

"That car was one of his true loves," Ruby agreed. "After me, of course."

As folks chuckled, Alice spotted Tiger Garrett in the group. The man looked dapper in a sports jacket, navy shirt, and black frame glasses that made him appear studious.

"We're all still in shock, Ruby," said Bridie, "but we want you to know that we're here for you if you need anything."

"And that's not just empty talk," Tiger said, slinging one hunky arm around Ruby's shoulders. "Good neighbors have to look out for each other. You know I'm here for you, girl."

Ruby nodded, obviously moved by the gestures of support. And maybe a little flattered by Tiger's attention.

*What a kind man*, Alice thought. She wondered if Tiger was single. Wondering for a friend, of course.

Leaving Ruby to thank the neighbors, Alice moved off to find more appetizers and engage in a little chitchat. She found a treasure trove in a platter of mini steak sandwiches with just the right slathering of horseradish on the soft potato rolls. A bit of crudité on the side made for a lovely plate to keep her energy up as she talked with George's colleagues and associates, trying to get a measure on how people felt about the deceased. Their answers were respectful, of course, though some city leaders were honest about the differences of opinion they had with George. Nothing wrong with that.

Alice was stashing her empty plate on a side table when Ruby joined her and leaned in close.

"People are asking if there's going to be a eulogy," Ruby said. "And I'm not doing a speech of any kind."

"You don't have to," Alice muttered through a forced smile. "Reverend Coltrane is going to say a few words, right? That should help wrap things up."

"How's the healing going?" said a voice behind them.

Alice turned to find Tansley Grand with her husband, Craig.

"Getting better. I kept it elevated most of yesterday."

"Glad to see you're on the mend," Craig said.

"Actually, ladies, I have a serious matter to discuss with you." Tansley leaned in closer. "It's about the items you picked up from George's office."

"All taken care of," said Ruby.

"The thing is, there's a problem." Tansley's perfect brows rose with concern. "I'm afraid our intern sent you home with some files that are city property. We'll need to get them back."

Alice's smile was guarded. She'd called this one.

"Of course," Ruby agreed, slanting a glance at Alice. "I'll get the files back, soon as I can. I've just been so busy, what with losing George, and work, and the wedding next week. You know it's still on. You folks are coming, right?"

"We are, indeed," Craig said. "Sent back the RSVP some time ago."

Tansley gave Ruby a sad smile. "I know you have a lot on your plate, Ruby, but we do need those records to be returned, ASAP."

"I'll help Ruby find them and get them back to you," Alice said. "I'm sure we can make it happen by Monday or Tuesday."

The mayor thanked them and said her good-byes. "Duty calls."

"There's a new boat club opening down on the river, and Tansley is cutting the ribbon," Craig explained.

"Thank you for stopping by," Alice said.

"You were right about the files," Ruby muttered as the mayor and her husband approached the gate.

"I'm going to really dig in this weekend so you can return them Monday."

Alice scanned the yard. She saw Taylor and Stone looking out from the deck off the kitchen. Probably taking a break. Violet was talking with the neighbors, in listening mode as Bridie Thompson chattered on. The barber was seated at the picnic table along with a handful of stragglers who watched the yard in silence, as if waiting for the show to begin.

As if on cue, Reverend James Coltrane stepped out of the crowd and extended his hands.

"My brothers and sisters . . ." A stout black man, the reverend wore a smooth navy suit and a sorrowful expression. "We are gathered here today to remember our brother, George Byrd."

As Alice stood watching, arm-in-arm with Ruby, her mind wandered to the flowers and trees, the bright blue sky. A minister's desultory voice could do that to her, and the meditative trance allowed a short break.

When the rev wrapped things up, the crowd began to stir.

"Looks like folks are getting on," Alice told Ruby. "Anyone else you need to spend some time with? How about George's coworkers?" She looked toward the cluster of admin people from city hall.

Cassidy was in an informal circle with many of the women Alice had met when she and Ruby visited George's office. The women were atwitter, obviously charmed by an animated man with thick golden hair, high cheekbones, and a smile that could get him cast in a toothpaste commercial.

This one must have slipped in the gate after Ruby and Alice had left their post.

Although Alice couldn't hear what he was saying, it was clear he was going for laughs and giggles. Inappropriate for the moment. Probably in his forties, he seemed to possess the mind and maturity of one of the teenagers making the rounds with appetizer platters.

"Who's that in the center? That man?" Alice asked.

"Actually, I'd say that's one person George was friendly with. His name is Jared something. You remember him. He's the head of that firm that used DNA testing to find the Cola Bandits."

"I'm sure I've seen him on TV before." Alice pulled Ruby over to the edge of the group and caught the attention of one of the young clerks, Asia. "Who is this man?" she asked.

"Jared Chase, from EYE-dentify?" Asia said, her gaze still trained on the man. "He's a local hero."

"Jared Chase." Ruby confirmed with a nod. "Yeah. Always was the life of the party."

"The man behind EYE-dentify." A handsome exterior, and entertaining. And probably fairly well off, as his firm was raking it in from the city of West Hazel. "He sure knows how to work a crowd."

Just then Jared noticed Ruby standing in his orbit, and he held his arms out, as if welcoming her onstage. "Ruby! Come over here, lovely lady. We've been reminiscing about old George. I have to tell you, it was an honor to work with George on that rash of burglaries that had the entire town of West Hazel on alert. This town is grateful to George. He stopped that crime wave."

People in the group agreed enthusiastically, almost on the verge of applause. But for Alice, it felt like a fabricated moment at a memorial like this.

Ruby stepped forward, nodding in acknowledgment as she took Jared's extended hand. "Finding the Cola Bandits was a huge source of pride for George," she said. "I know he considered it to be one of the highlights of his career. He was so proud."

"It was a true moment of leadership for West Hazel," Jared said. "But I have to admit, when I heard about George's murder, I wondered immediately if it was the work of one of those two culprits. Have Moynihan and Preston gone from burglar to killer?"

The mention of murder brought all conversation around them to a halt as people looked to the golden-haired man. Alice folded her arms, scowling at Mr. Jared Chase. George's violent death was too edgy a topic on this afternoon dedicated to his life.

But Jared Chase didn't seem to notice his faux pas. Either that, or he liked being the center of attention, awkward silence be damned.

"I'll bet the cops haven't even thought about these criminals as suspects," Jared said, as if a terrible injustice had been committed. "Where's my friend Detective Bedrosian? He should hear this. I'd say there's a strong possibility that George is dead because those burglars came back to get their revenge."

# Chapter Thirty

"**B**ut wait," Cassidy spoke up. "Aren't the Cola Bandits still in prison? They couldn't have come after George."

"I don't know if that's true," Jared said. "And we all know that a prisoner could easily hire some thug to attack George."

"Whoa, whoa, now." Tiger Garrett emerged from a gaggle of guests chatting by the emerald boxwood hedge. "That's an interesting theory, sir, but it's not quite so easy for inmates to exact revenge. Especially when you're talking about a pair of kids who engaged in nonviolent crimes."

Jared shrugged. "It happens more often than you'd think."

"I don't think we should target these young men." Violet stepped up, her shoulders back, chin up, looking every inch an educational warrior. "I've known Tony Preston and Jimmy Moynihan for years. I was their teacher when they were in fourth grade, and while these boys made some very poor choices, let's not paint them as violent monsters."

Violet now had the full attention of the people who had gathered around Jared. This was one of Violet's gifts, Alice realized. Poised and dynamic, she could hold an audience in the palm of her hand.

"Yes, Tony Preston had anger management issues," Violet said. "A blustery fellow. That boy was entitled and misinformed, but that's not a crime."

Alice remembered the accounts of Tony, Carrie Preston's son, upon his arrest. The kid had told police that his father would get him off the hook. Tony had been sure that charges would be dropped and he would be allowed to go off to the Ivy League college that had accepted him.

"And if you recall," Violet went on, "the other young man, Jimmy Moynihan, was really a gentle soul. Jimmy was a top high school athlete from a working-class family. His single mom worked two jobs to support him and nurture his talent in golf. He had earned a full-ride scholarship to Stanford, a scholarship that was gone in the blink of an eye with the guilty verdict. Such a shame."

Such poor judgment. Alice recalled her encounter with Tony's mother, Carrie Preston, at the grocery store. She understood the weariness she'd seen in Carrie's eyes, a mother's heartbreak when you couldn't pull your child out of a terrible situation. You tried to hold on, have faith, drag them out of the mire. In the end, you had to let go. Suck up the maternal ache, hope for the best, and really let go.

"None of us know what possessed those two young men to steal tens of thousands of dollars' worth of merchandise from the residents of West Hazel," Violet said, a sad lilt to her lips.

Memories of the old news photos flashed through Alice's mind: jewelry, golf clubs, artwork, cash, and bonds. The police had opened up a few bays of the Preston family's extensive garages and found a treasure trove of stolen items.

"The boys claimed that they stole for the game of it," Violet recalled. "There was a thrill in the act of getting away with something. But they were caught. They were prosecuted, and they have spent time in prison. In George's memory, we must move on. George would want us to put the past behind us and resist the temptation to scapegoat these young men for a new crime."

There was a smattering of applause as a few people voiced agreement and complimented Violet on her insights.

Not to be outdone, Jared Chase cut in one more time to bring the attention back to himself. "Don't you worry, Ruby. We're going to find George's killer. My company, EYE-dentify, is going to take the case on. We'll do our magic with DNA analysis. If anyone can find your husband's killer, we can."

"Add an eight hundred number and you can make this a TV commercial," Alice muttered under her breath.

Across the yard, Madison was waving, trying to get Alice's attention. She pointed toward the street and mouthed: "Gotta go."

"Go where?" Alice said aloud, and began to carefully make her way over to Madison. "Where are you going?"

"Ruby's house. The mouse took the bait."

# Chapter Thirty-one

"I'm going with you," Alice said. "I'll get Taylor to hold down the fort."

"If you come along, you can't let Ruby know what's up." Madison was looking at her phone, reading text messages. "Apparently Nicole is willing to talk, but she's threatening to clam up if she has to face Ruby."

"Smart woman," Alice said.

They went into the kitchen and gave Taylor and Stone a heads-up.

Taylor pulled her apron off over her head. "I'll go out back and keep Ruby company."

"Good luck," Stone said as Alice and Madison headed out the front door.

"Bedrosian is going to meet us there," Madison said as they got into the car.

"Where is he, anyway?"

"It's his day off. He's furniture shopping with his wife and kids. Something about getting a big girl bed for his daughter."

Alice smiled at the image of Bedrosian trying to corral children jumping on beds in a mattress outlet. "I suppose everyone's entitled to a day off."

"And please, when we see Nicole, just let me do the talking."

"I just have a few questions for her," Alice said.

"Gran, you're probably not supposed to be there. It's a police matter; she's under arrest."

There was something thrilling about that. They had found their culprit. "Don't worry, honey. I'll be discreet."

Madison let out a hard breath. "I don't know why I let you talk me into these things."

At Ruby's house, they found Nicole Bender sitting at the kitchen table, her left hand cuffed to the chair, while the officer stood leaning against the counter opposite her, filling out a form.

"I got her name and pedigree information," the officer told Madison.

"Thanks, Officer." Madison planted her feet, as if getting ready for a wrestling match. "I have quite a few questions for this suspect."

Nicole stiffened when she saw Alice with Madison. "You didn't bring his wife, did you? She's going to kill me when she finds out."

"She's not here," Alice said. "And she's not going to kill you." Though, Alice knew, Ruby would be sorely tempted.

"I can't believe this is happening!" Nicole cringed as she pressed her free hand to her forehead. "It's all freakin' me out! I'm gonna have a panic attack."

"Take a deep breath," Alice said. "And then another. You're okay. You're sitting in a chair with your feet on the ground. Do you want some water?"

Nicole shook her head. "No. Thank you." Tears started to stream from her eyes. "You know? I think maybe I wanted to get caught. I mean, it was stupid coming here today. And I was an idiot to come back the other day, when I ran into you, Alice."

*So true*, thought Alice, but she kept mum. Best to let the girl keep talking.

"Why did you come back, Nicole?" Madison asked in a calm, sympathetic voice.

"I was looking for my ring, but you know what? I think I really came back because the guilt was eating away at me. Maybe I wanted to get caught. I don't know. I'm ready now. I want to confess."

"Okay, then." Madison shot Alice a look that said *this is too easy* as she moved behind the woman. She took out her notebook, and then took a seat across from her at the kitchen table.

"All right, Nicole. Detective Bedrosian will be joining us soon. He's on another job, but I can start taking your statement. Let's begin with your relationship with George. You weren't being truthful the other night when we talked, were you?"

"I was too scared to tell the truth. But you must know, yes, I had a relationship with George outside the office. We saw each other a few times a week, usually at my apartment. We were saving and planning for the time when we could be together."

"So tell me what happened the night George's wife caught you with George," Madison said.

"I—I don't want to talk about it. It was so awful, I'll just start crying all over again."

Alice frowned. *Cry-schmy.* "You know, Nicole," Alice said, in a low voice intended to sound soothing, "difficult as this is, you're going to have to buck up, face the truth, and set the record straight. Now tell Officer Denham how you killed George Byrd."

"But I didn't kill George!"

Madison blinked. "Did you hit George with a candlestick holder?"

"I did! But I didn't kill him. I swear! I hit him, but I didn't kill him. He was still yelling at me when I left. He was back on that damn bike, ignoring me. I was mad at him, but I didn't want to kill him. I still loved him. Don't you see? We were going to get married. We were engaged."

"But George is married," Madison said. "You know that."

"He was getting a divorce. He promised me. He bought me an engagement ring, a pretty green emerald with little diamonds on the gold band. Sometimes he let me wear it when we went out together, but I had to give it back every time we parted. He said it was for safekeeping. But he promised I could have it as soon as he got his divorce from Ruby. He promised."

*So George was living a double life*, Alice mused. She thought of the things Violet had seen in Ruby's tarot card readings. Hidden secrets. The illusions and lies of the Moon card. Dammit, Violet had been right.

"We were going to get married and buy a house," Nicole went on. "I want kids, and he promised to make all my dreams come true."

Alice recognized one of George's signature lines: *"I'm here to make your dreams come true!"*

She was glad Ruby wasn't here to witness this. It would hurt her to know how George had been stringing this young woman along.

# Chapter Thirty-two

Bedrosian arrived, a bit annoyed to be called in on his Saturday off. Fortunately, he was able to click into the zone so that he and Madison could continue the interview.

From her seat adjacent to Nicole at the kitchen table, Alice told herself she was going to try to keep mum, mostly because she wanted to give her granddaughter the freedom to flex her interviewing skills. She only hoped Bedrosian would keep his irritation in check.

Nicole admitted that the affair had been going on for the past year. They had an arrangement in which George gave her one thousand dollars each time they were "together." "I deposited the money in the bank for our house. At the moment, we got more than forty thousand dollars."

"That's a lot of togetherness," Bedrosian said.

Nicole's lower lip jutted out in a pout. "Don't judge me. It wasn't that kind of a transaction. I was helping him save money, away from his wife's watchful eyes."

"Let's get back to Monday night," Madison said, "after Ruby burst in on you and George."

"That was horrible." Nicole contended that now that Ruby knew about them, it was time for George to leave his wife. But George said he wasn't ready. She was so angry, so frustrated, that she started to storm out. "Downstairs, I stopped in the kitchen to take my grand out of his wallet, but there was no cash. That was the last straw. I mean, I figured it meant he was planning to break up with me even before his wife showed up."

As Nicole let out a whimper, Alice wanted to tell her that George had come to the meeting with her money. It had been Ruby who'd snatched it out of his wallet in a fit of anger. Ruby who'd gone to the mall and spent the cash to get back at her husband.

"I was so mad." Nicole sniffed. "I wanted to hurt him like he'd hurt me. So I grabbed a candlestick from the display downstairs, stormed upstairs, and clunked him in the head with it. But I didn't kill him! He grunted and collapsed to the floor. He was quiet for a minute, and then he groaned and pushed up off the carpet and started calling me nasty names. I didn't deserve that! But he acted like I was nothing. He told me to get out, and I did."

"What did you do with the candlestick holder?" Madison asked.

"I left it on the carpet in his bedroom, right there behind the exercise bike. I know, you probably found my fingerprint on it. But I swear, I only hit him once."

"Were you worried that his wound was serious?"

"Not at first. I mean, the way he was yelling, he seemed fine. But after I left, when I kept calling his cell and he wouldn't answer, I got suspicious. At first I thought he was just busy with Ruby, but then when he wouldn't even shoot me a text, I knew something was wrong. I was up almost all night, worried. So when I didn't hear from him, I went into the office really early and called the police from the switchboard line, just in case my instinct was right.

And it turns out, it was." Her words dissolved in a sob, and Madison waited, handing her a box of tissues from the kitchen counter to dry her tears.

To Alice's surprise, Bedrosian also waited patiently. She would have expected him to railroad this young woman, push for answers. Perhaps he had some experience in drawing out a witness's story.

At last, Nicole blew her nose and took a deep breath. "I can't believe he's gone. I just hope I didn't kill him. It wasn't me, was it? I mean, maybe he had a heart attack or something."

"If you're innocent," Bedrosian said, "who do you think killed him?"

"No idea," she said. "George wasn't the most popular person at the office, but no one ever threatened him, not that I knew of. He didn't gamble or use drugs. He used to say that his big vices were fast women and hot cars. It was a joke. Get it?"

No one laughed. Alice frowned down at the table, recognizing George's old line that he'd often used to amuse Ruby. Yuck.

"Why did you return here?" Madison asked. "When we talked last, you told us you weren't here Thursday night, but that wasn't true."

"I was here. I needed to get my ring, but I knew I couldn't take the chance of that neighbor's camera catching me again, so I went in through the little park in the back, hopped the fence. The garage window was already unlatched, the screen off, so it was easy. I was in the house, looking for my ring, when Ruby and Alice came in."

"Do you realize you assaulted this woman?" Bedrosian asked.

"Yeah." Nicole scowled down at the floor, then looked

over at Alice, fear in her eyes. "I'm sorry I freaked out on you. I was just trying to get out the back door."

Alice rested her chin in her hand, realizing this was no time to scold Nicole. "Let's get back to the question. You were here when we arrived?"

Nicole nodded. "I was searching George's office when you came up the stairs. I squeezed into the closet between some boxes and held my breath while you came in and got his checkbook."

"Creepier than I expected," Alice said.

"I knew I had to get out of there before you two came back. So I tried to sneak out. But you got in the way. In the end, I had to run out the front door. And I know that neighbor saw me." Nicole raked her hair back from her forehead. "I was so stupid, I know I was! But no one under-stands what I went through, losing George. It was the end of all my hopes and dreams. My job here. My love. I just needed my ring, so I could go."

*As if forty grand wasn't enough,* Alice thought. The in-creasing drama was a bit much for Alice. The truth sounded emotional enough without the added soap opera notes.

"And then, when I saw my face on TV, making it look like I was a killer . . . it was too much. I knew I had to make a break. Get out of this town and start over some-where else. I was going to move to Denver or Tucson—anywhere else—just as soon as I found my ring. That's why I came back today. I figured I'd have time to look around while Ruby was busy at the memorial service. But still, no luck."

"We'll be taking you to the precinct to press charges," Madison said as she slid her notebook over to Nicole and put down a pen. "But just so I get it right, would you mind printing your name in my notebook? That would be most helpful."

Bedrosian's hands went up in the air, ready to object, but a stern look from Madison silenced him.

Alice, too, found Madison's request a little odd.

Nicole shook her head. "You'll have to take off these handcuffs, because I'm left-handed."

Madison unlocked the cuffs, then slid the open notebook and pen over to Nicole. "Here you go."

Nicole picked up the pen, printed her name in large letters on the pad, and then handed it back to Madison.

"Thanks for that. So . . . left-handed?" Madison said, and Nicole nodded.

"All right." Madison closed her notebook and turned to Bedrosian. "It looks like we won't be charging this witness with homicide. She's left-handed."

"Right," he said, catching on. "So the charges will be reduced to breaking and entering, and assault."

"Wait. What?" Alice blinked. So they were letting Nicole off the hook for George's murder?

# Chapter Thirty-three

In the mellowing sunlight of her backyard, Alice felt like she was holding court with her friends. "So you can imagine my surprise when Madison closed her notebook and announced that the police would not be charging Nicole Bender with homicide."

"Not charging her?" Ruby gaped. "Why not?"

"Because she was left-handed?" Violet held her G and T aloft as she considered the evidence. "I don't know why that matters, but I bet that's a clue."

"It is, indeed," Alice said. "The answer is in a detailed report Madison received from the coroner. Turns out that, while there were multiple contusions on the back of George's head, one minor bruise was different from the others. From the angle and location of the minor injury, it would have been caused by a blow from someone who was left-handed. All the other wounds were in a different location on the rear right of George's head. Caused by blows from a right-handed person. If head injury was the cause of death, the killer was right-handed."

"Wow. Our Madison really has her stuff together, doesn't she?" said Violet.

"She was amazing," Alice said. "Right on point." Alice leaned back on the orange deck chair, adjusted the cushion under her foot, and took a sip of her drink. A glass of Empress lavender gin with tonic seemed fitting because it was Saturday, Alice's leg was feeling better, the memorial was over and, oddly, the interview with Nicole seemed to close a chapter in the story of George's murder.

"Well, congratulations on solving part of the crime," Stone said, toasting Alice with his drink. He had played bartender for all the gals, not to mention keeping the food and drinks flowing until the guests found their way out.

"Thank you"—Alice chinked glasses with him—"for everything. You and Taylor made a terrific team in the kitchen."

Stone nodded. "She's a mighty good cook when she trusts her instincts."

"How did the neighborhood kids work out?" Ruby asked, looking toward the back door. The three teens were still on the premises, helping Taylor clean up the kitchen.

"Have you ever tried to corral kittens?" Stone asked.

The women chuckled. "That bad?" Violet smiled.

"Nah. They were earnest and polite. And they tried really hard to follow instructions. Can't ask for more than that."

"I appreciate you stepping up, Stone," Ruby told him. "But I have one more question. If Nicole was just the blond-wigged floozie, doesn't that mean George's killer is still out there?" Ruby's voice was uncharacteristically subdued as she posed the question.

"That's the takeaway," Alice said.

"And it appears that the killer is right-handed," Stone added. "Which rules out almost no one."

"Well, that's kind of scary," Violet said. "What are you going to do now?"

"Keep digging," Alice said. "Which reminds me, I need to go through George's files again before they go back to city hall."

Ruby nodded. "I want a look, too. There must be something juicy in there. Especially now that the mayor asked to have the paperwork returned. It's suddenly forbidden fruit."

"We can check them out in the morning," Alice promised.

The sliding door from the kitchen opened and Taylor stepped onto the deck. "Our catering helpers are all done. Somebody going to pay them?"

"That's me!" Ruby said, popping up. "Let me get my purse."

"And item two: someone left a gift on our front porch." Taylor held up a box wrapped in plastic. "A new puzzle!"

Alice groaned. "Who left it there?"

"Could be anyone," Taylor said. "We had dozens of people come by today."

"Put it down, and keep away from it," Violet said. "It could be laced with poison."

"Look at it," Ruby said from the doorway. "This one is in a box, and it's still sealed in plastic."

"It's from a Disney movie, Aunt Vi," Taylor said, handing it to her. "*Frozen.*"

Violet waved her off, but Alice reached for the box. The illustration showed the princess Elsa holding her arms up to cast a spell in her ice castle. The banner over her head proclaimed: "Let It Go!"

"Honestly? It's adorable," Alice said. "And very colorful."

Ruby leaned in to take a look. "I do love me some ice princess."

"Enough with the puzzle mystery," Violet said. "I say we donate the puzzle. Give it to the senior center."

"It's five hundred pieces," Alice said. "Could be the perfect amount for a Saturday night." She turned to Ruby. "But if you guys aren't comfortable . . ."

"I want to do it," Taylor said.

"Same," Ruby agreed. "Come on, girls. Life's too short to worry about poisoned puzzles. Stone, can you bring out the card table? I'll show you where Alice keeps it. It's turning into such a beautiful evening. We'll do the puzzle right here."

"I'm happy to help," Stone said. "And then I'm going to call it a night. The kitchen is closed."

Twenty minutes later, they had the puzzle pieces face up in the box and on the table, with most of the border constructed. Alice studied the art on the box, musing over the banner.

"Maybe this is too obvious, but do you think 'Let It Go' is the message of this puzzle? Is anonymous telling us to let go of trying to find out who killed George?"

"That interpretation is quite literal," Violet said, "but offhand I can't think of an alternative."

"Well." Alice picked out a few pieces that had the curlicues of black wrought iron. "I'm not giving up."

"Thank you, honey," Ruby said. "I'll be right beside you."

"I want to help, too," Violet said. "In fact, I'm going to do some cleansing to get us on a new path." No one questioned her when she placed her collection of blue pieces on the table and headed inside.

The puzzle work continued as Violet reappeared with a royal-blue velvet bag.

"Are we doing another ritual?" Taylor asked cheerfully.

"I'm not changing into that white bathrobe again," Ruby said without looking up.

"Just a little housekeeping. Not to worry, but we had lots of strangers passing through today, and I'm picking up on some negative energy that needs to be cleansed." A bouquet of dried herbs emerged from the blue bag. "This is just a sage stick, for cleansing. It will remove all energy, so we need to be sure and preserve everything positive and loving and fruitful." Violet lifted the sage stick, held a lighter to it, and flames traveled along the dried leaves. The ribbon of smoke that followed had a distinctive aroma. Not unpleasant.

"Just don't set off the smoke detectors inside," Alice said. "Do you need us to do anything, Violet?"

"Stir up some positive energy." Violet swayed around the yard, lovingly waving the smoking sage through the air. "Cleanse this home, white as a dove," she chanted. "Fill this yard with joy and love."

"That's sweet, honey," said Alice.

Ruby agreed. "A lot more comforting than summoning George back from the dead."

When the cleansing was brought to a close with three taps on a small gong, Violet seemed pleased by the results. "So much better."

"Wait." Taylor hopped out of her seat. "I've got a great idea." She disappeared inside, and returned a minute later with her guitar. "I learned this song at karaoke night, but if you guys don't know the words, you can join in on the chorus."

The sweet strains of steel strings came together in an impressive array, only made better when Taylor started singing. The girl did possess talent. But what was the song?

"Let it go!" Taylor belted out.

Ruby and Violet joined in, leaving Alice openmouthed.

How was it that she was the only woman who didn't know the words?

# Chapter Thirty-four

"In most murder investigations, there comes a point when you realize you've been chasing a red herring," Alice told Ruby as they sat in the kitchen nook enjoying coffee and some fruit tarts that were left over from yesterday. "We can't be discouraged by that. It's part of the process."

"So we made a mistake going after Nicole?" Ruby said.

"Not a mistake. When you work a case, you need to follow every lead, and Nicole was definitely involved."

"And you know this because . . . ? Alice, you sound like you just spent twenty years in the homicide division of NYPD."

"From reading mysteries, of course." Last night, alone in bed, Alice had put her current novel on her nightstand and dumped a few of her favorite mystery novels on the comforter. The books were well worn, the plots quite familiar. She'd skimmed them just enough to review the road map of the plots. "Twists and turns are inevitable in any investigation."

"Maybe that's how it goes in books," Ruby said. "In our situation, I'm hoping for a clear path ahead to find George's killer."

"Well, let's get to those files and see if I missed something the first time through," Alice said.

Ruby cleaned off the table and brought the two boxes over, while Alice topped off their coffees.

"Okay," Ruby said, rubbing her hands together in mock enthusiasm. "Show me what's what."

They sifted through the files together, Alice guiding Ruby's perusal of invoices, bookkeeping statements, and budget estimates and reports. Alice found the budget information to be quite juicy, but she could tell it didn't interest Ruby.

"I don't see anything that sticks out," Ruby said. "Honestly, I'm not a numbers person, but I go over the accounts for Ruby's House of Wigs every month. It's important to keep an eye on your money."

"Agreed. It's just interesting for me to see the big picture, beyond my own library budget."

"I get that, honey, but isn't most of this public information?"

Alice tapped a finger on the spreadsheet in front of her. "Good question. Let's see." She got her laptop and went to the city Web site to find the budget. "There it is. Should be simple to do a line-by-line comparison of the budget in George's files and what's posted."

Ruby lifted her coffee mug. "That noise you hear is the sound of my brain icing over."

"It's not that bad," Alice said as she ticked things off, line by line. "It matches up beautifully. All except . . . something's missing here."

"Don't tease me with anticipation," Ruby said flatly.

"Everything matches except the payments to EYE-dentify," Alice explained. "On the city Web site, EYE-dentify isn't mentioned in the line budget. Instead, the one hundred thousand dollars per month debit is attributed to 'criminal investigations.' Interesting."

"Significant?" Ruby asked.

"I think so. I'm guessing that George wanted to play down his astronomical payments to Jared Chase's company."

"Because people might object to their tax dollars going to the golden boy?"

"Something like that. I'm going to bring it up with the mayor," Alice said. "Along with the surprising amount of the payment to the outside vendor."

"There's a file for EYE-dentify here," Ruby said, "but it's quite slender."

"I saw that before. It's just a bunch of bills, right?"

"Looks like monthly invoices from Jared Chase's company. Those astronomical payments."

"Shouldn't there be monthly reports?" Alice asked. "DNA tests or something from Jared Chase? I mean, you pay a company more than a million dollars a year, you'd expect them to generate some hard information. What was EYE-dentify providing in return for all that money?"

"A good question."

"Maybe they delivered the product online," Alice suggested.

"Not if George was the client," said Ruby. "Remember, he didn't even own a home computer."

The rest of the files contained pages of fiscal data. Proposals from other vendors. Billing from IT consultants and other outside vendors.

"I never knew George's job was so dry and boring," said Ruby.

"At least his office files were organized," Alice said as they replaced the official files in the boxes.

"Probably the work of Nicole," Ruby said.

"From the looks of his home office, I suspect you're right." Alice went to the butler's pantry where she'd stashed the papers they'd removed from George's office at the house. "Before we return those files to the city, let's see if George's personal records tell the same story."

Ruby gasped. "Do you think there's a discrepancy? Like . . . wait. Do you think that hundred grand in his bank account is money he stole from the city?" She pressed a palm to one cheek. "Maybe he was skimming funds from West Hazel."

"Possibly," Alice said. "Though I think he was too smart to do something so obvious."

"I used to think he was smart. Now I'm really wondering."

George's personal papers were a mess. Alice sorted and skimmed for a half hour without any financial insights. "If there's a discrepancy here, I don't think we're going to find it."

"Did you see this folder, marked EYE-dentify?" Ruby asked. "It's got a list of names, and a bunch of copies of old newspaper articles."

"Hard to make sense of it, but let's take another look." Alice sipped her coffee as she studied the list. "Seven people?"

"Or maybe it's seven items," Ruby said.

"I think they're people. In George's notes, he's got phone numbers for some of them." Behind the list, there were individual profiles of some of the people, a few with phone numbers and other notes scrawled in George's handwriting. There were also printouts of old newspaper articles about West Hazel. Twenty to thirty pages.

"I'll need some time to read through these news accounts," Alice said, "but they seem to be from the crime blotter. A murder. A drowning."

"Some of the articles date back to the eighties," Ruby observed.

"Interesting." Alice felt like there might be something here. "I know George was not a regular library patron, but I'll bet he got these from the electronic records of a library. Maybe even the West Hazel branch."

Back to the list of names. Alice didn't recognize any of them.

J. Amichi

L. Haynes

J. Jin

B. Montell

A. Preston

A. Russell

D. Washington

Seven names, and a bundle of news stories describing maybe a dozen different crimes. Alice wasn't sure what to make of it. She was still skimming through the newspaper accounts when the slider from the backyard opened, and Madison appeared.

"Hey there." Guilt surged through Alice as she closed the folder quickly, as if she was doing something illegal. And maybe she was. Was her face red? It felt a bit warm.

Nothing like being caught in the act.

# Chapter Thirty-five

"I'm afraid I made a terrible mistake." With pale skin and shadowed eyes, Madison exuded misery.

"Honey, you don't look so good." Ruby pulled out a chair for her.

"Come in, sit down." Alice scooped the remaining papers off the table and transferred them to the kitchen counter. "Let me make you some cheesy eggs, scrambled just the way you like them."

"Gran, no. You're supposed to stay off your feet."

"I can stand on one foot while I'm cooking." Alice shoved the papers into the pantry and went to the fridge for eggs. "What's going on?"

"I don't want to talk about it." Madison put her head down on the table, and Ruby patted her back.

Alice proceeded to cook, knowing good food could unravel the tightest story.

Violet breezed into the kitchen and stopped short. "What's wrong? Are you ill?"

"She doesn't want to talk about it," Ruby said. "Now, who wants a mimosa?"

Having overheard the conversation, Taylor emerged

from the basement stairs. "I'll take a mimosa. It's Sunday brunch time."

"Can I get you a drink, Madison?" Ruby offered.

"No, thanks. I've got to go back to work. I just feel so bad about screwing up."

Taylor slipped an arm around her sister's shoulders. "You're a wreck. It can't be that bad."

"This is all my fault." Madison covered her face, her voice cracking with emotion.

The other women exchanged looks of concern. Everyone was immediately sympathetic to the girl who never made mistakes.

Alice buttered an English muffin and brought the plate of eggs over to the table. "Okay, head up and down the hatch."

"I feel like I've ruined a kid's life," Madison said. "I've destroyed Jimmy Moynihan."

"Who's that?" Ruby asked. "Some boy you just broke up with?"

Madison shook her head. "He was one of the Cola Bandits. After everyone was talking about the case yesterday, and someone suggested that the kids may have had a vendetta against George, I did a little research. I found that the Preston kid, the mastermind, is still in jail. But Moynihan, who pled guilty to lesser charges, was given an early release two weeks ago."

"So one of the Cola Bandits is out of prison," Alice said.

Madison nodded, swallowing a bite. "I mentioned it to Bedrosian, and we paid Moynihan a visit."

"And you arrested him because he confessed to killing George?" Ruby asked.

"No. It was all so awkward. Moynihan's mom, Patty, was freaked out to see the police at the house. She was sure we were there to take her son back to jail. She thinks the slightest hint of trouble will send Jimmy back to prison. It was hard to calm her down."

"Was Jimmy upset, too?" asked Violet.

"The kid was contrite and soft-spoken. We asked him if he had contact with George Byrd since his release from prison, and he said no. He wasn't even sure who George Byrd was."

"Well, my George wouldn't want to hear that," Ruby said.

"We explained Byrd was one of the people involved in DNA investigation for West Hazel. Jimmy just remembered one old guy, and one guy who was like a Ken doll."

"Yeah, Jared Chase does strongly resemble Ken," Violet said.

"Before we left, Bedrosian offered to call Jimmy's parole officer and vouch for his cooperation on our case. That really freaked out Patty Moynihan. When we left she was crying, insisting that her son is a good boy." Madison shook her head. "We shouldn't have gone there."

"You're conducting an investigation," Alice said. "Trying to find information."

"And your presence there didn't compromise Jimmy's future," Violet pointed out. "Trust me, I've dealt with plenty of overwrought parents, and this Patty Moynihan isn't thinking rationally. Her fears are unfounded. You did the right thing, going there."

"I hope that's true." Madison took another bite of eggs and sighed. "Sometimes it sucks to be me."

"Join the club," Taylor said. "I live in my grandma's basement."

Madison turned to Ruby. "How are you doing?"

Ruby squeezed her arm. "I'm okay, honey."

"Bedrosian wanted me to notify you that the police department has officially released the crime scene; you're free to move back into your home."

Ruby winced. "And here I've been focusing on moving my things out."

"You know, you can stay here as long as you like," Alice assured Ruby. "Alice's Palace has plenty of room."

"Thank you, honey. I'd like to stay for a while. I'm not sure where I'll go after this, but it won't be back to that house. For now, I'm happy here."

"Well, that's a bit of good news," Violet said cheerfully.

"So no one will have to go near the house during the wedding, I've booked a floor of suites at the Hazel Hotel for bridal party and family members."

"Your kids will love that place," Taylor said.

"So, Madison, I want to ask, if I may, the final outcome of the cases of the two Cola Bandits," Violet said. "They are former students of mine, and I was concerned to hear Jared Chase casting aspersions on their characters. Are you looking at them as suspects in George's murder?"

"They've both been cleared," Madison said. "Preston is still in prison, and Moynihan seems to be on a straight path now. Aunt Violet, you'll be happy to hear that Jimmy Moynihan is enrolled in community college starting in September. Until then he's got a summer job landscaping at the country club, where the golf pro is helping him with his swing."

"That's wonderful." Violet smiled.

"So I suppose they're off the suspect list," Ruby said.

"Aren't you the super sleuth," Alice said, nudging Ruby.

"Ladies . . ." Madison arose from the table. "In the future, I'd appreciate you leaving the investigation up to law enforcement. You know I'd hate it if something happened to any of you."

*Highly unlikely,* thought Alice. But then the gals had gotten a message to back off in last night's puzzle. Madison didn't need to hear that.

"We're just trying to get some solid answers," Ruby said.

"Exactly," Alice agreed. "The big question remains: Who killed George?"

# Chapter Thirty-six

After a brunch of eggs, bacon, fruit salad, and English muffins with spicy apricot jam, Alice thought it was time to take out the beachy Surf Shop puzzle that Stone had brought. She figured that everyone could use a bit of color, palm trees, foaming waves, and fun in the sand. The puzzle consisted of one thousand pieces, so Alice pulled out the small boxes used to divide pieces by color and border pieces.

Taylor immediately searched for the four corner pieces—her forte. Alice saw the technique as a means of getting quick gratification, but if that was her granddaughter's worst vice, so be it. Of course, there were occasional disappointments when Taylor discovered a puzzle with split corner pieces, but again, she needed to learn adulting.

"Give me all the pieces with royal-blue and white stripes," Ruby said, already forging ahead into the center of the puzzle. "I'm going to put together the area with these beach chairs."

"And I'm working on the palm leaves with blue sky behind them," Violet said, staking her territory.

As Alice collected beige border pieces and tried to construct areas of the sandy beach in the foreground, she thought back on the conversation with Madison.

"Something is bugging me," Alice said. "It's about the Preston family. Madison said the police dismissed Tony Preston as a suspect because he was still in jail. But what about the parents? Tony's father, JB Preston, is a million-aire with vast resources. JB could have hired someone to go after George if he wanted to."

"Wait, I met his wife, Carrie, right?" asked Taylor. "She didn't seem like a mobster's wife."

"Not at all," Alice said. "But a parent's love runs deep. Maybe the Prestons blamed George for their son's incar-ceration."

"Blamed him enough to have him killed?" asked Violet. "I'm not sure I buy that."

"It's a theory," Alice said, rising from the puzzle table and going to the pantry to retrieve the messy throng of George's papers. It was within the realm of possibility.

"I feel like I'm missing something." As the others con-tinued the puzzle, Alice settled back on the love seat with George's EYE-dentify papers in her lap. Once again she looked over the list. Jin, Montell, Preston . . .

Wait, that was one name she knew. But A. Preston? She knew Carrie, JB, and Tony . . . but Tony was short for An-thony? Was Tony Preston one of the people on this list?

"What does this mean?" she asked aloud.

"Are you talking to us?" Violet asked. "Or the Mother Goddess?"

"Anyone who will answer." Alice put the list aside and started to peruse the articles. Some were copied a few times, with hand-scribbled notes on some copies. Others had been folded and unfolded, as if stuffed into a pocket. A total mess.

But as she read on, she noted a common factor in each crime: potential homicide. Unsolved homicides. Some articles described bloody murder scenes, and many detailed discoveries of dead bodies.

"I wonder if any of these were solved after this coverage was written," Alice said, thinking aloud.

"What are you muttering about over there?" asked Violet.

"I'm looking through George's papers yet one more time. These news articles are about violent crimes, possible homicides. And they all happened here in West Hazel." While the other women kept working on the puzzle, Alice set her laptop on the kitchen island and started searching for more information on George's collection of crimes. "There's a reason George was interested in these cases."

"Maybe because he was a crime buff?" Taylor asked.

"I'm trying to find out."

She skimmed the account of a man knifed to death at three in the morning outside a bar.

A man shot and killed by intruders in his apartment.

A young man found dead of a suspicious overdose, with evidence at the scene indicating he had not been alone.

The body of a young woman found on the riverbank some twenty years ago.

The water tower baby, a tragic case of a newborn found dead and abandoned at the foot of the town's water tower.

She searched the cases individually, then found each one listed on the county law enforcement Web site under "West Hazel Cold Cases."

As Alice sorted the paperwork out on the granite island, she was able to decipher the handwritten notes written on the article about the drug overdose. It was a more recent case, from nearly two years ago. The victim's name was Harlan Powell, and the note read: "Contact JB Preston."

Tony Preston's father.

What was with the connection to the Preston family?

"I need to go," Alice said, closing her laptop and stacking the papers.

"Where are you going?" asked Ruby.

"To visit an old friend."

# Chapter Thirty-seven

Alice arrived outside the gate of the Preston mansion with a bouquet of sunflowers in hand. While at the store looking at flowers for her friend, she had recalled the painting class she and Carrie had taken at the library together. Carrie had been smitten by the emotion in sunflowers, the way their faces grew toward the sun like people yearning for light. Did Carrie remember those days fondly? She hoped so.

Alice hit the button on the gate, but the woman on the intercom told her Carrie wasn't available today.

"But I'm an old friend," Alice said quickly. "I just wanted to—"

"Call for an appointment," the voice said, and the intercom switched off.

Time to think of a plan B.

The broad, two-story brick mansion that loomed at the end of a vast green lawn seemed more fitting in the English countryside than here in a Portland suburb on a bluff overlooking a wooded lake. A structure like that lent itself to fox hunts and afternoon tea, not so much hops festivals, food trucks, and Pink Martini concerts.

Distant. Cold. Unapproachable. But somehow Alice had to get in.

Stepping back, Alice scoped out the iron fence, its pointed spires announcing that this family did not mess around with security. Besides, was it wise for a woman pushing seventy to scale a fence? Maybe there was some Olympian out there who could do it. Alice could not.

As she was scouting and deliberating along the fence, a van pulled up to the gate and the driver spoke into the intercom. It was the pool maintenance service, its bubbly splash logo declaring "Clean & Clear."

A moment later, a buzzer sounded and the gate started to swing open. Perfect. Alice walked in behind it, taking cover in back of the vehicle until it picked up speed and continued up the driveway.

Opting not to get turned away at the front door, Alice followed the van around back, past a rose garden and a tall stand of yews to the pool area. The water sparkled in the sun, promising refreshment on this hot, sunny day. While the pool woman unloaded her equipment, Alice moved forward, contemplating a dip of her feet in the warm spa when she realized someone was sitting by the pool. A strong-jawed man in dark glasses and a polo shirt. Was it JB Preston? She didn't really remember what the millionaire looked like.

"Sorry," she said. "I hope I didn't startle you. I stopped by to see your wife. I'm Alice Pepper."

"JB Preston." He reached out and gave her hand a firm shake.

"I think we met before, years ago. I met Carrie through the library. The West Hazel branch is my baby."

"Is that so?"

She asked if Carrie was in, but he didn't answer. A few

more questions were answered by him reintroducing himself or saying: "Is that so?" or "Sure is."

*Dementia,* she thought, sinking into a pool chair near him. But he was probably only in his sixties. He seemed too young for this.

Alice sat with him for a while, commenting on the pleasant weather, the rose garden, the hardworking pool attendant. Easy, pleasant topics. She was gaining new insight to why Carrie was so stressed these days. It was also clear that JB Preston was not a man who recently hired someone to extract revenge on George Byrd.

When Carrie came out and spotted her, she was annoyed at first. "Really, Alice! Did you ride in on the bumper of the pool van?"

"I needed to see you." Alice picked up the flowers from the side table. "I brought these for you."

Carrie's head tilted to one side. "Sunflowers."

"Reaching to the light."

"That was a good time, our painting class," Carrie said. "Seems like a long time ago."

The silence that followed was restful. A breeze rose, cool and chlorinated and green in the sun. Then JB Preston introduced himself to his wife, and the moment was lost.

Carrie turned away from her husband, switching gears. "So now you know our secret. We're trying to keep the business going . . . well, I'm trying. I'm in over my head."

Alice wanted to be sympathetic without casting pity. "Are you alone in this?" she asked Carrie. "You're going to need support, both emotional and fiscal guidance. Maybe legal, too."

"I have the best therapy money can buy."

"But there will be so many other things to handle," Alice said. "You know that."

Carrie nodded. "I face it every day."

"I know someone who can help. May I reach out to him on your behalf?" When Carrie frowned, Alice added, "If Stone can't help you with business matters, he'll find someone who can."

Carrie nodded. "I'll talk with him."

"Good." The tranquility returned as JB put his hand over Carrie's, and the only sound was the high whir of a hummingbird glimmering over one of the planters. "You have a beautiful place back here."

"In many ways, we're fortunate."

"I have to admit, I came here today with a different set of questions. I've been helping Ruby go through her husband's things, and I saw Tony's and JB's names mentioned in some of George Byrd's notes. Something related to EYE-dentify?"

Carrie's head jerked around, her eyes cold again. "I can't talk to you. Tony's going to be released in six months, if all goes well. He's having a hell of a time in there, and I can't do anything to compromise his chances of getting out."

"Nothing you say to me will change Tony's sentence. Listen, Carrie, I know George played a big role in your son's conviction, but George is gone now. Tony will be free and clear soon. You can talk to me."

Carrie shook her head. "Despite the way he spun his reputation, George Byrd was no hero. I'm sorry I ever talked to that man. He nearly destroyed our family. That's all I'm going to say about him."

Alice shifted in her chair, a bit discomfited by the strong words about George.

"I'm sorry to dredge up bad memories. I'm just trying to sort through this mess so the matter can be put to rest.

Can you explain why the Preston name was linked to the death of Harlan Powell?"

"Who told you that?" Carrie shot out of her chair so quickly, she knocked a table and a lemonade glass shattered on the concrete. "Did he tell you that?"

"No, no. No one told me. I read it in a file."

"Then shred it. Burn it. Whatever it takes to destroy it. My son had nothing to do with that young man's death. Nothing! Tony was Harlan's friend! Do you hear me?"

JB was cringing and squirming in his chair, his hands on his ears as if to block out the conflict.

"I do. I'm sorry," Alice said, wincing as she stooped to clean up the glass.

"Just go," Carrie ordered. "Please, just go. You've done enough damage."

This time, the walk down the driveway seemed to take an eternity as Alice's mind whirred with questions about George Byrd and his very strange, very disorganized files.

# Chapter Thirty-eight

"Where'd you go?" Violet asked when Alice walked into the house and checked on their puzzle progress. Parts of the palm trees, the beach shack, and the sand were beginning to take shape. "Nice surfboards."

"You're killing us with suspense, Gran," Taylor said. "Tell us everything."

"I'll catch you up," Alice promised. "But first, I need a moment with Ruby."

"All right. But let me know if you find any other pieces for the flower-power VW bus." Ruby rose from the table and followed Alice out to the back deck, where Alice was scooting into a chaise to prop her foot up.

"Come, sit. We need to talk. It's about George, honey. As I'm digging into his past transactions, I'm finding some details that paint George in a negative light. I'm beginning to question his integrity."

"Worse than infidelity?"

Alice shrugged. "Different. Carrie Preston just told me George ruined her family. I'm sorry, I don't have details on how or why. I mean, we know George was instrumental in the arrest of Tony Preston. But as I dig deeper, I want you to be aware that whatever comes to light about George might be hard for you to hear."

Ruby leaned back into the chaise beside Alice and stared straight ahead. "You know, from the day I met George, I thought he was too good to be true. Lots of laughs. Lots of fun. No sense of pathos or intellectual pain. After a lifetime with Darnell—who you and I know had the corner on existential crises—George's low-key attitude was refreshing. Easy." She shook her head. "Too easy, I guess. There's always a catch, isn't there?"

"I'm sorry, honey."

"It's disappointing. But you and I know the truth needs to come out. The illusion needs to fade, even if we find out George wasn't the man I thought him to be."

Alice nodded. For a moment they let the sad possibilities sink in as they took in the blue skies overhead and the cottony clouds lingering over the peak of Mount Hood. It didn't take long for the looming questions about George to nag at Alice. Why had he collected those news articles? What had he done to the Preston family to make Carrie revile him?

Alice swung her legs around and sat up.

"You're itching to get back on the prowl, aren't you?" Ruby asked.

Alice smiled. "You know me so well."

Ruby waved her off. "Get at it, girlfriend."

After Alice recounted her visit to Carrie Preston, the ladies seemed intrigued but confused. Alice admitted that she was still struggling to make sense of George's notes.

"What, exactly, did Carrie say George had done to ruin her family?" asked Violet.

"She didn't get that specific," Alice said. "The whole topic upset her. As did my question about this Harlan Powell, who apparently was Tony's friend. Look, right now I have more questions than answers. That's why I want to get back to George's list and see if I can extract information from other people named there."

"I'll help you, honey," Ruby said, sitting on a bar stool at the island, where Alice had left the papers.

"Let me take another look at this list," Alice said. "Maybe another name rings a bell."

"These papers are so disorganized," Ruby said. "Look at this—a menu for Gold House of Asian Fusion, stuck in with other important papers." Ruby fanned herself with the menu, and then paused to take a second look. "Actually, I've eaten there before. You know that restaurant in the shopping center down by the river? The one with the hardware store."

Alice nodded, going over the names. "Amichi. Haynes. Jin. Montell . . ."

Ruby was stuck on the menu. "They have great fish tacos and dumplings. And I've always liked eating there, because the restaurant was started by a woman who emigrated from Korea decades ago. What was her name? Oh, here's her story." She unfolded the menu. "Ara Jin. Says here she opened this restaurant to feed her family the food she'd loved as a child."

Alice put down a news clipping to look over at the menu. "Did you say Jin?" she asked. "Let me see that." She noticed that "Jin" was scrawled on top of the menu.

"Wait a minute. J. Jin is one of the names on the list."

"Not Ara Jin?" Ruby asked.

"No." Alice looked back at the article. In the top right corner, someone had written: "Jack Jin" along with a phone number. "Does this phone number match the restaurant?"

Ruby compared the two. "It does."

"So we're looking for a Jack Jin. Maybe he's married to this woman Ara."

"Maybe," Ruby said. "Should we call the restaurant and chat them up?"

"I think we can kill two birds with one stone." Alice went online to check out Gold House, which was open Sundays, no reservations.

"Ladies, put on your Sunday best," Alice announced. "We're going out to dinner."

# Chapter Thirty-nine

"Thank you so much," Alice said as a young woman, probably still a teenager, poured hot tea for everyone at their table.

"It's lovely having a warm cup of tea as soon as you sit down," Violet said.

"And the real flowers on the table are a nice touch." Ruby reached forward to delicately touch the tiny yellow rose in the bud vase at the center of the table.

"Just saying, you guys need to step out more," Taylor said, holding up a menu to cover her face.

Alice let Taylor's comment slide. Personally, she was pleased to be with such an appreciative bunch. With wooden tables, red upholstered chairs, and gold scrolled trim around the ceiling and windows, Gold House was a fairly basic restaurant with some charming touches.

"I hope they still have the soup dumplings," Ruby said, looking over the menu. "They are to die for."

"Good evening, ladies." A twentyish man dressed in a black T-shirt and pants stopped at their table. He had dark hair, a broad face, and a smile that tipped the needle to handsome. "Can I get anyone a drink?"

As they went around the table, ordering wine, Alice noticed Violet filling with excitement. "I'd like a glass of white wine, young man, and I hope you'll excuse the question if I'm wrong, but I do believe you were in my class at one time."

He blinked, lowering his notepad. "Ms. Pepper?" Now his smile positively beamed joy. "I thought you looked familiar. I'm Jack. Jack Jin."

*Copacetic,* Alice thought, sipping her tea.

"How have you been?" he asked. "I heard you left teaching, and I couldn't believe it. You were so good."

"I'm a vice principal now. Instead of corralling one class, I'm looking after every student in my school."

"I believe that. You were one of my favorite teachers. Really. You protected the nerds, and you made everything interesting."

"You're so sweet." Violet clasped her hands to her heart in a gesture of gratitude.

"Seriously. You're one of the reasons I'm going to med school. We were the only fourth-grade class that got to do science."

"And now you're going to med school?" Alice said. "Impressive." She was pleased to have a trusted connection with Jack Jin through Violet.

"That's wonderful, Jack," Violet said. "Good for you. Now, for the most important question, do you still have soup dumplings?"

"For you, of course!"

Everyone chuckled, and then Jack took their order, making a recommendation here and there.

"I'd better get your order in," he said. "But just so you know, I can give you a ten percent friends and family discount on your tab."

"You're the best," Violet said as he headed off to the kitchen.

When he was out of sight, Ruby shook Alice's arm. "He's it! He's the one!"

Taylor frowned. "Isn't he a little young for you, Ruby?"

"Not that. He's one of the people on George's list!" Ruby hissed, trying to keep her voice down.

"I'm well aware," Alice said, looking toward the kitchen. How could she get a quiet moment to speak with the young man in private?

"That's concerning." Violet placed her tea back on the table. "I can't imagine Jack Jin being involved in any criminal activity."

"Well, if you don't mind"—Alice arose, setting her napkin on the table—"I'm going to chat him up a bit."

Alice intercepted Jack at the beverage station and made a special request. "I'm wondering if I might get a brief tour of the kitchen. As a cook and former restaurant owner, I'm always interested in different foods and how they're prepared."

"Then you'll want to meet my grandmother." He pushed open the kitchen door and held it for her. "Come on back."

The kitchen was stainless steel tables and counters, woks and steamers and fry baskets. Jack introduced his grandmother, Ara Jin, who was forming dumplings by hand.

"Such a beautiful process to watch," Alice said.

"I learned from my grandmother." Ara rolled her eyes. "But who knew I would be making dumplings for the next thirty years?"

They talked about their special kale dumplings, as well

as other fusion items on the menu like spicy cauliflower tempura and barbecued chicken burritos.

As Jack brought her to the back of the kitchen, Alice came clean. "I confess, I was hoping to ask you a few questions that might be disturbing."

"Me?" He shook his head. "What do you mean?"

"I'm wondering what you can tell me about a former friend of mine, George Byrd."

"The guy who was just killed?" When she nodded, he squinted at her. "You a cop?"

"I'm not. I'm asking for a friend. That sounds ridiculous, doesn't it? But Violet Pepper is my sister, and I'm hoping you can help me out here. I'm trying to get information on George's business dealings before he was killed."

He shook his head. "I don't think you wanna know, Alice. George Byrd was bad news."

"How so?"

"He tried to get money from me. Blackmail. He acted like I'd get arrested for something I didn't do if I didn't pay up."

"He tried to blackmail you," Alice said. "What was the crime?"

"A homicide. This guy in the neighborhood got shot and killed in his apartment. And I had been on the scene that night. A food delivery, before he was killed. But the cops knew that. They saw the leftover food and our menus there, called here, and I told them about the delivery. The murder, it sounded awful. But honestly, I barely recall talking to the Henderson guy, and the police think the murder happened after an argument about selling drugs."

"I remember reading about the case." In truth, Alice had skimmed a news story in George's papers about a man gunned down in his own apartment.

"Anyway, I talked to the police the night of the homicide, and they believed my story. No issue. And then, two weeks later, George Byrd turned up here at the restaurant. He talked to my grandmother first, really upset her. He kept name dropping about that firm, EYE-dentify, how they'd found my DNA, and I could be in big trouble. He wanted money to keep quiet about the fact that my DNA was found at the murder scene."

"That's horrible," Alice said. "It's blackmail."

"Tell me about it," Jack said. "I smelled bullshit right away. I told George I was going to talk to the cops, straighten things out. And just like that, Mr. Byrd started backpedaling. Said he'd made a mistake. That I was all clear."

"You scared him off," Alice said.

"Seems that way."

"Did you tell the police?"

"Nah. Looking back, I wish I had. But then he dried up fast, and I never heard from him again. I wondered if it was just a mistake."

"Good for you for standing up to him," Alice said.

"I didn't feel like I had a choice. I'd worked hard all my life, and I wasn't about to let Byrd ruin things. You know, he really backed off when he found out I was premed at Green State. I think he assumed I was some lame kid who could be intimidated." Jack shook his head. "I wasn't. But he really scared my grandmother. That still makes me angry."

"It's unconscionable," Alice said.

Blackmail.

Alice tried to absorb the revelation.

George had tried to blackmail Jack Jin. Had that been his intention with the other people on the list? Use DNA from crime scenes, some of them very old crime scenes, to extort money from people who were involved? Even if those people, like Jack, were not guilty in any way?

She thought of Tony Preston, who'd been friends with Harlan, the young man who'd overdosed. What was the timing of that? She had to check, but she suspected that it had happened while Tony was out on bail. Even if Tony was innocent, the hint of impropriety, the suggestion that he had been there, maybe doing drugs with his friend, would have come out at trial. It would have increased Tony's sentence, for sure.

Had George extorted money from Carrie and JB Preston to keep Tony from being connected to his friend's death?

Blackmail. And Alice was in possession of George's list, seven people he'd targeted and tapped for money. Seven victims of George Byrd. Seven people with a reason to kill him and end the cash drain.

When Alice returned to the table, three of the appetizers had been served, and Taylor, Ruby, and Violet were in heaven.

"So delicious." Violet patted her mouth with the napkin. "So did you learn anything new from Jack and his grandma in the kitchen?"

"It was extremely informative." Alice picked up a soup dumpling and slurped it off the big porcelain spoon.

# Chapter Forty

"I feel like I'm onto something," Alice said, flipping through papers on the kitchen island. "I have a strong feeling that George was trying to extract money from everyone on that list."

"Are you going to call Madison and share your instinct with the police?" Ruby asked, sidling onto the stool beside her.

"Eventually. First, I need to make sure I'm on the right track." She flipped to the beginning of the stack and found the list. "Okay, the first name on the list, J. Amichi. I'm thinking he's the one mentioned in this article. Jeff Amichi, who may have been connected by DNA to the murder outside the bar."

"Is there any contact information?" Ruby asked.

Alice looked for a phone number, but found nothing.

Ruby turned the laptop toward Alice. "I got a Portland area Jeff Amichi on Facebook, but he hasn't been active for the last year." On the screen was a photo of a bearded young man, with bubbles of sympathy messages beneath it.

"This Jeff Amichi is dead," Alice said. "Killed in a motorcycle accident." An avid biker, and, from his friends' messages, a big partier.

"A bit of a dead end for this line of investigation," Ruby said, "so to speak."

"So to speak," Alice agreed. "Next on the list is L. Haynes."

Haynes seemed to be connected to the case of Alexa Patel, a teenage girl who was found dead on the riverbank some twenty years ago. At the time, authorities thought the girl drowned while swimming at night, but no one came forward with information. DNA, specifically skin cells, were removed from under her fingernails, but with no suspects, the investigation went cold. But George had connected Lana Haynes of Boulder, Colorado, to the case. "At least I'm assuming that Haynes is connected to the drowned girl, since Haynes's name, location, and phone number are jotted down on the Alexa Patel article."

Ruby squinted at the photocopy. "This does seem to be George's bookkeeping style. Scribble someone's name and number on something they're connected to."

"Should I cold-call this woman?" Alice asked Ruby. It was a Sunday night, but not quite eight p.m.

"Might as well give it a shot."

Alice placed the call. "It might not even be a current number," she told Ruby, but a woman picked up on the third ring.

"This is Lana Haynes."

It was a delicate dance, but Alice winced and spun out a greeting, trying to win the woman's trust by playing the hometown card. "We probably met years ago when you were a student and I ran library programs at the high school."

"That's doubtful." Lana was blunt. "I wasn't a great student. All I wanted in high school was to graduate and get the hell out of there."

"Everyone has their own unique path," said Alice. "What are you up to these days?" As if they were old friends.

"I'm a realtor now. Three kids. And I love Boulder."

"I'm wondering if you remember being friends with a young woman named Alexa Patel when you were in high school."

Silence.

Then, "Are you a cop?"

"No, I'm not. I'm still a librarian. But I'm investigating the handling of Alexa's death." Alice struggled to maintain the truth. "Did a man named George Byrd contact you about—"

"Yeah, that guy called me. Byrd, like a dodo bird. He said he worked for some DNA testing place. EYE in the sky, or something like that. What an ass."

RIP, George. "George Byrd said he was with EYE-dentify?"

"If you're looking for a rating for him, I give him zero stars. I thought he was hitting on me, but instead, he wanted money. Bribe money. He wanted me to pay him so that he would shitcan the evidence that I was with Alexa the night she died. Can you imagine? He thought I was going to care enough to shell out big money. First of all, I don't have that kind of money. And second of all, I'm thirty-seven and this happened when I was seventeen. Like, twenty years ago."

"That was a long time ago," Alice said, though she knew there was no statute of limitations on homicide.

"Yeah, I knew Alexa," Lana went on. "She was my friend. A lot of people knew what happened that night, but we kept it quiet. No one went to the police. Solidarity, baby. But basically, a bunch of us had been drinking and we went swimming in the river. Stupid, I know. But we all knew how to swim. Only the river was cold, and it was kind of shocking for all of us. Alexa struggled. She never said anything, but someone pointed her out. I went over and tried to help her, but she was all panicky. She was flailing, scratching me, pulling me down. Trying to climb on top of me. One of the guys also tried to help, but Alexa almost dragged him under, too. In the end, we couldn't save her."

"I'm so sorry, Lana."

"It was the worse night of my life. I'll never forget her. But my friends and I made a pact not to tell the police. Nobody needed that trouble. And we got by okay until I took one of those spit tests on Heredity Plus. My bad. But I wanted to see if I really was half Swedish, like my mom says. That's how Eye in the Sky got a match to my DNA. That George guy said my DNA was found under her fingernails. Well, duh, yeah. She scratched the hell out of me when I tried to help her. Anyway, my lawyer friend says nothing will come of the investigation."

"Your lawyer friend is probably right," Alice said. "As far as I know, the West Hazel Police are not actively investigating this."

"Well, good. And if you say anything about what I just said, I'll deny it. 'Cause no one did anything wrong that night. It was just an awful accident."

"I'm sorry that happened to you," Alice said. "And I'm glad you've been able to move on."

There was no justice to be served in the death of Alexa Patel. The police had ruled it an accidental drowning, and they'd been right.

"I appreciate you talking with me," Alice said. "I wish you well, Lana, and I'll be sure to pass on your zero-star rating."

# Chapter Forty-one

"Gran, I wish you hadn't played detective." The ceiling light in Alice's kitchen made Madison's gold badge twinkle as she leaned back in the stool at the island. "You called some woman in Colorado? Really? You might have compromised our investigation."

"On the contrary, I oiled the gears with Lana Haynes. If you get her to warm up to you, I'm sure you'll get her to tell you the same. But there's nothing to be gained in that tangent of the story. She told a clear story of George trying to blackmail her based on DNA evidence found at a crime scene. Jack Jin had a similar account."

"And you ladies pieced this all together?" Madison seemed gobsmacked as she looked at Alice and the others, now in their pajamas. Taylor had flopped on the couch next to Ruby, who was nursing a bourbon. Alice had poured a tiny shot glass of water to take with her statin drug and beta-blocker. The days of a nighttime coffee or even herbal tea were over for her; too much caffeine and too many trips to the "Ladies."

"We've been discussing everything," Violet said, cupping her mug of chamomile tea. "All of us agree that George was using that DNA investigator, EYE-dentify, to feed him information on folks who were within the periphery of deadly crimes."

"Even innocent people, like Jack Jin," Taylor said. "The poor guy happened to make a food delivery just before something bad went down. And the police understood that. But George threatened to stir up suspicion with the DNA evidence if Jack didn't pay. It makes me so mad." She turned to Ruby. "I'm sorry you were married to him, but George is turning out to be a real jerk."

"It's sweet of you to be concerned," Ruby said. "But I'm a big girl. He's gone, and I can't abide him taking advantage of folks. The truth has to come out."

Madison was flipping through George's papers on the island. "Where did you get this stuff?"

"George's home office," Ruby said. "The cops left it behind."

"I know it looks like a jumble of nothing—handwritten notes, news articles, and take-out menus—but there's information there," Alice said. "George seemed to record connections in his own sloppy code."

"Sloppy being the operative word," Madison said.

"But this is not just about George's blackmailing scheme." Alice stepped up to the island, positioning herself across from Madison. She really wanted to drive this point home. "We've been talking, and we're wondering if one of his blackmail victims was driven to kill him, to make him stop extorting money."

"As in, motive for murder?" Madison stopped flipping through the papers and picked up the list. "You think someone on this page killed George to stop the blackmail?"

"Exactly!" Taylor thrust an arm into the air from her reclining position.

"That's what we're thinking." Alice noticed the other women watching Madison, their eyes bright. It was the group effort that had brought them to this point. How fortunate to have smart, good women in her life.

"I like your theory," Madison said. "So let's go over this one more time. Amichi appears to be dead. I'll confirm that. Haynes is the Colorado realtor whose friend drowned. Jin is the manager of Gold House who made a delivery to the man who was later shot in his apartment. Preston is Anthony Preston, whom we know about from his burglary record. I don't see how he fits in here in the blackmail case."

"I believe A. Preston is Tony, but I think it involves another case," Alice said. She didn't want to get into the details about Tony's involvement in the Powell death until she learned more. "I've talked with his mother, but Carrie was too upset to discuss it. I'll get back to you on that one."

"And these other people on the list." Madison looked down at the paper. "So far you haven't discovered anything on Montell, Russell, or Washington? Correct?"

"That's right," Alice said. "And we think we know where the blackmail money went."

"George has a hefty bank account containing more than a hundred thousand dollars," Ruby said. "It's money he kept secret from me. If the bank would let me get access, I'd be able to see if deposits, possible blackmail payments, came from anyone on the list."

Madison nodded. "I think a judge might sign off on a warrant for detectives to examine George's account."

"Follow the money, baby," said Taylor.

"You guys have done amazing work," Madison said as she bundled up all the papers from George's home office and slid them into a paper shopping bag from Alice's pantry. "I'm taking these to the precinct for further inspection."

Alice stood up. "You what?"

"I need to sift through this carefully," Madison said. "Part of me is surprised that Officer Lang didn't confiscate these documents in his initial search, but honestly, this EYE-dentify file is a hot mess. I understand him assuming that it's not business related. But you figured it out, Gran. You guys did a great job. Kudos."

While Alice appreciated the praise, she didn't want the police to intrude. "Madison, honey, why don't you leave the papers here for now?" Alice couldn't bear to let this chaotic mess of a file go. There were still other names on the list, many avenues to explore. "I'm sure I can make some other connections."

Madison shook her head. "You've done a great job, Gran. Leave the rest to us." She paused at the door and nodded to the group. "Thanks for your help, guys."

"She's adorable and smart and totally ticking me off," Alice said after Madison left with the papers. "I shouldn't be surprised, but I thought we'd have more time with George's notes, more time to explore other connections." Now it felt like someone had just robbed her of a favorite hobby. When she'd discovered key points in George's papers, it had felt good to get the circuits connecting, the old wheels spinning.

She wanted more.

"I want those messy papers back," Alice said.

"Well, then, this is your lucky day." Ruby tapped the surface of her phone a few times, and Alice's phone buzzed with a message. "I just sent you a copy of the EYE-dentify file. I took snaps with my documents app before Madison got here."

Alice was astounded as she tapped her own cell phone and opened the attachment. "Ruby . . . how did you know to do this?"

"Honey, I watched you obsess over those papers all day. Yeah, they're a mess, but they're a juicy mess. And having run a successful business for two decades, I know that records are important. Always have a backup."

# Chapter Forty-two

*Monday*

The pallor of George Byrd's death seemed to have lifted from city hall over the past week. Alice noticed bright eyes and smiling faces as she wheeled a cart of boxes into the mayor's office on Monday morning.

"You brought back George's files." Tansley clapped her hands together. "Alice, you're a lifesaver."

"I'll take those," Cassidy said, as the mayor waved Alice into her office for a chat.

"I'm glad we got to see you and Ruby at the memorial Saturday," Tansley said. "Ruby seems to be handling things well, and the appetizers were terrific. Your doing?"

"My recipes, with help from my friends."

"It was a fitting affair." She looked over her shoulder. "Though I suppose I shouldn't say that word around here, after what we've learned about George."

"He was a man of secrets," Alice said. "And dreadful fiscal plans. Have you had a chance to talk with the city council about budget adjustments?"

"Yes! We're meeting next week, and it looks like we're

going to adopt a new budget. Everyone is in agreement that George's fiscal plan was too . . . austere. I think most of your library's budget will be restored. I can't make specific promises until the council meets, but for now you don't need to plan budget cuts. We're going to make amends for George's mistakes."

*Mistakes?* Did the mayor know about the blackmail? No, she couldn't. She must be talking about the budget, which was mistake enough.

"It's been a scramble, trying to piece a new budget together," Tansley lamented. "The online records are sparse. Apparently George's assistant, Nicole Bender, was responsible for most of his budget proposals, statements, and reports. She was a hard worker, all right. But now that Nicole is facing charges, we could hardly rely on her to step in. We've brought in an outside accountant, who's eager to see George's files."

*Good luck with that,* Alice thought. George had been more of a doodler than a record-keeper. "I hope the accountant can make some headway. I have to admit, I've gone over the city budget a few times this past week, trying to find things to cut. My eyes bulged when I saw the exorbitant consulting fee for EYE-dentify. How did that happen?"

"It was approved during our little Cola Bandits crime wave. George and the police chief rode the wave of fear that rattled the community during the rash of home burglaries. You remember how freaked out people were during that time."

"Only vaguely," Alice said. The case hadn't captured Alice's attention until the police released the names of the suspected bandits, and Alice saw that her friend's son Tony had been indicted. Immediately the community had begun pointing fingers at the "depraved" young men and their families. Cue the torches and pitchforks.

"Well, the Cola Bandits emergency prompted the council to approve funding to bring EYE-dentify in as a consultant. After the chain of burglaries was solved, no one had the nerve to cut crime-fighting measures, even extremely expensive ones. But we're planning to cut back now. In fact, I have a meeting with Jared Chase in a few minutes, so if you don't mind, I need to return a few calls."

"Of course." As Alice rose to go, she smiled. "I'm glad to see you looking healthier and happier since last week when we all got the bad news about George."

"It was a rough week, all right, but I do believe the worst is over." Tansley walked Alice to the door. "Thanks again for returning the files. I promise to keep you posted on budget adjustments."

Alice thanked her, headed out, and exited city hall into a sunny, blue-sky day.

A glorious day. A day that deserved attention for a few minutes while she cleared her head.

Moving past the bursts of fragrant color outside the flower shop, she strolled to the town square and found a bench across from the large statue of children flying around a globe. The sculptor seemed to be making a statement about the global community of the future, but it always made Alice think of Peter Pan and men who resist growing up. Men like George.

For once, Alice wished she had more of a math brain. She might have been able to employ forensic accounting and detect irregularities in George's official files. She wondered how vendors like EYE-dentify usually billed agencies.

Curious, she took out her phone and searched for the company's Web site. She landed on a home page that was sleek and hinting of justice, with an American flag on one side and a deep blue background punctuated by gold police shields. "Crime-Solving Is a Click Away" proclaimed a banner. Alice saw that the EYE-dentify offices were in San Diego, California, though the company was incorporated in Delaware, which, she had read, was a way to dodge taxes for many companies.

Another page of the site revealed a stunning photo of Jared Chase, his hair sparkling gold in the lighting. Under crime-solving services, the site listed Genetic Genealogy, Ancestry and Kinship Analysis, and Phenotyping.

Alice knew the firm had used genetic genealogy to identify Preston and Moynihan from the saliva samples they'd left on cola cans at many of their crime scenes.

Under other services, the site explained that DNA samples could be used to determine kinship out to six degrees of relatedness. And the DNA phenotyping service used DNA to predict the physical appearance and ancestry of an unknown person.

Quite a range of services. Alice wondered what the firm charged for these other services. And who were their other clients? Unfortunately, she could only get that information by calling or filling out a form, and she didn't want to share personal information with them. Alice was still exploring the Web site when someone invaded her personal space.

"Look at you, glued to your cell like a Gen Z-er," he said.

Jared Chase was smiling over her. Speaking of men who resisted growing up. He was probably pushing fifty, but his hair was still a golden honey blond. His stylist probably charged a fortune. But then, with his exorbitant fees, he could afford it.

She lowered her phone abruptly, not wanting him to see

his corporate logo on the screen. "You caught me. I find it hard to move on with my day until I crack the daily Wordle."

He laughed as if he enjoyed the joke, then grew serious. "Actually, I'm glad I ran into you. I heard you've been asking some questions about George Byrd, and it brought out some suspicions I've had for a long time."

She wondered how much he knew. "Suspicions about George?"

"Don't get me wrong, I liked George. The man could be a hoot to hang with, but I also had my concerns about the guy. I'm not sure his personal goals were consistent with the goals of law enforcement in this community. You don't want to dig too much into George."

"What do you mean, exactly?"

"I'm afraid George might have been on the take," Jared said, his blue eyes icy cold in the sunshine. "Extorting money from some of our good citizens." He nodded sadly. "Blackmail."

# Chapter Forty-three

"Really?" Alice feigned shock. "And what did you do about George? Did you try to stop him?"

"Any interference on my part would have been way out of line," Jared insisted. "You see, I provide a limited service. Genealogical techniques have proven to be a valuable tool in identifying criminals who have otherwise evaded law enforcement experts."

Alice felt her eyes glazing over, but she let him go on. "Take the case of Joseph James DeAngelo. You probably know him as the Golden State Killer. He terrorized victims in California in the 1970s and '80s. His capture, through DNA evidence, was an achievement in technology."

"We agree on that much," Alice said.

"So you see how important it is to identify a culprit. Narrow down the bad guy," Jared said. "That's my job. And once I hand over my data, I have to trust that law enforcement agencies do their part and use the information to find criminals."

"Actually, you don't always identify the culprit," Alice pointed out, thinking of Jack Jin, who'd delivered food to an apartment minutes before the crime had happened.

"Sometimes you're just supplying evidence that someone—maybe an innocent person—was on the scene."

"Well, sure, that's true, but it's a fine difference. My point is, I don't have detailed proof of corruption or anything on George Byrd. I'm just not sure whether George actually shared genetic evidence we provided with the police department."

"And you didn't copy the police chief on your reports?" Alice asked. "You thought it was adequate to deliver only to the city comptroller, the person who pays the bills?"

"We did what our contract required." That damned contract. Alice could see that George had bamboozled the mayor and the city council into a contract that compromised West Hazel.

"I've always been a careful, cautious guy," Jared said. "By the book. But George, he liked to play the rogue, bend the rules a bit."

Alice studied him, wondering if he was really so careful. Yes, he did seem calculating. Was he floating this information now to actually expose his "old friend" George? But what would Jared get out of that? She didn't understand this man, but she was willing to play along.

"So tell me, if you don't mind," Alice said, "what makes you think George was blackmailing citizens?"

"Let's just say that the Cola Bandits were the last criminals arrested based on DNA evidence. Since then, we've given George plenty of leads, but nothing's come of it. I think he must have been extorting money to keep quiet about evidence."

"Wait, you have solid leads?" Alice asked, looking over her shoulder. "There are criminals among us?"

"I'm not at liberty to give specifics, but yes."

"Seriously? Any homicide cases? Any I might have heard

of?" Alice took a breath, then threw a bit of flattery his way. "Everyone was amazed when you provided the key evidence in finding those Cola Bandits."

He beamed. "It felt great to crack that case."

"Can you give me a hint about any of the others?"

Jared rubbed his chin. "There's one case you might know. A sad one. Did you live here when that baby was abandoned by the water tower?"

The water tower baby. That case was such a heartbreaker. "I was here," she said, not wanting to fake enthusiasm anymore. "My daughter was a kid back then, but I remember. Do you have solid evidence on that case?"

He nodded. "And from what I've observed, George didn't pass it on to the authorities."

"Why do you think that?"

"Because the person who committed the crime is still walking free," he said, with half a shrug. As if they were discussing the weather or a baseball team.

"Have you considered going to the police now?" Alice asked. "With George gone, it's not as if you'd be overstepping professional boundaries."

"I just hate to cast aspersions on the reputation of a dead man. Besides, George was a friend. You get that, right? Being friends with his wife?"

"We are friends, yes."

"If you care about Ruby, you'll stop digging. George's loved ones wouldn't want to expose what's buried under the surface."

On that matter, he was wrong. Ruby was trying to prepare for a bitter truth, but Jared Chase didn't deserve to know that. Alice didn't trust him with personal information.

"You know, you're absolutely right," she agreed. "My

good friend is in mourning, and I don't want to make her pain any worse. Maybe it's best to let secrets remain buried."

"Exactly," he said, checking his watch. "Look at that! Time for my meeting with the mayor. You take care, now."

"Have a good meeting," she said as he walked off. Watching him go, Alice felt bolstered by his warning to keep mum.

Yup. She was definitely on the right track.

# Chapter Forty-four

That morning, by some fluke of luck, the library seemed to run as smoothly as a well-oiled machine. Alice was grateful, as it gave her time to review her encounter with Jared Chase, a meeting that had spooked her a little, as his advice to lay low had bordered on a threat. Or had it? The man was so phony, she had trouble picking out the grains of truth in their conversation.

For a glimmer of a moment, she wondered if Jared had been dropping off the puzzles at her house. The messages that George might have deserved to die and that the gals should let the investigation go seemed to match his views. But what about the avengers?

Alice didn't know if Jared had given them the puzzles. But if he had, she certainly did not trust his advice.

Around eleven Alice was at her desk, going over some of the cart orders for acquisitions when one of the children's librarians, Nancy Savino, came to her door. "Can we talk?" Nancy asked.

"Or course, Nancy. Come in."

Nancy had come to request a six-month sabbatical to care for her ailing mother. "You know I love this job,"

Nancy said, "but I just can't leave Gladys home alone any-more, and she wants to stay in her home of fifty years. She's eighty-two and her heart's giving out on her. Giving her a few months of my time . . . it seems like the least I can do."

"I understand." Alice thought of her last days with her father, the way stories had tumbled out from his failing body. Funny anecdotes. Sad memories from times of war. Beautiful moments of love. "I'll always cherish the days I spent with my father at the end of his life."

"Thank you for understanding." Tears glistened in Nancy's dark eyes. "I'll contact HR at city hall to work out the details."

"Let me know if you need me to run interference," Alice said. "You'll be missed. No one can strum the uke quite the way you do."

Nancy smiled. "Yeah, if the library science thing didn't work out, I could have been a rock star."

They chuckled together and the air seemed a bit lighter as Nancy left the office with Alice following behind her.

While making her rounds, Alice intercepted a group of rambunctious boys and sent them out to the library lawn for their game of tag. She moved stealthily past a snoring man in the quiet section. Then, seeing the line at the re-search desk, she helped out their specialist Charles and worked with a few high school students who needed help finding research materials. Alice had a fondness for these kids, who'd given up the beach and camp and vacations to take classes at Portland Community College. Hard work-ers, attending summer session.

During her lunch break, she sat down at a computer with her yogurt and Googled her way to the county crimi-nal investigation Web site. She'd visited the site before, but today there was a specific case she wanted more information on.

The water tower baby.

The county Web site gave her the date and stats on the case.

With that information, she did a second search and came up with several news reports for the case.

On a winter morning in 1988, a newborn infant had been found dead and abandoned on the gravel road beside West Hazel's water tower. The secluded, unpaved driveway was near the high school. Teens traditionally drove there to be alone. It had been a cold, wintry day when the infant was found on the gravel with a scarf tied around his neck. Despite a search, the police were not able to locate the mother who left the baby there to die. Such a tragedy.

Of course, the media at that time had exploited one of the big unknowns of the case: How had the newborn died? Had the infant died of natural causes before its body was abandoned? Or had the mother left the baby to die in the cold? Some reporters had even speculated that the child's mother had used the scarf around its neck to asphyxiate the baby. Thus a tragic death had been inflated and twisted, amplifying the tragedy.

Alice remembered hearing about the case on the TV news at the time. She'd been in her midthirties, a busy mom, trying to juggle her career as a librarian, her daughter, her husband, and squeeze in a few moments walking or doing yoga with the girls to maintain her sanity. It had always bothered her that the police were searching out the mother as the suspect, as Alice believed the woman must have been delirious to have abandoned her child that way. *Blame the mother*, she thought, flashing to her own daughter's questionable choices. Mothers carried so much blame and guilt as it was; they didn't need laws that drove the nail deeper.

Her research was interrupted by a call from Madison.

"This is a welcome distraction," Alice said, closing the windows on the computer. "What's up?"

"I just got a call from Dr. Jane, and I'm looking at her updated autopsy. She noted that George's lips were blue at the crime scene, and so she tested for fentanyl. Early tox screen results were positive. He was injected with a fatal dose."

"Fentanyl? There's nothing good about that."

"Jane found an injection site on the neck. It's not final yet, but she believes it was the drug injection that stopped his heart and killed him. The blows to the head didn't cause a fatal amount of brain swelling and blood loss. The right-handed blows were probably an afterthought."

"So the killer came prepared with the toxic injection, and then hit him in the head to distract from the real means of killing," Alice said.

"Seems that way. Jane said the levels of drugs in his body make it clear that someone wanted to be sure George was dead. It's ironic, but the media has labeled this murderer the 'candlestick killer.' But they're probably wrong."

"A much catchier moniker than the 'syringe psycho' or 'death by OD,' " Alice said.

"Gran, those sound like book titles," Madison said. "Really bad books."

"Don't get me started on book reviews. I wonder who could have come prepared to murder someone with a syringe. I wouldn't know how to do it. Where do you get the syringe, or the lethal dose of medication?"

"With the Internet and street drugs, I don't think it would be too hard for a devious person to get the tools,"

Madison said. "But of course, it would be easier for a doctor or nurse."

"Who do we know in the medical field that had a vendetta against George?"

"Gran, you're racing ahead," Madison said. "And you're not a detective."

"Killjoy," Alice said. "Admit it, you called me with this info because you want my input on this case."

"I—I thought Ruby should know about the overdose."

"But you called me, not Ruby." Alice got up from her desk and tossed the empty yogurt container into a trash can. "I'm thrilled. And I'll help in any way I can."

"Gran, you're not supposed to–"

"I love you, too, but I've got to get back to work." Alice ended the call and headed out to the reading room with a smile on her face.

She was in.

# Chapter Forty-five

Alice leaned into the pharmacy counter and gave a little wave toward Craig Grand, who stood behind a distant counter dispensing pills. He gave a nod, then looked down to finish what he was doing as Alice waited to pick his brain.

An Internet search of fentanyl had lacked information to explain the logistics of preparing a syringe and stabbing a man in the throat with it. Alice had decided to stop at the store after work and consult with an expert.

"What can I do for you, Alice?" Craig asked, looking at her over the short reading glasses that sat low on his nose.

"I'm wondering if you stock fentanyl here in the pharmacy."

His frown was full of concern. "I have dispensed fentanyl patches in the past. Had to special order them, though they've only been used for palliative care." He removed his glasses and studied her, assessing. "Is this for you, or Gildy?"

"Neither, thank goodness. It's research. I'm wondering how someone would go about getting a syringe of fentanyl to kill someone."

"As in a mystery novel?"

"Something like that."

"Well, liquid fentanyl is not something we stock. It's a hundred times stronger than morphine, and if someone requires that level of pain relief, they're generally hospitalized or in hospice care. Doctors I know don't want to go anywhere near it."

Alice nodded. "So aside from buying on the streets, the bad guy would need to purchase the drug online."

"Illegally." He nodded. "Opioids are readily available through the Internet, the dark web, they call it. They say you can order anything, pay with cryptocurrency, and have it shipped from China. In the past few years, there've been crackdowns, but they change the formula and start selling a new variation." He shrugged. "I don't need to tell you that it's a huge problem. You and I both know how opioids can ruin lives. And with these mail order products, the varied quality makes it easy to overdose."

"Well, in this case, overdose was the objective."

Craig squinted at her. "We're not talking about a mystery novel here. Is this about George?"

She nodded. "The coroner just got results. It seems that an injection of fentanyl killed him."

He whistled through his teeth. "And you're trying to figure out who might have had access to a syringe of fentanyl?"

"Exactly. I was thinking it would be someone with medical training."

He nodded. "Could be a medical assistant, a former army medic. A diabetic."

"A pharmacist?" Alice added.

He shrugged. "Well, sure. We administer vaccines, but I'm still in a bit of shock. A fentanyl injection? That would indicate that the murder wasn't spur of the moment."

"It was premeditated," she said. "Pretty scary."

"Quite frightening. You want to stay out of it and let the police figure it out. Keep safe, with your good friends and jigsaw puzzles. How goes the puzzle club?"

"All good, but you know the puzzles are a hobby. I'm still in the library business. Maybe not for long if the city council keeps cutting our budget. And you can tell Tansley I said that."

"Don't get me started on city politics," he said. "I know it can be tough working under any administration. Are you feeling burned out? There's always retirement. I think about it at least once a week."

"Sounds tempting." The truth was, she couldn't afford to do that. Not after her ex, Jeff, cashed in most of her 401K in an attempt to save Alice's Restaurant. So much for leaving the business finances in the hands of her husband the CPA. But she wasn't here to discuss her failures in life.

"Thanks for your time, Craig." Alice was about to turn away, but paused. "I meant to ask you about syringes. Can those be ordered online?"

"You can buy them at most pharmacies. I usually talk with customers about how they will be used, mostly so we can be sure they're purchasing the right type of syringe. Most of my customers use them to treat diabetes. But really, anyone could buy a syringe."

"Well, then, you're well-versed in this modus operandi," she teased.

And though they both chuckled, she was only half kidding.

# Chapter Forty-six

"Help!" Ruby called from the front door, where she was pushing one box in with her foot and trying to carry another.

"Careful, honey." Alice hurried downstairs to help slide the three boxes inside. Happy to be home, she'd just changed into joggers and a T-shirt in anticipation of a relaxing evening. "The mother of the bride is not supposed to be doing heavy lifting the week of the wedding. What is all this?"

"Candy. Enough candy for a hundred and fifty people." Ruby opened up one of the boxes and lifted a gallon-size plastic bag full of turquoise M & Ms.

"Did you have a sudden craving?"

"It's for wedding favors. Celeste ordered M & Ms in her colors—cream and teal—but they need to be placed in little bags and tied off with teal ribbon." Ruby gave a slight pout. "Can you help me?"

"A hundred and fifty favors?" So much for a relaxing evening.

"I was thinking it would take my mind off George and the fentanyl thing. And the fact that I still have to have a final fitting on my dress, and find a place for the rehearsal dinner."

"You're welcome to use the backyard," Alice said.

"Too small for our big crowd. And you've done so much already. I'll figure it out, over hours of bagging candy."

"Let's set up in the kitchen nook," Alice said, lifting one of the boxes. "We'll get an assembly line going." She headed into the kitchen, calling, "Violet! Taylor! It's going to be a pizza night!"

The task of bagging M & Ms in little cylinder bags tied off with ribbon was tedious work, but Alice, Taylor, and Violet were happy to contribute to Celeste's perfect day. As they worked Alice relayed her encounter with Jared Chase, and the women conveyed their varied opinions of the man.

"Jared Chase is dynamic and good-looking," Ruby said as she tied off a small transparent satchel of candy with a teal ribbon. "He's got the goods, but unfortunately, he knows it."

"With that gold, boy band hair, he's too fakey fake to be attractive," Taylor said. "I like a guy who's real."

"Despite his smugness, I admit to being impressed with the level of work genetic technicians can contribute to crime solving," Alice said. "Though Jared's firm is way overpriced."

"Has Jared come up with any DNA matches in George's case?" asked Violet. "During the memorial, he was bragging about how he was going to solve George's murder."

"Really?" Alice tilted her head, considering. "That's odd. I mean, it makes perfect sense, since his firm is on retainer. But Madison never mentioned DNA analysis, and Jared claims that he turns his reports in to George, that there's no contact with the police."

"Well, that's not going to work anymore." Violet had a knack for stating the obvious.

"No, it's not." Alice picked up her cell phone and dropped out of the candy assembly line. "I'm calling Madison."

When Alice gave a quick recap of her conversation with Jared Chase, Madison was intrigued.

"I haven't heard anything about EYE-dentify running labs for us. As far as I know, none of our DNA samples has been outsourced to their lab. But I'll double-check with Bedrosian."

"That was a good call, Violet." Alice sat down at the table and proceeded to fill bags with cream and teal candies. "For all of his big talk, and his big invoices, Jared Chase doesn't seem to be producing any product lately. Madison's checking on it."

"What's next for you, Gran?" asked Taylor.

"Good question. I'm not sure where to go with the fentanyl thing. But I do feel the need to resolve some unfinished business. I hate the way things were left with Carrie Preston yesterday."

"I've been thinking about that family, too," Ruby said. "I don't know them well, but I hate the idea that George might have been bilking that family out of money, especially considering the physical state of Carrie's husband."

"We still don't know that George was blackmailing them," Alice said, "but I'm going to pay Carrie another visit and see what I can find out."

"Are you going right now?" Taylor asked. "She's probably in her jammies."

"Tomorrow," Alice said. "Right now we have an important wedding task to complete. How could I walk out on Ruby and the M & M factory?"

# Chapter Forty-seven

"I can sing a rainbow. . . ." Taylor's voice was bright, the strains of her guitar sweet as she led the Tuesday morning toddler hour.

The kids sang along, some energized enough to dance, others rolling on the floor in their own worlds. When the tune ended and Taylor started a more upbeat tempo song about a bunny with long, floppy ears, everyone got up to hop and sing along.

Watching from the back of the children's section, Alice folded her arms. Taylor would make a fine temporary replacement for Nancy Savino. Temporary and probably part-time, as Taylor didn't have a library science degree; she wasn't capable of taking over the significant duties of ordering new books. Still, a good song leader was hard to find. Bravo, Taylor.

During the music segment, two of the moms and one of the grandparents moseyed back to join Alice.

"How is Ruby doing?" the mom named Sari asked. "Have they found the killer yet?"

"Ruby's holding up. And no, the police are still working the case."

"It's so awful," said the other mom, a wispy chickadee with straw hair. "I'm afraid to even run to the store after dark. It's that bad."

"I'm sure you can stay safe when you zip out for milk," Alice assured her. "You know, I've always had a policy; I won't let fear dictate how I live."

"You're a strong woman," said Grandma, a woman with jet black hair, silver hoop earrings, and a dour expression. "And good on you for taking in your friend and supporting your granddaughter, up there. I know you own that big, micro-chip guy's house on the hill, but still, to take folks in at your age. Very generous."

"At my age?" Alice squinted at the grandma, who was probably not much younger than Alice. Though she was quite liberal with that midnight black hair dye. "Really, how old do you think I am?" Alice teased, putting Grandma on the spot.

"I . . . I couldn't say, but—"

"I was just kidding. Age is relative, and I enjoy having family and friends around." Though it reminded her, it was time to give Taylor another kick in the fanny. And maybe time to put some platinum highlights in her hair. She moved toward a glass wall and studied her reflection. Were her silver locks looking dull and gray? Was the silver all in her head?

Age and beauty truly were relative.

As planned, Alice paid a visit to the Preston mansion during her lunch hour. This time she had called to invite herself over. Carrie made all kinds of excuses—"It's not a good day to come over. JB is having a bad day."—but Alice wouldn't take no for an answer. She arrived with a box of cookies from the bakery, and she flashed the rainbow assortment of macarons toward the security camera at the gate. This time, Carrie buzzed her in.

"Thanks for letting me in," Alice teased at the front door.

"I answer to macarons." Carrie gestured her to come inside. "JB is out by the pool, but we can sit in the sunroom. Iced tea?"

"Sounds great."

They sat on wrought iron furniture in a bright room overlooking the pool area and the green bushes and trees that rose up to frame the backyard. Alice didn't know how much acreage the Prestons owned, but from here, it seemed that they inhabited a private, isolated universe.

"I've learned a few things since I was here last," Alice said. "It's become clear that George Byrd was using DNA evidence to blackmail people. Was he taking money from your family, Carrie?"

Carrie nodded, but didn't speak.

"I found some notations in George's files," Alice went on. "Very messy files, by the way. I made a guess that Tony was involved with Harlan Powell. Although the police have the file now, they're not going to draw the same conclusion. They seem to think that Tony is named in the file because of the DNA found in the Cola Bandits case. And George didn't pass the DNA evidence on to the police."

Carrie sighed, her body sagging in relief. "I've been so keyed up about Tony. He's suffered depression and anxiety attacks in prison. He really hit rock bottom there. I've been so worried, Alice. Sick about it. But things are getting better. Tony says he's had a change of heart. He's working out and taking a class. He's found a new peace."

"That's wonderful. I'm so happy . . . for both of you."

"Now that he's approaching release, the future seems hopeful, and I don't want the scandal of Harlan's death to delay Tony's release. Tony tried to help Harlan. My son was not a drug user, but he mixed with a wild crowd. But you see, with one conviction, no one will see his innocence. At least that's the way George presented it when he came to us, demanding money to keep our son's friendship with an overdose victim confidential."

"George probably figured that a wealthy family was a lucrative target for blackmail."

"He always said that blackmail is such a strong word. He said ours was more of a business deal. The only problem was that the terms were too fuzzy. George wouldn't put anything in writing, of course."

Alice pressed a hand to her heart. "I'm sorry for everything that you've been going through." She had more questions. How long ago had the blackmail started, and how much had the Prestons paid? But she didn't want to push too hard. "You've got your hands full with JB, and it's been a long haul with Tony. I know how heartbreaking it can be when a child seems to be on a path of destruction."

"Your daughter," Carrie said.

Alice gave a nod. "I also appreciate how attentive you are with JB; he seems contented."

"You know, it's funny. For all of JB's confusion, he still likes puzzles. Simple ones. Isn't that surprising? It seems to calm him, finding a place for each puzzle piece to fit."

"You should bring him to the senior center, if that wouldn't put him off too much. There's a dedicated puzzle corner there. There are folks who puzzle together, people in various frames of mind. People like JB."

Carrie nodded, tears in her eyes. "He used to enjoy going out. He might like that."

"And Wednesday night, seniors get a free dinner with wine."

"Wine included? I'd have to be a fool to say no to that," Carrie teased, looking like the old friend Alice remembered.

# Chapter Forty-eight

"You might say this is where we begin the anger portion of grieving." Ruby was raging, clearly on a rant. "I'm so angry at George for blackmailing the Preston family. If he were here right now, I'd kill him a second time." She turned the wheel of the car with such a fury, Alice held on as they swung onto a highway that led out of West Hazel.

"Rage on, honey," Alice said, going with it. "Just be careful when we get to the ridge road. I'm not quite ready to join George this evening."

"I'm being very careful." Ruby drew in a breath, easing the clench of her hands on the steering wheel. "To be honest, I'm a little angry at myself for falling for that man."

"You didn't know about his fatal flaws."

"No, I did not. But maybe I should have. I could've saved some people a lot of harassment, money, and anxiety."

"What do we really know about our spouses? Forty years with Jeff, and I woke up one morning and found myself married to a self-absorbed stranger. What I'm saying is it's not your fault George turned out to be a loser."

"How is it that men do horrible things and it's the women who feel overwhelmed with guilt as we pick up the pieces?"

"Amen to that, sister."

"You're making me feel better," Ruby said. "And thank you for agreeing to come along this evening. This'll be the fourth restaurant I've hit today, and so far nothing will work for the rehearsal dinner. If I strike out this time, we'll be doing a tailgate rehearsal dinner in the parking lot of Arby's."

"Now, that would be a party people would talk about for years." The dense trees and lawns that they passed were a familiar and soothing sight for Alice. This was the road she'd taken every day for a year or so on her way to work, back when they had the restaurant. There was the farmhouse with the big bell in front. And a half mile ahead they would pass a sprawling ranch with a wishing well in the side yard.

A familiar road that she hadn't traveled in months. Wait. She turned to Ruby. "You're taking me to Alice's Restaurant?"

"Don't worry. Jeff isn't there. I checked, and it's his poker night."

Alice pressed her hands to her cheeks as Ruby turned into the restaurant parking lot. "Oh, no. Oh, no. No, no."

"It'll be fine. We can see if the food is still up to your standards."

Alice sagged in the passenger seat. She hadn't been back for a meal since she'd walked out of both the business and her marriage on the same night. Fed up.

Her husband had taken her dream of cooking for people in her own restaurant and run wild with it. Jeff was Mr. Host, the guy sitting at the bar at the front of the restaurant, popping up to greet people and chat, while Alice managed the kitchen, cooking, and working expo. Counseling workers who couldn't get to work on time. Doing inventory and scrubbing behind stoves. Working with markets and vendors to obtain high quality fruits, meats, and seafood.

All while Jeff sipped wine and played host.

"I was born to this job," Jeff had told her countless times. Unlike the CPA position he had quit six years earlier because he was too stressed and worried about an ulcer. He'd come to love the restaurant so much, he'd cashed in most of her 401K to save the business when they fell behind on bills.

The debt, the work, the ordeal had broken Alice, and somehow Jeff didn't understand why.

So when it came time to split things in the divorce, Jeff got the restaurant and Alice got her beloved Northwest palace home. To make it a clean break, Alice had sworn off the business. It was Jeff's now, God bless him. She had been overjoyed to return to her beloved library, her home, her friends, and the town that had been her home for decades.

Alice opened her eyes to find Ruby standing next to the passenger side. Ruby opened the door and leaned in. "You coming, honey?"

"As if I have a choice," Alice muttered. She emerged from the car and stood tall and rigid, a formidable foe to the beast.

But oh . . . taking in the structure on the lake, the patio, the little boardwalks out to the water, she felt a twinge of nostalgia. The setting, overlooking Waluga Lake with party lights zigzagging overhead like stars in the inky sky, was divine. Guests could take out paddleboats from the launch after they dined, and the three docks leading out to separate gazebos on the lake offered privacy and charm.

"It's still lovely."

"You built a beautiful place," Ruby said. "Will you be mad at me if I book it so Celeste and Jamal and their friends can have an Oregon summer night to remember?"

How could she say no when the question was a tribute to the dream Alice had built? Besides that, it would be the perfect location for the two families to gather before the wedding.

"Let me buy you dinner, Alice. We can have a nice little meal and critique the food. Which won't be as good as yours, but no chef ever is. You can take some time to think it over, and if you can stand it, I'd really love to have the rehearsal dinner here."

Even before the appetizers arrived, Alice relented. She had put so much into this place; it would be a wonderful reward to have Ruby's family and friends enjoy it. She lifted her wineglass and gave her friend a nod. "Book it, Ruby."

After a delicious meal, Alice and Ruby returned home looking forward to the family night at the restaurant. While Ruby went into the house, Alice went to fetch the mail in the lingering peachy golden light that bathed the street. These last moments before the sun dropped below the horizon, before the gray of dusk fell over the land, were such a marvel.

Hiking over to the group mailbox, she smiled, thinking that the mail—and the inevitable bills—no longer gave her that tar of dread in the pit of her stomach. With the added income of Ruby and Violet boarding in the house, she had more than enough to make her monthly mortgage payment and expenses. It was a temporary arrangement, but for now, she was relieved and grateful.

Alice was walking back from the mailbox right when she saw someone lurking on her front porch. The porch lights weren't on yet, but in the shadowed light of twilight, she was able to make out that it was a man. He was leaning over the little white wicker chair by the door, and as he stepped back, she saw that there was a plastic bag there.

A new puzzle.

Who was this man lurking in the shadows? Could it be the killer?

# Chapter Forty-nine

Alice's heart beat hard in her chest as fear twisted inside her. She took a step closer, but was careful to remain out of striking range. "May I help you?"

A tall, graying man turned and stepped out of the shadow of the covered porch. "Hello, Alice."

She braced herself until she recognized Craig Grand.

The pharmacist? The mayor's husband. "What are you doing here, Craig?" Alice was sure she'd seen him adjusting that bag on the chair. "Have you been dropping off puzzles for our little club, puzzles that contain messages about George's death?"

"Puzzles? Oh, no, I'm just here to make a delivery for Ruby. A prescription refill. I understand she's been staying here since she lost her husband, and I wanted to make sure she got her meds." He patted the pocket of his jacket and then removed a paper bag with a white tag stapled to the top. "That's it. Would you see that she gets it?"

"Of course." She accepted the bag and nodded as he walked toward the street. "I'm sure she'll appreciate the special delivery." She was not smiling.

"No problem," he called as he moved away.

Watching him drive off, Alice sensed that something was up with Craig. Suddenly she wasn't sure that her trusted pharmacist was trustworthy at all.

Violet and Ruby were lounging on sofas in the TV room when Alice handed Ruby the medication.

"What's this?" Ruby asked.

"Your prescription renewal. Special delivery from Craig Grand, our pharmacist."

Ruby squinted at the label. "It's my beta-blocker. But I don't need it for another few weeks. Weird."

"And there's this." Alice dropped the puzzle bag on the coffee table. "I saw the pharmacist leaning over it. I think he dropped it off. Which would make him the person behind the anonymous puzzle clues."

"Why would Craig Grand, our fatherly town pharmacist, warn us not to look into George's murder?" asked Ruby.

Violet held up a finger, as if eager to answer the question first. "The obvious answer would be that Craig is the killer, and he doesn't want us to discover that."

"That sweet man?" Ruby pouted. "Why would he kill George?"

Alice plopped into the overstuffed chair near her friends. "I don't know the motive, but I have two things to say about Craig. First, he's a pharmacist with the know-how and access to give George a toxic cocktail. He even joked about how easy a lethal injection would be. And two, he's married to the town mayor. Who, like it or not, had some involvement with George. What if Tansley knew what George was up to and looked the other way?"

Violet winced. "You think Tansley knew George was blackmailing people?"

Alice scratched her head and sighed. "I don't know. It's just a thought. Where's Taylor tonight?"

"Miss Taylor is out on a date," Ruby said.

"With Jack Jin." Violet smiled. "Such a nice young man. Is it wrong to wish for something to happen?"

"Love is grand," Alice said. "But my first wish is for Taylor to find her passion in life and learn how to make enough of an income to support herself. Isn't that how she should be prioritizing?"

"I guess." Violet sighed. "But I do like Jack Jin."

"I suppose there's only one thing we can do now." Alice arose from the comfy chair and lifted the bag with the puzzle. "Find the message in our new puzzle."

"Straight from the laboratory of the mad pharmacist," Violet said, tinkling her fingers as if casting a spell.

Ruby plodded over to the kitchen nook. "I am so sick of rushing these puzzles to figure them out for clues."

"I, on the other hand, work best under a deadline." Violet opened the bag and began spreading out pieces. "This can't be more than two hundred fifty pieces. It's child's play."

"Mmm. Looks like we've got some blue ocean," Alice said. "Or is it sky?"

"And a ship. And some print." Ruby smiled. "You're right. This is an easy one."

The images began to take shape quickly. There was a churning blue ocean with a pirate ship in the background. In the foreground was a montage of characters from the *Pirates of the Caribbean* movies. The banner was a movie title: "*DEAD MEN TELL NO TALES.*"

"Is that a threat?" Alice asked, more annoyed than frightened. "Is Craig saying that we'll wind up dead if we don't stop investigating?"

"Speak for yourself," said Violet. "You're the real investigator in this mix. We're all just your sidekicks."

"Don't you worry, honey," Ruby reassured Alice. "If the ship is going down, I'll be right beside you, fending off the pirates. Except that Captain Jack Sparrow. Any woman would be a fool to fight him off."

# Chapter Fifty

Wednesday morning Alice was about to grab one last coffee to take to work when she found her dining room taken over by tiny cakes in delightful shades of pink, peach, lavender, white, sparkling gold, teal, and chocolate, chocolate, chocolate.

"The dessert fairies were here!" Alice announced as Taylor and Ruby rushed in from the kitchen.

"I was just getting a fork." Taylor sashayed over to the table as if she'd just won the lottery. "Cake for breakfast!"

"Write down your response to each cake," Ruby instructed. "They have names and numbers. You have the scorecard I gave you, right?"

"Got it." Taylor was already seated, eyes closed in buttercream ecstasy.

"What's going on?" Alice asked.

"Celeste never did her tasting." Ruby paced beside the long table, on cake patrol. "We've got to pick a wedding cake for her, and today is our last chance. Please stay! We need every taste bud we can get."

Alice hesitated; she'd been calling out a lot at work lately. "What about Violet?"

"She left for school before the cakes arrived. Please, give a taste. Celeste arrives tomorrow, but that's too late."

There was only one thing to do. Alice held out her hand. "Fork me."

It was a tough choice when everything was so delicious. Alice helped narrow it down to lavender honey, German chocolate, vanilla-Oreo cream, and classic carrot before she headed out the door.

The two finalists were Oreo cream and lavender honey.

"You have to go with Oreo," Taylor insisted. "It's America's cookie."

Alice left the two women to decide with a call out to Celeste to break the tie.

But in her heart, lavender honey was the one.

Alice arrived at the library feeling well buttered and ready for a busy day.

Julia caught her up on a staff meeting she had missed that morning, and then she popped into a session of Needle Knockers, the yarn club that drew moms of young children and retired folk. Alice had enjoyed crocheting as a child, had never gotten back to it, but she liked popping in on these meetings to check the progress of projects. A retired teacher named Martha showed off a pink shawl she had knitted to raffle off at a breast cancer fund-raiser.

"Love the color!" Alice said.

Jennette Turck had just begun crocheting a soft yellow throw as a Christmas gift for her son's girlfriend. "I'm a slow worker, so I had to start in July! And I hope Mac is still dating the same girl in December. She's a keeper!"

A gentleman named Leon, who had started a small online business selling knitted covers for throw pillows, showed off some new creations in rainbow stripes.

"A fine achievement," Alice told him. "You know, I love to stop in and monitor the progress of this group. It reminds me that the world is spinning forward when so many things in life seem to be stuck in the muck."

The women chuckled. "You're not around when we drop a stitch and have to backtrack."

Leon gave her a thumbs-up. "One stitch at a time, Alice."

With a new spring in her step, she was heading back to the office when Julia intercepted her on the stairs.

"There you are. The mayor's office called and she wants to see you ASAP."

"Sounds serious." Alice checked her watch. Not quite eleven, and she had a coffee date with Taylor and Ruby at lunchtime. "I'll head over now, and try to intercept her before lunch."

At city hall, Cassidy cleared Alice to "go on in" to the mayor's office, where Tansley sat at her desk, working on her computer.

"Alice!" Tansley waved her in. "Thanks for coming over on short notice."

"No problem." Alice took a seat across from the mayor's desk. "I imagine you want to talk to me about all the comp time I've been taking in the past week. It's just a temporary state of flux, as I'm trying to help Ruby deal with George's death and her daughter's wedding. I'll be back to work full-time next week."

"Of course. I have no issues with you taking time off. I know you have vacation time to spare. But I did get a call from the chief of police today. Chief Cushman is worried that your probes regarding George's death are compromising the police investigation."

"Really?" Alice was surprised. The chief of police was worried about a silver-haired librarian asking a few questions? Besides, she would have expected Madison to tell her to back off long before the issue got to the top cop.

Tansley removed her glasses to give Alice a sympathetic look. "I know you've been acting out of concern for your friend, but the police are conducting the investigation, and I'm sure you don't want to interfere."

"Of course not." The automatic response didn't stop Alice's thoughts from whirring ahead. Where was this coming from? "Wait. Isn't the chief on vacation for the month? He and his wife are off on a European cruise. Nearly impossible to reach."

"Right." Tansley nodded and turned to look out the window, adding, "And he wasn't happy to interrupt his leisure time to make the call."

"Wow. I'm sorry to interrupt his time on the beautiful blue Danube. Or is he on the Mediterranean?"

"I'm not sure." Tansley put up her hand. "The important thing is for you to stay in your own lane. You're a valued employee, Alice. But you're out of line, involving yourself in this investigation. It really has to stop. You're the town librarian, for goodness sakes. West Hazel couldn't hope for a finer librarian. But you have no place in law enforcement."

Although Alice forced a smile, she felt annoyed by Tansley's condescension, as well as her order to step out of the case.

Alice let the silent pause increase her power before she spoke. "I haven't broken any rules or laws."

"No one's making accusations. Your inquisitions just have to stop."

Alice pressed against the armrests, straightening in the

chair. "I'm just asking questions of a few people. Nothing extraordinary. Just trying to help bring closure for my friend."

"It has to stop," Tansley railed, rattled by the resistance. "This order came from the top cop."

"But I don't work for him."

"Please!" Tansley barked like an aggravated pit bull. "Just do as you're told."

# Chapter Fifty-one

Alice took a breath, trying to make it a calming breath as Tansley vented about people needing to do their job and stay in their lane.

*The mayor is throwing a tantrum.*

Alice didn't know where Tansley's anger was coming from, but she possessed the grace to know that this was no time to argue. Holding tight to the armrests, she remained silent as Cassidy appeared in the doorway and Tansley ranted on.

"I would think someone with your education would have respect for the chief of police, as well as the chain of command in an organization like—" Tansley noticed her assistant. "What is it?"

"Sorry." Cassidy winced. "But your mother is on the phone asking for Tammy."

Tansley sucked in a breath and let it out with a grunt. "Leave it to my mother." She cupped her face with her hands, suddenly personable again. "I've worked hard to shed that hillbilly name."

"Tammy?" Cassidy said. "I think it's kind of cool in a country-western way."

"You're both too young to remember this," Alice said, "but I recall a wonderful Debbie Reynolds movie about a country girl named Tammy. As a kid, I used to watch it with popcorn whenever it came on. There was a sweet love story."

Tansley nodded. "My mother made me watch it. Years later I saw Debbie Reynolds in a cute Halloween movie with my own kids. She was awesome."

"I used to know you as Tammy Stransky when you were in high school," Alice said, relieved that the scolding was over. "It seemed like a normal name at the time."

"Except that Stransky made me a plum target for kids who had a repertoire of Polish jokes." Tansley lifted her phone from the receiver. "I was very happy to marry Craig Grand. It's a wonderful name." She lifted her chin. "Thank you for coming in, Alice."

"You can tell the chief I got the message," Alice said as she left Tansley to take the call.

*Message received, though I don't think I'll take his advice.*

Alice bid Cassidy good-bye and resisted the urge to take out her cell phone until she got outside the building and down the block. This riverfront piazza was the perfect place to meet Taylor and Ruby. The plaza with outdoor seating was shared by a pizza place, a bakery, a Thai restaurant, and a high-end burger joint. From her umbrella-shaded table, she overlooked two large beds of flowers and the sparkling Willamette River in the distance. She declined a pastry—easy, after all that morning cake— and ordered a double latte, though she would have liked something stronger to take the edge off after that dressing down from the mayor.

As soon as the server left her table, she called Madison.

"I just got called into the mayor's office. Scolded, really. She gave me a message from your police chief. Claimed my snooping around is interfering with your investigation into George's death."

"Wait, what?"

"So it *is* news to you." Alice tapped the table, calculating. "I thought as much."

# Chapter Fifty-two

"The chief is on vacation, out of touch," Madison said. "How would he even know you're looking into the case?"

"My question exactly."

"I'm going to check with Bedrosian to see what he knows. But really? The mayor told you to butt out?"

"In very specific terms. She told me to stick to being a librarian."

Madison laughed out loud. "I'm sorry, but that shows how little she knows you. Gran, you do not respond well to direct orders."

"You figured that out, did you?"

"All kidding aside, I don't like the sound of this. What does the chief know that Bedrosian and I haven't heard? It doesn't make sense. I'm going to ask around and see what I can find out."

"Call me back when you know more."

Alice was sipping her iced latte, trying to figure out what had put Tansley Grand in such an imperious mood, when Ruby and Taylor arrived together.

"We're here for our coffee date!" Ruby was so frantically cheerful. Would she tip Taylor off? Taylor didn't know this date was a ruse concocted to double-team her about getting a job.

They sat down and placed their orders. "Anyone want a pastry?" Alice asked. "The almond croissants are divine."

"I'm still stuffed from wedding cakes," Ruby said.

They chitchatted about various flavors of cake until the drinks arrived, and Alice took control of the conversation.

"I'm glad you could make it today, Taylor. I have a proposition for you that I think you'll find appealing."

"Uh-oh." Taylor pursed her lips. "Here goes trouble."

"No, honey, it's all good. You know I've got a children's librarian going on sabbatical, and we've opened up an assistant's position that would be perfect for you. You could play guitar for the story times, and supervise the children's activities like craft hour and Lego club. The kids do love you, and you really shine when you're entertaining them."

"A job." Taylor nodded, as if this were a totally new concept.

"We've talked about this before. It's the next step for you, a move toward independence."

"Adulting." Taylor jabbed the straw in her drink. "Ugh."

"And if the library doesn't work for you, I can create a spot at my office," Ruby said. "You don't have experience, but if you're willing to commit I could teach you all about the world of wigs, hairpieces, and toppers."

"Thanks." Taylor pushed her coppery hair back, her eyes indecipherable behind her sunglasses. "That's nice of you guys to offer, but those jobs really don't work for me."

Alice was floored. Two jobs, and she couldn't pretend to be interested?

"Well, you know you need to pursue a career," Ruby said. "What do you think might interest you?"

"Actually"—Taylor shrugged—"I was out with Jack Jin last night, and his excitement about starting med school was infectious. He's so into it. Helping people feel better, and even saving lives. So now I'm thinking of becoming a doctor, too."

Alice gripped the table with her hands to keep from slapping her forehead in amazement. A doctor? Far be it from her to discourage such a noble pursuit, but she knew her granddaughter. No follow-through. No way.

"That's a fine calling," Alice said, trying to exude patience, "but you need to focus on the kind of job you could do now, while you save money to finish college. Or even med school, if it truly calls to you."

"Something more immediate," Ruby agreed.

"Work is an important part of our lives," Alice said. "It improves our self-worth, establishes relationships. It's important for you to have a job, honey."

Taylor let out a huffy breath. "No matter what I do, I'm always being compared to my sister, who, yes, has a full-on career. But admit it, her life is a bore. And still, all I ever hear about is Madison's job, Madison's career, Madison's independence."

"Now that's not fair." Ruby nudged Taylor. "Alice and I haven't mentioned Madison. Not once today. We're focusing on you being your very best self."

"Yeah . . . I don't think that's going to happen."

"Don't be down on yourself," Alice said. "Every woman needs to follow her own path."

"Gran, that's so corny."

"I know." Alice took a sip of her latte, thinking that a change the topic would be good before Taylor launched into a diatribe about the mercenary nature of capitalism. "So remember the weird drive-by that Craig Grand did last night? Well, today his wife, my boss, called me into her office and ordered me to stop investigating George's death."

"What?" Taylor gaped. "She can't do that!"

"She said the order came from the police chief."

"That's ridiculous," Ruby said. "You're a citizen. You have rights."

"There was no room for discussion of that today." Alice started telling them how the situation went down. As she described how Tansley threw a fit, Madison walked onto the plaza and came to their table.

"Madison? What are you doing here?" Alice asked.

"I walked from police headquarters. Actually, I went to the library first, and Julia told me you'd be here. I have terrible news." She sank into the empty wrought iron chair.

Was that a pout? It seemed incongruous with her dark, crisp uniform and shiny badge.

"Aw. You look upset."

"I'm so disappointed. I just had two very different conversations with Bedrosian. First, he told me that my grandmother could conduct her own investigation until she was blue in the face. His words, not mine. Then, not even ten minutes later, he came to my desk and told me that the chief had just called in from vacation, and he wanted me bumped back to patrol. From now on I'm not allowed to help Bedrosian with the homicide investigation. Starting tomorrow, I'll be either in a patrol car answering radio calls, or working the front desk at the precinct, taking complaints."

"Did Chief Cushman give a reason why you were demoted?" Ruby asked.

"No reason, no explanation, but then, he doesn't have to. But it feels unfair." Madison frowned and scanned the tables around them. "I probably shouldn't even be seen in public with you guys at this point. Especially you, Gran."

"I, too, am technically barred from investigating, so I don't see that I can corrupt you," Alice said. "Beyond that, I am your grandmother. We are permitted to grab a coffee together."

"That's really awful." Taylor's eyes were warm with compassion.

"It's not fair at all," Ruby said.

"At least Detective Bedrosian was sympathetic." Madison took Alice's water, gripping it with both hands as she took a drink. "He said I didn't do anything wrong, but I keep wondering. Was there something I did, or something I missed?"

"With the work you've done, you can hold your head high. You've moved ahead with the investigation in leaps and bounds. You're the one who put Bedrosian onto the fact that George was blackmailing people."

"I guess."

"It must be a bad day in the universe," Taylor said. "I think Saturn and Jupiter are kind of facing off. Gran also had a weird confrontation at work."

"I heard." Madison nodded. "The mayor pulled the boss card."

"Had a bit of a tantrum," Alice recalled. "It was odd. One minute she was flipping out, telling me to mind my business, the next she was personable again, recalling her childhood name, Tammy."

"She didn't grow up as Tansley?" asked Taylor.

Alice shook her head. "She was Tammy Stransky. I knew her when she was a young student. A bit of a loner."

Something about the name resonated with Alice.

*Tammy Stransky, Tammy Stransky.* She was sure she'd come across it recently.

"You know . . ." Alice wagged a finger. "That name rings a bell. I think I saw it somewhere in George's garbled papers."

"Did you?" Madison asked. "Too bad I confiscated them from you. Now we'll never know."

"Although . . ." Ruby tapped Alice's cell phone, which lay flat on the table. "Someone might have an electronic copy."

Alice pressed a finger to her lips. "That's right!" She found the app, and then the link to the papers Ruby had scanned.

"Too bad you're not allowed to investigate," Taylor said.

"Mmm-hmm." Alice barely listened as she scrolled through the paperwork, squinting to make out George's scribble. There it was, on a sheet with various rows of numbers. "Tammy Stransky Payments."

Alice leaned over the table and showed the phone screen to Madison. "George must have used the mayor's maiden name for a code. Under her name there are entries of payments. Ten-thousand-dollar payments made six times over the last eight months."

"Why would the mayor be paying George off?" Taylor asked.

"Who knows?" Ruby said wearily.

"But look at this." Madison pointed to the phone. "George is subtracting the payments from a one-hundred-fifty-thousand-dollar total. Seems to indicate he's the one making the payments to Stransky."

"Why would George pay off the mayor?" Ruby asked.

"So that she would keep quiet about his scheme?" Alice suggested. "Maybe George was paying for her silence."

"Was that why Tansley ordered you to stop digging for information?" Ruby asked Alice.

Alice nodded sadly. "Because she didn't want me to discover that she and her husband were running their own blackmail scheme."

"This is *huge*," Taylor said.

"Totally huge." Madison looked around cautiously, as if someone on the plaza was watching them. "I'm dying. I've got to tell Bedrosian."

"Best keep it to yourself for now," Alice warned. "It's just a theory, and you're off the case."

"I know, but—"

"I hope it's wrong," Alice said. "Please, can it not be true? I didn't want to find a crack in Tansley's armor. A person needs a clean record to be elected mayor in a town like West Hazel, and Tansley Grand has a reputation for being tops at everything. Class valedictorian. Law review. Head of the Women Leaders Charity Group. I'm so disappointed."

"I know, honey." Ruby rubbed Alice's arm. "It's sad."

Alice had been so pleased to see a good woman rise to a position of power. But here was evidence of her hero's mistake. A huge crack in the facade.

It was just a matter of time before it all came tumbling down.

# Chapter Fifty-three

Wednesday was turkey tetrazzini night at the senior center. Not a dish that Alice made at home, but here at the senior center she always enjoyed the salty, creamy flavor.

After the falling dominoes of the day, it had been hard to summon her usual enthusiasm. While Violet and Ruby visited with Aunt Gildy during the cocktail social, Alice couldn't help but pull herself away to stare out the window and try *not* to think about the case.

"Can I get you to help me serve?" Stone asked. "We're a little shorthanded tonight."

"Of course!" She followed him to the kitchen pass-through. "Anything to take my mind off everything."

"You do seem a bit glum."

"I'm disenchanted."

His eyes held concern. "I'm sorry to hear that." He handed her two plates loaded with noodles and turkey, green beans, and applesauce. "Let me know if there's anything I can do."

"Smells good," she said, moving off to start serving.

By the time she had finished serving, Alice felt on a

more even keel, ready to socialize. Unfortunately, Aunt Gildy didn't let her slide.

"What's going on with you?" she asked. "You're such a gloomy Gussy tonight."

Alice took a sip of water, stalling to phrase her answer.

"Alice had a rough day," Ruby said. "She deserves a pass tonight."

"Buck up, bucko," Aunt Gildy said as she plunged a fork into noodles. "Your bad mood is a buzz kill for the rest of us."

Alice swallowed and nodded. "Sorry. You're right." If Aunt Gildy could incorporate "buzz kill" in her vocabulary, certainly Alice could get past her blues.

"What's wrong, anyway?" Gildy asked.

"Have you ever felt like you're losing control of things?"

"Ha! All the time!"

While Gildy went on to talk about her ailments, Alice's mind wandered to the things that seemed to be slipping away from her. Her restaurant and her marriage were gone. Her savings had been nearly drained by her husband and daughter. Her house was mortgaged to the gills now. Her snooping had gotten Madison kicked off her first case. Her investigation of George had opened a can of worms, making Ruby face her husband's dark side, even as it was uncovering crimes committed by seemingly good people.

Gildy squeezed Alice's arm, tugging her out of her reverie. "So really, pumpkin, what's eating away at you?"

"It's not one thing, Aunt Gildy. I have many regrets."

"Regrets are good for the soul," Gildy said.

"Aunt Gildy is right," Violet said. "Regret gives us a chance to look back and learn from our past actions. But it's good to realize that this is a phase, as the planets move through our universe. Saturn, the great teacher, has a lesson for you, whether you like it or not."

"Saturn needs to realize that I'm pushing seventy," Alice said. "I'm running out of time to make major course corrections."

"That's nonsense," Gildy said. "You ever heard that Chinese proverb? The best time to plant a tree is twenty years ago. But you missed that, deary. So when's the second-best time to plant a tree?"

Alice shrugged. "I don't know, when?"

Gildy pointed a finger to underscore her answer. "Today."

Ruby hooted. "And Aunt Gildy drops the mic!"

Alice nodded as she took a bite of casserole. Put in her place by her dear old aunt. She noticed a bluesy Steely Dan song playing in the background, and looked over at Stone, who controlled the music through an app on his phone. He was trying to meet her vibe, as Taylor would say. He was a good guy.

As they cleaned up the dinner things, Alice confided in Stone, sharing some of the things she'd learned. She told him that George had been using his position on the city council to blackmail people. And to top that off, her boss had had a meltdown in the office and told her to stop investigating George's murder.

"Your boss, the mayor?" Stone asked.

"I thought she would remain anonymous if I didn't name names."

"Small town. So did you inform her that this is the United States of America and you have the right to investigate any murder you choose?" He touched his chin. "Did you assert your rights?"

"I tried, but Tansley was not having any of it. She was

acting weird. Not like the woman I've come to know and admire. Actually, I'm beginning to wonder if I ever knew her at all." Swearing him to secrecy, she shared her suspicion that Tansley and her husband might have been involved in George's blackmail scheme.

"It's all a huge mess I've unleashed," she said. "And now it's too late to put the genie back into the bottle."

Stone snickered. "I've never seen you as a person who'd tamp down the truth. Maybe it's time for you to find your inner genie. Leave the bottle behind."

Alice smiled. "I like the image."

"More wine?"

"Please." Alice accepted more wine from this dear, wise, handsome man. He was right. This was no time to back off. Onward and upward.

# Chapter Fifty-four

*Thursday*

"Life is good," Alice said aloud as she stood in her robe on her bedroom balcony and breathed in the mountains, the trees, the sunshine. Things did look better after a good night's sleep. Not fabulous, but tolerable. And she was taking all of Thursday off to help with wedding errands, so she was breathing the air of a free woman on a mini vacation.

As she was scanning the flowerpots along her walkway, she saw a car drive past and pull into the back driveway by the garages. Who was that?

If it was Thursday morning it must be . . .

"Celeste!" She hurried down the hall, slowing to protect her foot on the stairs. She made it to the front door just as Ruby and her youngest daughter were embracing.

"Ooh-wee, my beautiful girl!" Ruby exclaimed, rocking her daughter in her arms. "It's so good to have you home."

"It's so good to be here, Mom. We've all been so worried about you. How you doing?"

"Hanging in there, baby girl."

They separated, and Celeste noticed Alice standing by. "Auntie Alice!"

"Here comes the bride," Alice said, hugging Celeste. "We're so glad you're here."

"I'm grateful to you for taking care of Ruby after everything with George. You've been through a lot, Mom. You're an amazing woman, letting us go ahead with the wedding as planned."

"The wedding is a welcome distraction, though, as I told you, the house is off the table. I'm just not comfortable hosting there. I don't even like going in there, but I've still got some clothes and shoes to fetch. Anyway, I've got you all booked at that luxury hotel on the lake, with a very nice pool. And you can walk to all the downtown restaurants from there."

"Sounds perfect. But first things first. Let's go over to the house and I'll keep you company while you get your things. It's my turn to help you. I know you picked up the slack for me, doing the cake tasting and wrapping the favors."

"Sweet tasks," Alice said cheerfully.

"We can go over to the house," Ruby said. "Honestly, it would be good to get that errand done. When things settle down after the wedding, I'm probably going to put it on the market. Too many bad memories."

"Mother, you're talking to a double-diamond realtor. Let's go take a look at your property, Ms. Milliner."

"Give me five minutes to change and I'll drive you over," Alice said. "My car has a good-size cargo bay, for wig boxes and shoes."

Ruby let out a small laugh. "You know me so well."

"A first-floor office with a closet, could be used as a bedroom. Nice." Celeste moved gracefully down the hall, touring the house with an experienced eye. "Not open concept, but there's a light, airy atmosphere."

"Don't mind the powder on the walls and such," Ruby said. "Fingerprint dust. I haven't had time to get the cleaners in."

"Not a problem, Mom. I can look past those things. What I do see is that your house has good bones, and it's in a wonderful, much sought-after neighborhood."

Ruby smiled. "Sounds like a listing."

"Exactly. After the honeymoon, I'm going to come back and help you sell this place. And then we'll find you a wonderful new house that will suit your new single lifestyle."

Ruby shot a hesitant look to Alice. "I'm not sure I'm ready for a new house, though I'd love to get this place sold. Over and done with."

Celeste smiled. "I'm happy to do that with you."

Ruby squeezed her hand. "I have the best daughter in the world."

Celeste headed toward the stairs. "Show me the upstairs, and we'll help you grab your stuff."

"If you don't mind," Alice said, "I'd like to look through George's office one more time."

"*Not* looking for clues for the case you're *not* working on?" Ruby winked at Alice. "Have at it, honey."

While Ruby and Celeste went to the primary bedroom, Alice surveyed George's office yet again. The two framed prints on the wall, hunting scenes with horses and hound dogs, seemed pretentious, here in a home office outside Portland, Oregon. On the credenza, next to the used mugs, was a wedding picture of George and Ruby. Alice shook her head at it. "You were so funny and affable, George. Who knew you were greedy at heart?"

She opened the closet, a sloppy mess, though there were a few puzzles and board games that might prove to be fun.

The shelves held a few small, dusty statues and bowling trophies. Some ridiculous sports bobbleheads. The knick-knacks were mundane. Nothing that would excite on *Antiques Road Show*.

She did find an opaque purple vase that had some potential. It would be cute with small flowers in it. Maybe daisies.

Taking it down from the high shelf, she took a closer look and found a small, black suede box inside the vase. A ring box.

She popped it open, and a dark green emerald stone glimmered among tiny diamonds.

Nicole's ring.

# Chapter Fifty-five

Alice rang the doorbell a second time, the ring box bulging from the pocket of her summer dress. Her intel, based on reports from the girls at city hall, indicated that Nicole would be home, as the young woman had taken to being a hermit since the day of her arrest.

She was about to knock on the door when the lock clicked and the door opened.

"Alice Pepper?" Nicole smoothed her hair back behind one ear and peeked outside, as if making sure there were no police or reporters.

"This isn't a trap. I've brought you something."

Nicole squinted, confused, but she allowed Alice to come inside.

It was a pleasant apartment. The main room was filled with a gray sectional, but it looked cozy with orange pillows and a fluffy white throw that had been balled up. If Nicole had been forced to be a hermit, Alice was glad to know she had a decent place to hide.

"I don't know how your case is going, and I can't get involved with that, so I'll cut right to the point." Alice reached into her pocket and held out the black box. "I think this belongs to you."

Nicole gasped. "My ring?" She opened the box and burst into tears.

Alice felt a tug of emotion. She wondered at the oddity of a world where you wanted to cry along with the woman who'd been having an affair with your best friend's husband.

"Ruby thought you should have it."

"She did?" Nicole sobbed.

"She did. George's death has hurt many people in many ways, but Ruby has come to see that George was hurting people while he was alive, and that's inexcusable. She thought you should have the ring. It's no compensation for George's manipulations, but it's rightfully yours."

"I don't know." Nicole swiped at her eyes. "I pegged Ruby as the type to destroy a woman who came after her husband."

"Ruby is moving on, dealing more with regrets than grudges. She's not blaming you, not anymore."

Nicole slid the ring on her finger and stared at it sadly. "Will you tell her thank you from me? I know that sounds cheesy, so maybe don't. Don't say anything. That's what my lawyer told me. No comment."

"I can't speak to your legal issues, but I do want to tell you that the police do not know the ring was found, so mum's the word." Alice closed her hand over the ring on Nicole's fingers and looked her in the eyes. "It's your ring. You told me that clearly. It was lost, but now it's found. End of story."

Nicole nodded, letting out a shuddering breath. "I miss him, you know. I even miss all the work I had to do at the office. George didn't know how to use Excel or any of the accounting programs. I did it all. I took good care of the business records. I miss the office, but not the other women there. Everyone's turned against me."

"That can happen in office scandals."

"I guess."

"Have you heard from the mayor?" Alice asked. "I understand George was especially close to the mayor."

"What?" Nicole twisted the ring on her finger. "No way. It was just the opposite. Tansley and George were always arguing behind closed doors. It was a strained relationship."

"Did George get along with anyone at city hall?"

"Not really. George's only real friend was Jared Chase, that guy from the genetic research place."

Interesting. Alice recalled Ruby saying they were friends. "Funny thing about EYE-dentify. We weren't able to find any official records from the company. Where did George keep the information he got from Jared Chase?"

"I wasn't in on those meetings. It was always between George and Jared. I think George might have had stuff on his phone, or maybe at home." Nicole frowned. "That's a lot of questions about George. Are you working for the police?"

"Oh, no. No, no, no. I'm just a curious woman who tries to help her friends."

With one more look at the ring on her hand, Nicole misted over. "I really do miss George. Without him, I'm so lonely. My friends don't have time for me. As soon as I clear up the charges here, I'm thinking about moving to Vegas, where my cousin lives. I've heard you can get a job there, no problem."

"But then you'd be living in Vegas."

"That'd be fun, right?"

"It's something I'd investigate before investing in a big move."

Nicole's lips twisted in a tortured frown. "I guess you're

right. I don't want to be there, really, but I can't stay here."

Face to face with the young woman who had assaulted her, Alice couldn't deny feeling genuine empathy for her. Loneliness was a cruel state for any person.

"Wherever you land, I wish you luck." She slipped her a card. "But if you do stay here, check out the library Web site. We have lots of free activities, reading groups, clubs, lectures, crafts."

Nicole was studying the card as Alice moved toward the door. "I used to knit."

"We have a yarn club. Something for everyone nearly every night of the week. Come on down."

# Chapter Fifty-six

B ack home, Alice helped Ruby pack for the hotel, where she'd be staying along with the wedding party.

"It's only for three days," Ruby said, "so I should be able to fit everything in one suitcase."

"Take two," Alice advised. "You don't want to be running back and forth because you forgot something."

"And that would give me a wider choice of wardrobe." Ruby rolled out a large suitcase made of soft, amber leather. "Are you sure you don't mind doing the airport runs?"

"Not at all. I've got your son Isaac and family coming in at eleven thirty, and then cousin Xavier around three."

"Perfect. I so appreciate you doing the limo service so I can spend more time with Celeste."

"I'm happy to help. It'll give me a chance to catch up with some of your family. I don't think I've seen cousin Xavier since the old days back in Queens."

"He's doing well. Teaching at a college in California." She rolled open a dresser drawer and paused. "I've been really comfortable here, all moved in." She turned to Alice, a hopeful light in her eyes. "I have a new proposal for you. After the wedding, I'd like to move into this suite permanently. And maybe take one of the other rooms for a home office? I'll pay rent, of course. And we'll work out a generous amount because I want to feel like it's my home, too. I want to be a permanent resident of Alice's Palace."

"Oh, honey." Alice teared up at the offer. She needed the financial help, and right now Ruby needed the companionship. "It's the perfect arrangement."

"I knew you'd agree. I'm so happy here. It's fun being one of the gals," Ruby said. "Like a constant slumber party."

"Remember when we used to have sleepovers back in Queens?" Alice smiled. "When we made fudge?"

"I do, indeed." Ruby grabbed a stack of slacks from the dresser. "Thank goodness we switched to making real meals. One more batch of fudge and I'd be in a diabetic coma."

After Ruby left, Alice took the time to brew herself one more latte, complete with foamed milk. With an hour or so before she needed to head out on her airport run, she called Carrie Preston to see if it would be okay to stop in. Now that Carrie was beginning to trust her again, Alice wanted to extract more information about the blackmail scheme. She particularly wanted to see what Carrie knew about Tansley Grand's involvement.

Unfortunately, Carrie was in a flustered state. She refused when Alice suggested a visit. "Stay out of this, Alice. You really don't want to get involved."

"But I am involved."

"I can't talk to you," Carrie snapped. "Don't come by, and don't tell anyone we talked."

Hearing the quaver in Carrie's voice, Alice asked if they

could meet in a public place. "Maybe at a coffee shop or . . . or at the library?"

"I can't leave my home. I'll . . . I'll never be safe again." Her voice broke, but Alice couldn't be sure if it was frustration or fear that was plaguing Carrie.

"I thought it would stop, but it's still going on. It's as if George is hounding me from the grave. I know I must sound paranoid, but I'm not safe anywhere and I've had it. I'm going to call Tansley and put an end to this."

"Tansley?" Alice said. "Is she the one who's been extorting money from you and JB?" Alice listened, but there was no answer. "Carrie?"

The dead silence indicated that the call had been disconnected.

# Chapter Fifty-seven

Something was wrong with Carrie. Alice could feel it. Taking a deep breath to tamp down the surge of adrenaline that made her pulse race, she called 911 and requested a welfare check at Carrie's house. When they asked for her identity, she gave them her information. What the hell. She was willing to go out on a limb and get in trouble with the boss if it meant helping Carrie.

"Can you get someone there quickly?" Alice asked the operator.

"We've already dispatched a patrol unit, ma'am."

Alice grabbed her phone and car keys and headed out the door. She was going straight to Carrie's house. As soon as she hit the porch, she realized the problem in her plan. She ran back inside and flung open the basement door.

"Taylor? I need you, honey. Can you—" She gave up and texted her niece to come upstairs pronto. A minute later, Alice had transferred her still-warm latte into a travel cup, and Taylor appeared at the top of the stairs.

"What's up?"

"I need you to drive to the airport and pick up Ruby's son and his family and deliver them to the hotel. Isaac and

Angie and sundry children. Eleven-thirty arrival. Don't argue; it's an emergency. I'll explain later."

"Are they old?"

"Their children are younger than you."

Taylor rolled her eyes. "Aw, Gran. You're killing me."

"And there's another pickup at three. I'll text you the details. We'll need to switch cars, as they're quite a crew." Alice unclipped the Audi fob from her ring. "Get me your keys to the bug."

"Only good part of the deal," Taylor muttered, grabbing her keys from a hook inside one of the kitchen cupboards. "Remember, for reverse you have to press down really hard and go forward and left toward the dashboard. Don't break the stick."

Alice sighed. "I wish you'd move on from that car."

"I'm broke. And I'll never give up Anastasia." She smiled at the Audi fob. "But I don't mind driving your car."

Normally Alice would have argued about the ridiculous habit of naming cars, but she had no time to waste. She struggled with sticky seat adjustment in the Beetle and ended up putting an old phone book from the floor behind her back. Was that what the book was meant for? The car fired up on her first try, and she worked the gears like a pro, trying to ignore the worn-through part of the floor where she could see moving pavement. Travel in a tin can, but it moved.

Alice arrived at the Preston estate just as Carrie was being taken away by ambulance.

"Gran . . . I heard you called this in." Madison emerged from the front door of the house and touched her arm gently.

"Are you working with Bedrosian again?"

"The detectives aren't here yet. I was one of the first responders."

"Is Carrie okay?"

"She's unconscious, but vital signs are good. We found her on the dining room floor, bleeding from a head injury. She was attacked, apparently hit by a candlestick holder."

"Again with the candlestick holder?"

Madison shrugged. "It's either a copycat or the trademark of George's killer." She nodded toward the house. "Do you want to come inside? We were just about to interview the housekeeper, Svitlana, who was out of the house with Carrie's husband when the attack happened. She's distressed, and struggling to calm the husband down."

"JB. He's quite reliant on Carrie. This is going to be tough on him."

"They're out by the pool. I was going to talk with them once the husband calms down."

"I might be able to help with that." Alice lifted her chin defiantly. "If I can stay for the interview."

"Fine with me," Madison said. "For now, this is a brand-new case, wink-wink."

Out by the pool, Svitlana was trying to soothe JB in a rapid-fire barrage of what Alice assumed was a mixture of English and Ukrainian. It was a noble attempt, but JB seemed annoyed by it.

"It's a beautiful day, isn't it?" Alice said, approaching the man.

Svitlana looked up and took a breath. A relief to have quiet restored.

"Sure is." He turned away from Svitlana and extended his hand to Alice. "JB Preston."

"It's a pleasure to meet you," Alice said, shaking his hand. "And this is Officer Denham."

"JB Preston."

"Nice to meet you." Madison shook his hand tentatively.

"Let's get you some lemonade, JB," Alice said. "I know you like lemonade. And I'm sure there are some cookies inside."

"Is that right?" he said casually.

The housekeeper rose, staring at him in relief. "I'll get them." She hurried into the kitchen.

A few minutes later, with JB Preston calmed and staring out over the pastoral yard, the women moved to the far side of the turquoise pool where they could keep an eye on him but not disturb him with the conversation.

"So, you took Mr. Preston to the park around what time?" asked Madison.

"Around eleven, I think." Svitlana touched the little gold ball in her earlobe. A woman in her forties, she had light brown hair, brown eyes, and a full face that now seemed ghostly with concern. "You know, when she sent us out, I thought Mrs. Preston was expecting someone to come over, a guest she didn't want the staff to see. It's unusual for Mrs. P to be alone in the house, but she dismissed the groundskeeper for the day. She gave Mr. P's caretaker the afternoon off, and sent me off to the park with Mr. Preston. I didn't like leaving Mrs. P alone in this big house, but Mr. Preston doesn't do well when his schedule is thrown off. He needs his trips to the park."

So it was unusual for Carrie to be alone in the house. Alice wondered if Carrie had been attacked by her "visitor."

Madison asked Svitlana a few more questions about the timeline of the day, then it was Alice's turn.

"I'm Alice." She smiled. "I was here earlier this week, visiting Carrie. I know you've had a rough day, and I appreciate your patience."

Svitlana frowned, raising her gaze to the sky. "I pray to God she's all right. She's been so upset lately. She worries about her son. I want her happy, and Mr. P, too. He needs her."

"Has Mrs. P mentioned the mayor recently?" Alice asked. "Tansley Grand is her name."

"Tansley, yes." Svitlana nodded.

"Do you remember what she said about her? Has Tansley come to the house?"

"No, she doesn't come here. But Mrs. P kept saying she had to call her today. Said she just couldn't take it anymore."

"Did she tell you that?"

Svitlana shrugged. "She talks to Mr. P, but he doesn't really listen. She talks to herself, I think. But something was bothering her. Something bad."

"Do you know what that might have been?" asked Madison.

"This I don't know."

With no more questions in the air, Svitlana went into the kitchen to start JB's lunch.

"It doesn't add up for me," Alice said. "I find it hard to believe Tansley Grand clocked Carrie with a candlestick holder, but that's where the evidence is pointing."

"How so?" Madison asked.

Alice quickly brought Madison up to date on her theory that Tansley was involved in George's scheme, receiving a share of the blackmail money. "We think Tansley's husband, Craig Grand, is in cahoots with Tansley. He's the one who's been dropping off puzzles at the house, puzzles with the message that we'd better back off from investigating George's murder."

Madison levered her hands up and down, as if weighing

things. "Threatening puzzles don't really amount to much in the criminal world."

"It shows intent, or a possible cover-up."

"Madison?" Their discussion was interrupted by the other patrol cop, Jorge Perez. "The housekeeper had the codes for the security cameras. I got access. Some good pictures from this morning." He slanted his iPad toward the women.

The images showed a person decked in black leaving the compound. The height, body build, and stride made it clear to Alice that it was not the mayor.

"Seems male," Madison said.

"Definitely a dude," Jorge agreed.

"Is that the mayor's husband?" Alice squinted, wishing she had a handy pair of reading glasses. "Is that Craig in the video, wearing dark sunglasses, a surgical mask, and hoody?"

"Could be," Madison said. "Hard to nail a conclusive ID. I guess we could find out if Craig Grand has an alibi."

"Excellent way to corroborate," Alice said. "Did he go to work today? Did he slip away for a long lunch?"

Officer Perez followed their conversation, his head moving as if watching a Ping-Pong match.

Alice waved Taylor's pompom key ring in the air. "I'm going over to the pharmacy to find out."

"No, Gran." Madison linked her arm through Alice's and guided her away. "Excuse us a moment," she called back to Jorge Perez. When they were out of earshot, she spoke softly. "Let me send a patrol cop. It'll be faster, more efficient. Besides, you're supposed to be laying low, right? The last thing you need is for the mayor to catch you snooping around again."

"I hardly care about getting caught when the mayor

might be the killer," Alice whispered sternly, not wanting anyone to overhear.

"We don't know that yet," Madison growled back. "And if you dip your toe in too deep, you're going to get me bumped off patrol, too. I'll be swimming in paperwork. Permanent desk duty. Back off. I mean it. No more poking around!"

# Chapter Fifty-eight

Poking around . . . the description seemed demeaning, but it was true. Alice thought she was getting rather skilled at investigating, but this was no time to argue with her granddaughter.

"I'm going to the hospital to check on Carrie," she told Madison crisply. "She'll have no one there, no advocate. No person should be alone in a hospital."

"That's a good idea." Madison nodded. "Hoping for the best."

As Alice carefully inserted herself into Taylor's tiny car, she realized there was one other thing to check. She would go to the hospital, but first, she wanted to take one more "poke." She left the grand drive of the Preston estate and cajoled the little VW straight to city hall.

Outside the mayor's office, Alice was happy to find Cassidy at her desk.

"Hi, Alice." Cassidy stopped typing and looked away from her monitor. "Do you have a meeting with the mayor today?"

"Today is actually a day off for me," Alice said, smoothing down her dress. "But I wanted to touch base with Tansley about a mutual friend of ours. Do you think I can steal a minute?"

"Your timing is good. She's just back from lunch."

"Lunch with . . . ?"

"A working lunch in the conference room. With that new budget person, going over numbers."

Just trying to make sure the mayor wasn't slipping out to extort money from people on George's list.

"It was so boring I thought my ears might bleed," Cassidy moaned. "I had to take notes."

"You poor thing. It's been a busy morning?"

"Lots of meetings, but you're good now. You can go on in."

"Thanks." Alice paused in the doorway and knocked on the open door. "Sorry to drop in. I just . . . well, something's happened to a friend of ours, and I wanted to let you know."

Tansley's initial disinterest became concern. "Come in. What happened?"

"You know Carrie Preston, don't you? I'm afraid she was attacked in her home today."

"That's awful." Tansley seemed genuinely shocked. Alice tried to play the devil's advocate, reminding herself that Tansley could be acting. "Do you have details? Is she okay?"

"She was unconscious when the ambulance took her away. It appears that she was attacked in her home, hit on the head. She's at Riverwood Hospital now."

"Oh, my gosh." Tansley closed her eyes and curled forward in her desk chair. "I have to see her."

Alice remained still as Tansley rose out of her chair, grabbed her bag, flew out the door. "Cancel my afternoon appointments," she called to Cassidy as she hurried down the hall.

Trying to escape? Alice didn't think so.

That was the reaction of a woman who was genuinely concerned. Crestfallen.

As Alice was on her way out of city hall, she got a call from Madison.

"Not that you're investigating," Madison said.

"Poking around?"

"I just wanted to let you know that Craig Grand's alibi checked out, so you don't need to worry about him. He was at the pharmacy for the past six hours."

"Good to know."

Alice wasn't surprised.

Tansley and Craig Grand were guilty—but not of attacking Carrie.

# Chapter Fifty-nine

The Beetle stalled twice on the way to the hospital, causing Alice to notice that the gas gauge was dangerously low. She pulled into a station for twenty dollars' worth of regular, and suffered the praise of a young dude who was stoked that her car was "classic" and "retro!"

At last she pulled into the parking lot at Riverwood, a private hospital that offered all the services a person in the suburbs needed, but still was small enough to navigate. She knew she'd arrived in the right waiting room when she saw Tansley crying in her husband's arms off in the corner. Such a sad sight.

She checked in at the medical desk, where she needed to bob and weave to get information. "I think I'm her closest relation in town," Alice told the attendant, who gave her next of kin paperwork to fill out. A nurse told her that Carrie was still unconscious; her stats were being closely monitored in the intensive care unit. For now, it was a waiting game. No visitors in the ICU.

Alice thanked the staff and turned away with the clipboard of paperwork. Of course, she wouldn't dare put her little lie in writing.

On the other side of the waiting room, Tansley and Craig

were talking in low tones. Surreptitiously, Alice moved closer, within hearing range. Close enough to hear Tansley tell her husband she should have done something.

"Carrie was so scared when she called." Tansley sobbed. "I should have protected her."

"It's not your fault," Craig murmured.

"I should have done something. I could have saved her."

Tansley's despair was no act. And it was becoming clear that Tansley and Craig were not the killers. Though Alice was sure they sent the puzzles. But she still couldn't piece together their involvement in George's scheme.

Alice crossed the waiting room and took an empty seat near the couple. "Tell me something," she said. "Why did you drop those puzzles off at my house? I mean, I think I got the messages. Let justice be done. The point that George Byrd deserved to die, though that varies from the rich themes of the *Mockingbird* novel. Let the investigation go, and the most obvious but frightening *Dead Men Tell No Tales*. I've always enjoyed the mythology of pirates, characters like Captain Jack, but there's no denying the savage underbelly of that lifestyle."

"Yeah, those puzzles . . ." Craig rubbed his chin. "I apologize for being menacing, but we were trying to protect you and your friends. Tansley and I read the article about you helping Ruby, and it was clear that you were going to do everything you could to prove your friend's innocence."

"And we knew that involvement would draw you into George's crime world," Tansley said. "George Byrd spent the past year using information from that DNA firm to go after people who had some connection to crime scenes. He created a hot mess, preying on people who didn't want their personal details revealed."

"Preying on people like you, Tansley," Alice said. "I

thought you were extorting money alongside him, but I was wrong. You were a victim. He was taking money from you, wasn't he?"

Tansley and Craig exchanged a worried look, and Tansley nodded.

"So George was blackmailing both of you?"

"It was me he was shaking down," Tansley said.

Craig turned to her with a pleading expression. "Please, sweetheart, don't say anything else." He turned to Alice, rubbing his brow. "We've come so far and Tansley didn't do anything wrong."

"Maybe I did." Tansley's voice was ragged with sorrow. "We were paying George to keep quiet. I had a secret, something in my past that's so horrific . . . I knew it would ruin my career if it got out. There was a possibility that I'd even be arrested, even though I was just a kid at the time."

Alice drew in a breath as the realization hit her. "The baby at the water tower was yours."

Tansley nodded, her eyes shiny with tears. "I was his mother." She sniffed. "But the investigators were wrong. I didn't leave my baby to die. He was stillborn, and I . . . that's why I left him there, all alone. I didn't want to, but only because he was gone. He had no heartbeat. His little body was cold already."

Alice pressed a hand to her heart. "I'm so sorry."

"They thought I choked him with the scarf, but I wrapped him up to keep him warm. He was dead, I knew that, but I couldn't bear to leave him in the cold without something to keep him warm." Her words dissolved into a sob, and Craig consoled her as the tears flowed.

*Have a good cry,* Alice thought, her throat tightening with sorrow and sympathy. If she thought too much about the situation—the plight of a confused and desperate young woman, the sad loss of an infant—she was going to start crying, too.

When Tansley calmed enough to take some steady breaths, Alice pressed her palms to her heart. "I'm sorry you had to go through that trauma."

"It was the worst day of my life. My parents didn't even know I was pregnant. I didn't understand it. I was sixteen and in denial. It was a nightmare, but I got past it. I kept working hard at school, and got a scholarship to college. I had kids and built a life and then, decades later . . . some pop genealogist comes along, connects me to my poor baby, and threatens to ruin everything that matters to me."

"It happened so long ago, when she was a kid," Craig said. "Tans thought about coming forward, but I talked her out of it. I figured a few payments to maintain the status quo would be worth it in the long run. I was wrong. It was getting so bad, so stressful, believe me, I thought about killing George myself."

"Craig, don't . . . don't even say that," his wife warned.

"It's true. You've surmounted huge obstacles in your life, sweetheart. You were so happy. We were happy. And then this schmuck came along and tainted everything. Why, so he could rake in some cash?"

Tansley let out a heavy sigh as she raked back her hair. "We budgeted money from our savings. In the beginning, it seemed worth it to make the trauma go away, keep it buried in the past. But George didn't stop, and the payments were beginning to cut into our savings. I've got two kids headed to college, and Craig isn't far from retirement. It was just too much."

"And then, by some dark miracle, George was killed," said Craig. "We thought it was over. Our problems solved. But we were wrong."

Alice nodded as the details sank in. Their problems didn't end with George's death, because George wasn't the only person who possessed compromising information.

Like rivers, all problems had a source.

"The trouble couldn't have ended with George's death. You still had his killer to contend with." Alice leaned closer and confided, "Jared Chase."

# Chapter Sixty

Craig and Tansley exchanged a look of surprise. "Do you really think Jared murdered George?"

"He's the obvious choice," Alice said, scanning the waiting room and the nearby medical desk. No one was near them, and no one seemed to be paying attention. "I hear they were buddies; I suspect they bonded over money and their scheme. And sometimes when a partnership involves money, one person will do anything to get the upper hand. Remember, Jared was the one with access to the information about you and the other folks who'd left DNA evidence at crime scenes. He could have easily stepped into George's shoes."

"Here's the thing," Tansley said. "Jared didn't plan to step into George's blackmail scheme. At the memorial for George, Jared told me he wouldn't dream of stooping so low, asking money of the 'unlucky individuals' on George's list. I was so relieved."

"Really?" Alice was intrigued. "So what changed his mind?"

"My fault. When I met with Jared Chase to renegotiate the city's consulting deal with EYE-dentify, he totally flipped. I didn't fire him; the city was simply reducing the services of his firm. But Jared went cold. He argued with me, saying he would sue for breach of contract, which wouldn't have gotten him anywhere.

"Then, he threatened to reveal George's blackmail scheme and implicate me for knowing about it and letting it continue." Tansley winced. "He had me on that one. It was my duty to stop him, but I was scared. I couldn't have my past revealed. It would ruin my career, my kids' lives. . . . But despite his repeated harassing phone calls, Jared never mentioned my baby. A while back, George promised me he'd take my name off his list. I don't think Jared knows about me. He doesn't realize I was once Tammy Stransky. That's why he attacked Carrie, to put pressure on me as mayor. He wants his big contract back. Until he gets his way, he's threatened to go after the people on George's list, starting with Carrie. She recently started getting anonymous calls about Tony, how his prison release would be delayed if people knew the truth about his involvement with Harlan Powell. Carrie was crumbling from the stress. I suspected Jared was behind the threats, but I had no idea he would go so far as to attack Carrie."

"This thing has snowballed out of control." Alice held her head in her hands. "This Jared is a wild card."

"Gone rogue. Right now he won't even meet with me. I think he's wary of cameras and witnesses at city hall. But he won't leave me alone, keeps calling me. Says he'll negotiate if we can meet away from city hall, but I don't trust him."

"I wonder if it's time to take this to the police," Alice said.

"I thought of that, but what hard evidence do we have on Jared? Unless the police have evidence pointing to Jared in Carrie's attack or George's homicide, the evidence boils down to my word against Jared's, a he said, she said."

"We do have George's files," Alice pointed out, "but they're sloppy and inconclusive."

"I say we continue to keep the police out of this," Craig said. "I'm afraid they'll charge Tans as an accessory in the blackmailing. That they'll reveal her connection to the water tower matter."

"I'm not sure how the law works, but she was a victim," Alice said. "She didn't make any money on the scheme."

Craig clasped Tansley's hand tighter. "Exposure will ruin us, and hurt our kids."

"I am ready to step up." Tansley pulled her husband's hand to her heart and looked earnestly in his eyes. "Sweetheart, it's time to have the past revealed, damn the consequences. I'm not going to spend the next few decades hiding from the truth."

"I don't want to lose you," he said.

"You will never lose me. You just might need to visit a facility to see me." Tansley turned to Alice. "How can we snag this guy?"

"He's tricky," Alice said. "Jared once told me how he played within the rules. Seems he's been quite careful not to leave a paper trail or get caught."

It was time to get Jared Chase to reveal himself. "He's been taunting you to meet him outside the office," Alice said. "We can make that happen. If you're game, I know the perfect place to meet."

"I'm not sure about this." Craig shook his head. "It might not be safe."

"I'm sick of playing it safe." Tansley straightened in the chair and gave a hard nod. "I'm in."

# Chapter Sixty-one

The appointment with Jared Chase was for drinks at eight p.m. The Thursday evening dinner crowd was waning at Alice's Restaurant when Taylor, their spotter in opaque sparkle makeup and one of Ruby's A-line cut wigs of pink hair, sent word that Jared Chase had pulled into the parking lot. Taylor had convinced her grandfather to let her handle this little "gag," and she was playing waitress in the outdoor bar area, where Tansley was seated alone at a two-top, sipping an iced tea.

Jared had refused to meet Tansley in her city hall office, but he agreed to meet at the restaurant Tansley suggested. In the hours before the meeting, Alice did some quick preparation, finding disguises and recording devices. Tansley was nervous, but Alice felt confident the mayor could extract some kind of confession from him.

On the small lamp at Tansley's table, Stone had planted a tiny microphone. He would record the conversation and monitor it live from his earbuds. Alice had been amazed that he possessed such spy technology. "It's from the year I spent as a bodyguard in Hollywood," he said. "A long story for another time." Indeed, she was learning that Stone had lived more lives than a cat.

With the operation in motion, Stone slouched at a near-by table, disguised in a baseball cap and a glued-on silver beard, which he'd admitted was quite uncomfortable. Alice shared his table, with her back to Tansley's table, and she was disguised in a wig with dark hair piled high. Another wig from Ruby, and though Alice thought it was an effective disguise, it made her feel like Cher or Elvira. Or maybe that was the heavy makeup Taylor slathered on her face. If someone stuck a microphone in her face, she was going to break out into a chorus of "If I Could Turn Back Time."

Jared strolled in, seemingly unaware that he was being watched. Taylor guided him to the table, where he took a seat and ordered a beer. After a cool greeting, he cut to the point. He didn't want to be in the business of collecting blackmail money. "All I want is to have my corporation's consulting contract reinstated. You can do it. You've got the power."

"My job is more about corralling the city council than making decisions on my own. And I resent the hell out of you hurting Carrie to get to me. Do you know you put her in the hospital?"

"I heard that Carrie walked in on a burglar," he said. "You'd think someone that wealthy would have a better security system at home."

"You'd think a consultant who stays in a hotel when he's in town wouldn't know about a local resident's security system."

"Good one," Jared said. "Score one point for the mayor."

"Here's your beer." There was a bit of chatter as his drink was delivered. A pause. And then Jared started in again.

"Carrie Preston is tangential," Jared said. "I need to

protect my company. This is a business deal, all above-board. Peace will be restored in your little hamlet as long as you reinstate our deal and retain EYE-dentify at the highest monthly rate of service."

"You call it service; I call it extortion."

"I don't care for semantics. I'm just here to close the deal."

"The old deal is off the table. I took an oath to serve the town of West Hazel, and a big monthly payout to EYE-dentify doesn't serve the community well."

"You're not listening; I don't take no for an answer. Look where that left your friend Carrie."

"Is that a threat?" Tansley's voice hardened. "Are you going to hurt me, Jared? Kill me over money?"

He snorted. "That wouldn't get me what I want. I need to keep you around so you can keep me in with the board. I know you've got the charm to do it. But if you don't co-operate, I have a strong incentive program. Carrie understands that now. Next it will be someone closer to you."

Alice stiffened, straining to listen. This was illegal, right? This sort of menacing threat?

"Something could happen to that adoring husband of yours," Jared said smoothly. "Maybe one of those kids. The older one is in high school, right? Lots of independence at that age. Lots of chances for things to go wrong."

# Chapter Sixty-two

Alice's jaw dropped at Jared's threats. She clenched her fists, infuriated.

Stone gave her the "cool it" sign with one hand. With a deep breath, Alice twirled the stem of her lemon drop martini glass, which looked wonderful, but was off limits while she needed to keep a clear mind. She listened as Tansley punched back.

"Don't be foolish and dig yourself in deeper. I know you killed George," she said, "and the police are catching up to you. If you're as smart as you say, you'll turn yourself in now."

Jared scoffed. "If I did kill George, the police have nothing on me. I'm careful. A little attention to detail can get you out of all kinds of scrapes."

"Your grace period is about to expire," Tansley said. "My advice is that you leave this town now. Take the money you made and run, before the police come knocking on your door."

In the silence that followed, Alice sensed that Tansley's advice had hit home. Perhaps he hadn't realized how close he was to being caught.

When he did speak, his voice lacked its usual cockiness. "Thanks for the advice and the beer," he said. "And truth be told, I can't wait to leave this town—as soon as my contract is reinstated."

The shuffling noise behind Alice indicated that he was getting up from the table. Alice stared down at her drink as he walked by. When she looked up, she accidentally caught his attention, a searing glare in his eyes. She quickly broke eye contact, murmured something nonsensical to Stone, and took a deep sip of her cocktail, feeling the heat of Jared's gaze.

Did he recognize her?

Not that it would be the end of the world. She didn't think he would come after her. But she would hate for him to know that people were probing his behavior, wise to his crimes. Finally, Stone murmured that he was gone. Everyone stayed in place, waiting for Taylor to give the word that his car had pulled out.

"And that's a wrap, folks!" Taylor called out so that some of the real customers heard her and looked around for cameras. "That was so fun! Maybe I'll go into acting."

Alice turned around to face Tansley. "You did a great job."

Craig emerged from the kitchen and rushed to Tansley's side. "How did it go?"

"He didn't confess!" Tansley's head hung low with disappointment.

"He said some incriminating things," Alice said.

Stone pushed back the baseball cap and held his phone up to Tansley. "And I recorded it all. We need to pass the recording on to Detective Bedrosian."

Tansley's eyes were wide and rueful. "I'm just afraid he's going to be out there forever, menacing our family, and hurting people like Carrie."

"We won't let that happen," Alice vowed. "We'll keep closing in on Jared Chase until we have solid evidence of his crimes."

"And maybe the police already have something?" Stone said. "They've been moving forward with their investigation. Even the most careful perpetrator makes mistakes."

Alice nodded. It felt like they'd come so close to nabbing their culprit. Just not close enough.

"Well, I guess I'll find out soon enough what the police know," Tansley said. "I'm going to go in and make a full confession, and see where that leads. Just as soon as I stop at home and check on the kids." She shot a look of concern at her husband. "Jared's threats to our family were downright creepy."

"Go," Alice said. "You need your peace of mind."

Tansley thanked Alice for her help, squeezing her arm affectionately. "If this is how you spend your days off, I can't imagine the fun you have on a full-fledged vacation."

The Grands headed out, and Stone wasn't far behind them.

"I would go with you to meet Bedrosian," Alice said, "but I feel like that might get Madison in more trouble."

"I can handle this one alone," he told her, a trace of a smile under that beard. He scratched his jawline and shook his head. "This thing has to go."

"Unless you want to join ZZ Top," Alice called after him as he walked off. "Or maybe you've already done that."

He turned to wave at her and then disappeared beyond the patio gate.

Alice picked up her lemon drop and moved with it to the outdoor bar. Such a lovely place she'd built. Might as well enjoy it. Across the patio, she saw Taylor at the bussing station chatting with some of the staff. It was good to see her granddaughter out of the basement and interacting.

"Fancy meeting you here." The voice of her life, so familiar. And yet, cloying.

"Jeff." She turned to find her husband on the bar stool right beside her. Sneaky devil. "Thanks for letting us use the place today. And the wedding rehearsal dinner tomorrow," Alice said. "It's a stellar week for Alice's Restaurant."

"It's great to have you here," he said. "You've stayed away."

"I have."

"Something I said?" he teased.

"A million things."

"Sorry for that. Times a million." He cocked his head at her. "You're not laughing."

She forced a smile. Had his charm worn off? Or had she built up a strong tolerance for it? A Jeff immunity. "I'm a little preoccupied with trying to catch a killer."

"Yowza. Serious stuff. They've really stepped up your job duties at the library."

She turned away from him and took a deep sip. "Don't you have some hosting duties to attend to?"

"The dinner rush is over." He came around her stool, in her face. "Besides, I've been wanting to talk to you. Truth is, the business is hurting without you. I may have to let it all go if I don't find a decent chef soon. These cats coming through our kitchen, they've got mad talent but no sense of commitment. Not like you."

"I guess it's hard to find good workers these days."

"No one can match your artistry in the kitchen, Alice.

Would you ever think about coming back? You could help me save this place."

Translation: come back and work your fingers to the bone while I take the credit and schmooze folks and comp drinks.

Alice shook her head. "No." There was no helping Jeff.

"We worked so well together."

"Definitely not." She slid off the bar stool. He took her arm to try to hold her there, but she brushed him off, slapped him off. "No, no, no!" She'd lost this place once. She couldn't go through the turmoil and disappointment of losing it again.

"Okay, okay." He held his hands up, as if surrendering. "I didn't mean to rush you. Maybe you want to take some time to think about the offer. Sleep on it."

She sucked in a breath, annoyed with herself for letting him get to her. Apparently her Jeff immunities weren't as strong as she'd thought.

"I could sleep for a hundred years, and the answer would still be no." She slugged down the rest of her drink. She was tempted to slam the empty glass on the bar, but it would have been a shame to smash a lovely martini vessel. Instead, she handed him the empty glass and patted her tall, black wig. "Good night."

"Wait. Does that mean you'll think about it?"

Without looking back Alice stormed off the patio and headed toward the lake. She cut a steady path along the boardwalk to one of the gazebos on the water, looking for fresh air and peace.

*Save the place?* He'd already cashed in most of their savings to cover his financial mistakes. And she had spent so many days and nights working her fingers to the bone in that kitchen. *Save the place!*

Jeff was a seething idiot! A charming moron.

This restaurant was a part of her past now.

The new Alice was a librarian, and happy to be part of the town she loved.

End of story. Period.

# Chapter Sixty-three

Daylight waned as Alice sat alone in the gazebo staring at the moon's reflection on the water. It was the in-between time, when sunlight lingered but the moon hung bright in the sky. Alice savored the long Oregon summer days when more daylight meant more time to live life.

Shaking off her irritation with Jeff, she took out her cell phone and saw that she had a voice mail from Madison. Police news?

"Gran, I'm calling to warn you to be careful." Madison spoke quickly, her voice animated with excitement. "We've got a new lead on Jared Chase. One of Ruby's neighbors came forward after recalling a strange encounter the night of George's murder. The neighbor was walking his dog in the park behind the house when he saw a hooded man jump the fence from Ruby and George's yard. The neighbor asked if he was okay, and—get this!—the guy's hood had fallen back to reveal thick golden hair!"

Alice gasped. "Jared Chase."

"I'll give you more details when I see you, but basically, we think that blond man was Jared Chase, escaping out the back way after killing George."

Alice smiled. The thrill was undeniable. "Gotcha!"

She wondered how Madison had gotten the info. Was she back on the case? She placed a call to her granddaughter as, in the distance, a man left the restaurant patio and headed down the pier toward her.

Jeff again, trying to badger her to save his sorry ass. She watched him approach as the line rang and went to voice mail.

But it wasn't Jeff. Instead, a tall, handsome man strutted down the pier toward her. The low rays of the sun cast a glimmer on the golden streaks in his hair, and his smile seemed phosphorescent in the waning light.

*Here comes the killer.*

# Chapter Sixty-four

Alice shot a desperate look to the restaurant onshore, which was nearly empty now. Would anyone hear her if she screamed and shouted? Probably not. She was trapped at the end of the dock, with Jared closing in on her. A dangerous prospect.

But then, Jared didn't know that she'd been digging into George's blackmail schemes and comparing notes with Tansley. How would he know?

In as calm a voice as she could manage, she spoke into the phone. "I'm at the restaurant gazebo, Alice's Restaurant, and I need—"

The phone beeped in her ear. The message had been cut off.

Panic time. Well, Madison was too far away, anyway. Taylor was closer.

"Is that you, Alice?" he called as he approached. "Or have I come upon the ghost of Amy Winehouse?"

"You flatter me," she teased, patting the stacked wig that had become more comfortable as the night air had cooled.

"I thought I recognized you earlier on the restaurant patio." He seemed amused. "Costume party tonight?"

"Sort of." His footsteps were getting closer as she quickly typed a message to Taylor.

"Help. Gazebo. Now." Cell phone in her lap, she touched the SEND icon, but couldn't be sure it delivered. Or that Taylor would see it. She would have to keep him talking.

When she looked up, he was right upon her, looming over her.

"Aw. You're not calling nine-one-one or anything, right?" As he spoke he snatched the phone from her hand, looked at it, shoved it in his pocket.

"That's a little rude," she said in a chastising tone, hiding the fear that clenched her heart. "And you've always been so civil and polite. I've been impressed by your maneuvers here in West Hazel. You made a tidy profit for your corporation. You hobnobbed with the city council and mayor. You almost got away with murder."

"Almost?" Jared smiled as he took a seat on the bench beside her. "Come on, now. I think I did get away, except for you. But I should have never tried to trick a librarian. Where did my story fall apart?"

"The candlestick holder threw me off. Why such a messy, brutal method of murder when you came with a loaded syringe?"

"That was me, bobbing and weaving after Nicole left the bronze holder on the floor. I figured if I whacked him a few times, it would look like Nicole was the killer. Originally I planned George's death differently. The injection would kill him, and then George's body was supposed to topple down from the small balcony off the main bedroom. I figured most people would assume suicide, that George had jumped. I even had a note to leave behind for good measure."

Alice was unimpressed. "It's been determined that you came in the back way, over the fence from the park."

"Yeah, but I got there early and hid in the main bedroom closet. I knew George and Nicole would come inside, finish their business within the hour, and she'd be out of there. She usually took an Uber. I knew their routine. George loved to brag. He was big on the kiss and tell."

"Not surprising."

"But the plan got twisted when Ruby popped in unexpectedly. Nicole cried on and on in the bedroom. She was so annoying, I thought about killing her, too, and making it look like a murder suicide. But I wasn't prepared for that."

"You only pack one toxic syringe at a time," Alice said.

"Exactly. And believe me, dealing with fentanyl is pretty scary. You can't mess around."

"You make it sound effortless," Alice said.

"I felt bad at first, but it's not like I had much of a choice. George had gotten pushy. He wanted a share of my monthly consulting fee, and that wasn't the deal. George was supposed to get his money from the criminals he was blackmailing. Folks on the list. George loved his lists. And for me, that was the beauty of the scheme. George had all the risk; he was the one breaking the law. And my actions were completely above board."

"But you killed a man," Alice said. "That's illegal, and immoral, too."

"George brought that upon himself when he got so greedy," Jared said, harsh lines straining his face now. "And that's my secret. No one is ever going to find out about it."

"Well . . . I know."

"Of course you do." He rose and took a step to the gazebo opening, blocking her access to the pier. "You know too much. More than the police. More than the mayor. You put together all the puzzle pieces. That's why I'm here for you, Alice." He reached into his pocket and removed a capped syringe. "I'm sorry, but I can't let you ruin everything I've worked for. It's time for you to go."

# Chapter Sixty-five

*Talk your way out.*
*Stall.*
*Bait him.*
*He's a sucker for witty repartee.*

"So you've got a toxic injection for me," Alice said, rising from the bench cautiously. "One problem with that: the police will connect my death to George's, and then you'll be imprisoned for two homicides."

"The police don't know I killed George."

"They do, Jared. It's just a matter of time before they come for you. They've got evidence pointing to your presence at the murder scene. And video of you at Carrie Preston's house."

"They won't have enough to make a case against me. I'm a careful guy. Detail oriented," he said, moving toward her.

"So you say." She stepped back, moved to the side.

He matched her step for step, and they began an odd dance in the gazebo, with Alice trying to evade his advances.

"Listen, I don't want you to feel any pain, Alice. If you just hold still, this will be over soon."

"How generous of you. But for a man of detail, you haven't thought this through. What would you do with my body?"

"You're going into the lake. An appropriate resting place, just beyond the patio of your charming restaurant."

"Don't be ridiculous. You can push me over, but the fall is only a few yards, and I can swim. Not to mention the water is less than eight feet deep in most parts of this lake. I might stub my toe on a rock, but that'd be all."

"They'll think you drowned."

"I'm an excellent swimmer," she lied. "No one will believe I drowned."

"It's a plausible theory. It'll buy me enough time until the tox screen comes back and shows that you've got a lethal dose of morphine in your body. Not fentanyl this time. I'm mixing it up." He held up the syringe.

"Clever." She sidestepped toward the water. "But they'll trace it to you."

"By then, I'll be long gone, drinking mai tais on the beach in Bora Bora or knocking back vodka in some Icelandic hot springs. The mayor was right. I'm getting out of Dodge. Taking my million and running with it."

He lunged toward her and she scrambled toward the exit. Her gaze was set on the boardwalk leading to the restaurant—escape!—when he grabbed her from behind and lifted her off her feet.

Panic set in as the air left her lungs. "You're crushing me!" She pulled at his solid arms, trying to wrench free.

"It'll just be a minute," he said, releasing one arm.

She flailed in response to the loosened hold, but his arm

clamped her tighter. She managed to turn her neck a bit and saw him fumbling with the syringe.

He needed two hands to get the cap off. Ha!

Struggling in his hold, Alice thrashed, shifting wildly, as if she could fling him off. Her heartbeat was thumping wildly in her ears, and the stillness of the night was broken by the shriek of birds.

"Get off me!" she groaned, slipping in his grip, only to have him clamp one arm painfully around her neck. She tried to shout, but it was hard to get enough breath in through his tight choke hold.

They struggled in the gazebo, casting this way and that. Still, there was the pounding as she twisted and thrashed, trying to break free. When she paused to try and sneak in a breath, she saw him fumbling to uncap the syringe with his thumb, and then straining to bring it to his mouth to remove the cap with his teeth.

*This is it!* She thought as the pounding of her heart grew louder. She used her free hand to smack away the syringe, unsuccessfully, as she opened her mouth and sank her teeth into the arm around her neck.

"Aaaghh!" he bellowed, his grip weakening. She let his arm slip from her jaw. Then, suddenly, he was peeled away from her.

Alice stumbled back, trying to regain her balance as she took in the force that had overcome Jared Chase.

Stone.

He stood behind Jared, restraining him by the neck and one arm, as Taylor snatched the syringe from Jared's other hand.

"Alice!" Jeff was now running up the boardwalk pier, a little late. Alice suddenly realized that the pounding noise had not been her heart, but footsteps on the wooden pier.

"How about a little inoculation?" Taylor asked, mocking Jared. "If you count to three, it won't hurt a bit." She pointed the syringe at his arm and went in for the jab.

"No! Don't! It'll kill me," Jared begged.

"Oops!" Taylor sighed as the cap of the syringe glanced off his skin. "Who's a big baby about shots?"

# Chapter Sixty-six

Adrenaline still coursed through her body as Alice watched Jeff and Taylor bind Jared's arms and ankles to a patio chair with many layers of butcher's twine from the kitchen. "Be sure to triple knot it," she said.

"Here's where my old scout rope badge comes in handy," Jeff said with a grin. Still showing off. Still merry. Eternally Jeff.

They had moved Jared up to the patio, where the lighting was better and the police would find them faster. Alice lifted a water glass to drink and saw that her hand was trembling. Still shaky.

Stone knelt beside her chair to study Alice's arms and face. "A few scratches. You feeling okay?"

"You came back?"

"I barely left the parking lot. Bedrosian couldn't meet me till later, so I sat in my car peeling off that beard. When I finally pulled out, I passed Jared Chase on the road. I smelled trouble. So I turned around. Had a feeling you would need me."

His words brought tears to her eyes. Was he speaking of a greater sense of togetherness, or just supporting her in this investigation? "Thank you," she said. "I'm going to be fine."

By the time the police had arrived, they were under the full veil of night, and the rolling blue and red lights of the law enforcement vehicles cast an eerie glow over the patio, slope, and lake.

"Gran!" Madison cast aside professionalism to give her a hug. "Are you okay? I was so worried."

"I'll admit, I got myself in quite a pickle," Alice said. "Don't know where I'd be without help from my friends." She touched Stone's arm. "Stone was a hero, and Taylor held her own, too."

Taylor gave a quick smile, but remained standing off to the side. Now that the commotion was over, she had receded to the background, as much as any person with a hot pink wig could fade.

"You're all heroes in my book," Madison said. "You caught the killer."

Alice looked over at Jared, who stared down as Bedrosian informed him of his Miranda rights. "I do hope this will provide enough evidence to put him away. He did confess to me."

"We've got the witness testimony from the neighbor in the park," Madison said. "And earlier this evening we executed a search warrant of Jared's hotel room and found a hefty piece of evidence. The candlestick holder from Ruby's house."

"And you bragged about being careful!" Alice scolded Jared, who scowled and stared down at the patio tiles.

"Some killers can't resist keeping a trophy," Bedrosian said.

"You can't prove that the candlestick holder doesn't belong to me," Jared snapped.

"Well, if you own it, you'll still need to explain why there would be traces of George's blood and hair on the bronze." From the glimmer in Bedrosian's dark eyes, Alice sensed that he enjoyed going toe to toe with Jared Chase. "Dude, we got you on the murder of George Byrd. Homicide *and* assault. You went after Carrie Preston, too."

"Carrie . . . how is she?" Alice asked.

"She regained consciousness, and we were able to speak with her," Madison said. "The prognosis is good for a full recovery, but it's been traumatic for her."

"Not surprising." Alice frowned. Now that she had reestablished contact, she would reach out to Carrie and invite her to some events around town after she was feeling better. She could help Carrie beef up her home security to ward off future incidents. "How did you connect Jared to the attack?"

"Some of our officers did a wider canvass of the Prestons' neighborhood," Madison explained. "They found video evidence of Jared Chase parking his car outside the neighbor's gate and pulling on gloves and a ski mask before proceeding to the Preston home."

"Apparently, not quite clever enough," Alice called to Jared.

"Yeah, well, I was a lot smarter than George," Jared said. "I got the legitimate contract, the big bucks, while he went shaking down losers."

"For all his crimes and faults, George was not a violent criminal," Alice said. "You crossed that line, more than once."

Jared rolled his eyes. "Can we go? I don't need to sit here and get dressed down by Grandma."

Bedrosian pointed to one ear. "You should listen to what she has to say, chump. And considering where you're going, you might want to take in the fresh air. Hard to enjoy such a beautiful evening in a cell." Bedrosian nodded at Madison. "But, yeah, we can go." He looked down at the string bonds. "Anybody got a butcher knife to release this goose?"

Taylor held up a pair of kitchen scissors.

"That works." Bedrosian clipped the string from one wrist, and then cuffed Jared's hands together before continuing.

"Not to embarrass you, Officer Denham," Alice said quietly, "but I'm glad you're back on the case."

"Me too. The chief is still on vacation, out of the loop, but he trusts Bedrosian's judgment. Now we realize why the mayor wanted me out of the loop."

Alice nodded. "How is that part of the investigation going?"

"Still sorting it out. But the district attorney put a freeze on George's bank account after they found large deposits from Carrie Preston, Tansley Grand, and two other people on the list. We're thinking some of his victims can be compensated for their financial loss."

"So Carrie and Tansley might recoup their payments?" Alice asked.

"Looks that way," Madison said as the detective called her to go. She leaned in close to Alice to whisper, "Love you, Gran!" before heading off with the prisoner.

"Nothing quite as satisfying as justice served," Stone said.

As the police loaded up their cars, Taylor stepped forward, enveloped Alice in a hug, and burst into tears. "That was such a close call! I'm sorry for being such a pain in the ass."

"Honey, you are many things, but pain in the tush is not one of them."

"I'm going to figure my life out." Taylor sniffed and swiped at her eyes. "But for now, I've got a job. I've been talking to Gramps and I'm going to work as a manager here. He needs the help, and I'll do some kitchen stuff, too. But you can't pin down a social butterfly like me in the back room. I need to fly free!"

"I support your journey and your flight pattern, whatever it may be." Finally, her granddaughter seemed to feel the love and support around her. Alice scanned the grounds of the lakefront restaurant. Not hers anymore.

"I'll be back here tomorrow for the rehearsal dinner. After that, I hope you won't expect me to visit while you're working."

Taylor nodded. "I'm cool with that."

"I've moved on," Alice said. "And I need to nurture my life away from this place."

*And what a fine life.*

# Chapter Sixty-seven

Saturday dawned with cooling breezes and bright blue skies.

"The perfect day for a wedding," Alice told Taylor and Violet as they hustled out the door, all dolled up for the event.

After Jamal and Celeste exchanged vows in a beautiful ceremony, Ruby and Alice shared a hug.

"Thank you, thank you!" Ruby rocked Alice in a warm embrace.

"I'm supposed to be congratulating you," Alice said, taking her friend's hands. "This is your day. Your last baby girl is married now."

"I know it, and I'm so grateful to you for everything you've done. You took care of me during this bad patch, and you've given me a new home. Not to mention you solved George's murder, allowing folks in West Hazel to feel safe again."

"The investigation started with you, honey." Alice smiled. "I couldn't let my best friend get pegged with a murder charge."

"Oh, please!" Ruby rolled her eyes. "Seems like that was years ago. I must have aged ten years in the last two weeks."

"Not at all. You're a lovely mother-of-the-bride." Alice noticed Celeste motioning from across the lawn of the club. "Looks like you're needed by the fountain. Family photos."

Ruby looked over her shoulder and sighed. "Okay, but I will see you on the dance floor, honey!"

"Absolutely."

As the wedding guests milled about, Alice talked with Tansley and Craig Grand, who appeared to be in a calmer state. Everyone was relieved to know Jared Chase was being held without bail.

"I guess you heard that I resigned as mayor." Tansley's eyes appeared brighter, and the smattering of freckles beneath her foundation was endearing.

"I did hear that rumor."

"I've been in meetings with the police to help them piece together the blackmail scheme. And I told Bedrosian the complete story about the baby. No more secrets."

"You've displayed true integrity," Alice said. "I admire that, Tansley. What was the detective's response?"

"First, he had to look up the case. After a long interview, he referred the incident to the district attorney. Bedrosian has been kind. He doesn't plan to charge me as an accessory since I was also a victim. The attorneys are sorting that out."

"How are you feeling?"

Tansley took a moment to consider the question. "So relieved. Happy to be home, spending time with my kids, for now." She smiled. "Eventually, I'll need more. Maybe volunteering at the women's shelter? We'll see."

\*   \*   \*

After a buffet headlined by carved roast beef, salmon, and fried chicken, the deejay opened up the party with the rock anthem "Celebrate!" Alice and Ruby moved onto the dance floor, an enchanted area surrounded by flowers and shrubs and strings of lights. Alice loved to dance, despite the fact that she often towered over everyone on the dance floor.

Next the deejay played Neil Young's "Harvest Moon," and Jeff asked Alice to dance.

She stared at him as the old feelings swirled inside her.

Here was Jeff, her first love, the father of her child, the affable man she thought she'd be partnered with forever. The old desire, the longing for him to see her as her, the hope that they might find each other again—all the attachments that had tortured her for years gave one last tug and then dissipated to nothing.

Nada. Mere memories.

"No. Thank you, anyway," she said, turning away.

Jeff moved down the line and asked Ruby.

"Sure." She gave it a go, laughing at Jeff's corny jokes. And that was that.

Across the room Alice spied Stone chatting with Celeste and Jamal.

*Just friends,* she'd told him. It was the right choice, but that didn't make her feel any better about it now.

Taylor came along. "Hey." She stopped short, followed Alice's gaze, and figured it out. "Oh, Gran. You got it bad."

"We're just friends," Alice insisted.

"Uh-uh. I've witnessed otherwise. He's crazy about you. What is your major malfunction?"

Alice shrugged, without an explanation to give.

She was saved from having to answer when the Emotions' "Best of My Love" came on, and Taylor pulled her onto the dance floor. Ruby, Celeste, Madison, and Violet rushed to join them for an all-girl dance. Aunt Gildy pushed out on her walker and wagged a finger, keeping time to the music.

They laughed, sang along, pumped fists in the air. It was a joyous moment in which Alice was happy to be alive, surrounded by women she loved.

When the song ended they were smiling and short of breath. The dance floor cleared, and Alice took a seat when the ELO song "Strange Magic" began to play. As Violet painted wide swathes of awe in the air, Alice felt a shiver run through her. Was it regret? Sadness? Not for the loss of Jeff, but for the way she'd pushed Stone away.

She still believed in magic. Yes, indeed. What had she done, closing the door to magical possibilities? As if she were too old to fall in love again. That was the sort of thing an old, shriveled nincompoop would say.

As the song wound down, she pushed back from the table and decided to take a walk in the garden to sort out her thoughts. Once on her feet, she found her path blocked by a large figure of a man. She looked up and her heart ached.

Stone.

"I strongly suggest that you dance with me." His low drawl held a note of whimsy. And he was so darned attractive, standing near her in his black suit with a lavender shirt.

It killed her, but she shook her head no.

"I figured you'd say that. But this next song is for you. Special request by your granddaughter."

Alice glanced over at the deejay, where Taylor stood with a broad smile and a thumbs-up. "She didn't."

"She did," Stone said. "And I was quick to agree."

As the music began, Alice recognized the intro to a classic jazz song redone by Michael Bublé. She let out a laugh. "I know this one. How can I refuse?"

Stone held out his arm to her. But Alice stepped forward, folded her arms across her chest, and lip-synched the first line, "I won't dance . . ." She strutted away from him, moving in time to the music.

Playing along, Stone mouthed the next line to the song, and soon they were both lip-synching as they danced around each other, jitterbugged, tangoed, and swung into each other's arms.

They moved well together, light as two feathers in a breeze. He twirled her, then brought her back into his arms. It was divine confirmation that Alice was a fool. She'd been wrong. But she suspected Stone would forgive her. He seemed to have breached that gap already.

But that was a conversation for later. For now, she was swaying joyously in Stone's arms. In his embrace, she felt the warm glow of magic.

"I could get used to this," she admitted.

Pressing his lips to her ear, he answered: "Good thing."

# Acknowledgments

Alice and her friends have brought me many months of joy and challenge, and I can't let this one go without thanking the people who were fundamental in this creation.

First there's John Scognamiglio, my brilliant editor, who planted the seed for a mystery solved by women of a certain age drawn together in love and friendship. How do you do it all?

I am forever indebted to my writer friends, who fuel the fires of creativity and also know when it's time to kick back and enjoy life.

I am grateful to Margaret Barnes for taking me through the paces of a day as the director of a library. Every day should be librarian appreciation day.

Many thanks are due to the amazing women of my book club, who put up with my meandering descriptions of Alice Pepper and friends as I was weaving this story together. You ladies understand story, character, and entertainment on so many levels. I lift my glass of Chardonnay to many more good times and shared adventures in reading.

Thanks to Robin Rue, my agent, my rock, always just a phone call away. I can always count on your support.

And love and thanks to my family, my real-life characters, who give me the space to create and work and lose myself in the made-up characters.